To
& Harriet

To Irene—
Best regards

by

Don Pardue

This story is a work of fiction, with the exception of recognized historical characters, events, and institutions. Names, characters, and incidents are products of the author's imagination. Any resemblance to actual persons is entirely coincidental. The names of places are used only as a means to establish the locale of the story.

Library of Congress Control Number: 2006901694

ISBN 0-9755892-1-0

First printing - February, 2006

Additional copies of this book are available by mail.
Information / Ordering sheet located inside novel.

Printed in the U.S.A. by
Morris Publishing
3212 East Highway 30
Kearney, NE 68847
1-800-650-7888

Dedication

To all who are old in body,
but young in spirit.
- Don Pardue

~ Cover design by Victor Pardue ~
~ Editing by Victor Pardue and Donna Pardue Thompson ~

Acknowledgments

I owe a debt of gratitude to a countless number of fellow senior citizens for providing indirect contribution to this work. The need for brevity, however, dictates special mention of only specific individuals for their notable assistance:

My son, Victor, and my daughter, Donna, who worked as a team in editing the book and also provided continuing encouragement and an inexhaustible supply of creative ideas.

Joan Buell, a friend and fellow artist who not only extended literary advice, creative suggestions, and technical expertise, but also offered constructive criticism with obvious patience as well as tolerance of my stubbornness.

And finally and most importantly, as always, Barbara, my wife of fifty years, whose optimistic, youthful spirit has been my constant source of motivation and inspiration.

Chapter 1

The accumulation of people was beginning to grow larger, expanding into a huge gathering that consisted of complete strangers to me. As I scanned the crowd, I didn't see a member of the male gender among them, for it seemed that the group was made up exclusively of chattering women and giggling teenage girls. Being the only man in the congregation of people, I felt alien to the others. *Why are we assembled here? Is it a picnic, a family reunion, or perhaps a graveside service?* I suddenly felt the urge to urinate.

As the swarm of females grew to gigantic proportions, my bladder discomfort became almost uncontrollable. I looked around the area for a building that might have a restroom, but we were assembled in a large, empty field, devoid of any kind of structure. The group of females pressed closer, completely encircling me. In desperation, I visually explored the area in search of a tree to hide behind long enough to relieve myself, but when I gazed in every direction I could only see endless stretches of a level, grassy field.

I awoke just in time to avoid the first dribbling, thankful that I was lying alone in my bed instead of standing among hundreds of females in that eternal expanse of empty prairie. I rose quickly, because whenever I have the urge it is imperative that I immediately respond. Luckily, the bathroom was only ten feet away. My rapid rise from the bed made me dizzy, causing me to almost black out. My doctor had warned me to rise slowly when I stood after lying in bed.

I relieved myself in the bathroom and tried to remember whether this was the second or the third time I had gotten up to urinate. A year ago, Dr. Stevens had confirmed that my prostate was slightly enlarged, but fairly normal for a man of my age of sixty-eight. But that was twelve months ago, when I was getting up only once during the night. If it is now necessary to urinate three or four times a night, I concluded that my prostate gland must be as big as a basketball.

I climbed back into the bed and squinted my eyes in attempt to read the glowing numerals on my bedside clock, but the vision was only a luminous blur. I reached to the nightstand for my glasses, but after unsuccessfully groping around the tabletop in the dark, I realized that I had misplaced them… Again.

I squinted my eyes and moved close enough to the clock to see that it was 3:45 a.m.: Too early to get up, but more than likely too late to go back to sleep. I was probably facing the dreadful, but familiar ordeal of lying awake for three or four hours dwelling on the negative past experiences in my life or possibly remembering things that I had forgotten to do: *Did I take my Lipitor and Synthroid medication last night? What about my Metamucil?* I couldn't remember.

I again got into bed and crawled under the covers. In an effort to induce sleep, I tried to think of tranquil pleasant scenery: Winter sunsets, beautiful autumn harvest moons, the deep, dark woods on a lazy summer afternoon; but wait…it was in the woods that I had been bitten by a snake when I was a child. The memory of the event aroused an anxiety that made it even more impossible to go to sleep.

It is the curse of the elderly, this inability to sleep at night. Sometimes during the day we are able to cat-nap, but at night haunting memories join forces with aching bodies to rob the mind of the serenity necessary for sleep. When I was a younger man, sleep came easy for me…but that was before I lost Jennifer. Dear, sweet Jenny—the love of my life. Breast cancer had stolen her from me when she was only fifty-seven. She had given me forty years of her life as well as two daughters: Melissa, now forty-nine, named after my maternal grandmother, and Marsha, forty-seven, who was given the name of Jenny's mother. Because she considered it to be too common, she never liked her given name.

Both Melissa and Marsha had taken their mother's death hard, and for the first two or three years after her passing they had been a great emotional comfort to me. But, as the saying goes, "time heals all wounds;" consequently, for the past seven or eight years, their lengthy visits to me had changed to frequent but brief stops.

Time had healed their wounds, but not mine.

Damn it! These are negative thoughts! If I am going to be able to go back to sleep I need to think of pleasant memories and peaceful scenes...Mountains during a golden autumn, placid lakes, the first stars blinking in the twilight sky, a manicured, dew covered golf course on a beautiful summer morning... How long has it been since I played golf? Let's see...I guess the last time was a couple of months ago when I played with my best friend, Dick. I had played so terribly that following the round I had taken a solemn oath to never again pick up a golf club.

Damn! More negative thoughts!

In search of a pleasant train of thought, my mind drifted back to Jenny, for I love remembering her. We were married hastily when I was only eighteen and she was seventeen. Although her father never threatened me, I guess the event could be called a "shotgun wedding," for after a brief courtship, Jenny had become pregnant by me. We both had just graduated from Northridge High School, and my courtship with Jenny had begun a result of my rebound from my passionate lost love, Harriet Dawson, who had jilted me. I had loved Harriet with a passion. And although we were very young, it was not "puppy love," for it was several years after I married Jenny that I finally recovered from my broken heart.

Although Jenny was a lovely girl and very affectionate, I had not yet felt the passion for her that I had experienced with Harriet. But over the years I grew to love Jenny. She was vivacious and optimistic and made a wonderful wife and mother. As I lay in bed thinking of her, I realized how much I still missed her.

We had wed in a simple ceremony in a small local church with only a handful of guests attending. After pronouncing us husband and wife, the minister introduced us to the attending group, "I now proudly present to you Mr. and Mrs. Thomas Spencer." My friend Dick Noble had been best man, as well as our closest friend throughout our marriage.

Over the years Dick had become a very affluent and generous man; and knowing that I had little money, he even offered to pay for part of the funeral when Jenny died. Since my semi-retirement began three years ago, I had begun to miss the presence of Jenny even more. Living by myself in this empty house made me terribly lonely.

I've gotta stop digging up these sad memories or I'll never go back to sleep. If only there was an on/off switch to the process of thinking; but I considered that the brain is perhaps the only human organ that never rests. Even the heart is able to rest between beats, but the brain is always at work. During sleep, it is still busy conjuring up dreams, some of which are more depressing and terrifying than reality.

In most of my dreams I am once again a young man.

When did I become old? Is there a certain chronological milestone in the span of life in which one can declare himself old? At what age does one become old? Our perspective on the passage of time is mystifying. When we are younger, time seems to move forward at such a creeping pace that it is almost imperceptible. Becoming old is such a distant future event that we give it little thought; but suddenly we are old. When did it happen?

When looking back over our lives, the passage of time that links *young* to *old* is so incredibly rapid that we are terrified by the accelerated pace. Our perception tells us that the older we become the more rapid is the pace of time.

As a young man, I smugly assumed that when I became old I would accept it with complacent resignation. With most of my life behind me, I would have no dreams of the future. I would be content to consign myself to a rocking chair and relax. Failing health, diminishing eyesight and hearing, forgetfulness, a wrinkled, sagging face, hair loss, and an extinct sex drive would inhibit any desire and remove any expectations of living a useful and exciting life. At my age, I am supposed to assign such lofty dreams to the realm of the young.

But such is not the case. For the elderly, the dream may be tempered to some extent, but longings and aspirations still reside in the heart of the aged; and because our time on earth is dwindling, we sometimes feel a desperation to fulfill some of our earlier aspirations before we pass on. Although our deteriorating bodies may sometimes hinder our plans, our minds continue to possess the dream. Old people still retain a passion for life, a longing for adventure, hopes for the future, a desire for companionship, and yes, even a craving for sex. Unless we have developed dementia, our minds are the same as when we were young, only wiser.

With these pleasant thoughts, I considered that I might be able to drift off to sleep; but the pain in my left ankle prevented it. Yesterday, I turned my ankle during my daily three-mile jog. I wondered how long it would be until my ankle was well enough for me to jog again. I may not be able to jog for a week—maybe even longer.

Damn! A sore ankle...and depressing thoughts about it too.

I turned over onto my right side and tucked a pillow between my legs; for some reason this seems to make me more comfortable.

I need to go to sleep!

A glance at the bedside clock told me that it was now 4:30 a.m. If I could only sleep for a couple of more hours I could get up and make coffee. *Did I remember to buy coffee?* Oh, yeah, now I remember–Marsha brought over a pound of coffee yesterday, along with my medication that she had picked up for me at the pharmacy. Both Marsha and Melissa are very helpful in providing the items that I always seem to forget. Marsha never has a lapse of memory. *She is Mrs. Efficiency.*

Although alike in their headstrong natures, my daughters are mostly a study in contrasts, both in personality and appearance. Marsha is pretty and fair-skinned and wears her blonde hair cut short in a pixie style. She married a man named Jason and bore him a son, Patrick, now twenty-four. Petite and shapely, Marsha is fastidious in her manner of dress—usually wearing a stylish and expensive business suit when working at her job as a secretary for a prestigious Knoxville law firm. She has a degree in social science, but has aspirations to obtain a law degree. Well-mannered and soft-spoken, she is articulate in her speech and expressions. Her character is impeccable to the point of self-righteousness, and she is very discerning in her judgments. Marsha chose an appropriate line of work, for in her evaluation of human behavior, her thinking is like that of an attorney; a person is either innocent, or guilty; there is no middle ground. In all ethical matters her judgment is rendered with uncompromising certainty. In her political beliefs she is a right-wing conservative, and her moral world is painted in black and white. She is a devout yuppie and a neat-freak; also, she is a technology whiz—she loves computers, cell phones, camcorders and all types of technical gadgetry. Although her intellect is superior, she lacks the creative inclination possessed by her more uninhibited sister. Like her father, she is structured and well organized.

Melissa is very pretty and dark-skinned. Her silky, long raven hair is usually combed straight back, flowing in long tresses down her back and to her waist. Twice married and divorced, she has no children. She is undisciplined, spontaneous, and unstructured. She lives for the moment, enjoys life, is flirty and promiscuous, and worries the hell out of me. If she is not spending time with one of her numerous boyfriends, she can be found at some peace rally or demonstration against the war in Iraq, an inclination that stands in stark contrast to Marsha's hawkish stance concerning the war. She is a genuine throwback to the hippie generation of the sixties. Inheriting my talent in painting, she has a fondness for abstract art, expensive wine and outlandish clothing. Although she graduated from college with a degree in philosophy, she owns and operates a small flower shop in the suburbs of Northridge while working on her master's degree in sociology. In her carefree nature, she is more like her mother.

Both she and Marsha, although drastically different in most every respect, are unified in their efforts to direct my life. When did they become the parents—and when did I become their child?

I've got to get some sleep. How can I stop reliving my life in my head? I think I'll get up and take a sleeping pill—maybe two. After all, I don't have any early scheduled appointments. I can sleep until 8:00 if I wish. That will give me almost three more hours of sleep. To hell with working today in my small sign shop; after all, this is Saturday, and my shop is only a part-time retirement business anyway. I should close it—go out of business; but I need the small income that the business brings in to pay the utility bills, insurance, and property taxes on the building. I have tried to go out of business before, but empty buildings attract vandals; consequently, only a short time after closing, the windows were all broken and graffiti was painted on the outside walls, forcing me to reopen the business. My small company resembles a perpetual motion machine: I work only to enable me to have a place to work. It's like a neighbor I had when I was a child. He owned a pair of mules that he kept complaining about having to feed. When I asked him why he needed the mules, he replied, "I need the mules in order to plow that crop of corn." He pointed to the cornfield.

"Why do you need the corn?" I asked him.

"To feed the mules," he replied.

"Why don't you sell the mules? Then you won't

have to raise corn," I suggested.

"I've got a sentimental attachment to them," he replied.

It was the same with me in regard to my studio building—I have a sentimental attachment to it.

I slowly got out of bed, and in the darkness I groped my way to the bathroom. After turning on the light, I plucked from the cabinet a small box containing a new bottle of sleeping pills. It was a different type from my usual brand, so I needed to read the directions in regard to the prescribed dosage; however, I remembered that I had previously misplaced my glasses. I squinted my eyes in an effort to read the print, but I couldn't make out a word on the label.

Oh, well, I'll open the bottle and take just one pill…That can't hurt me.

I opened the container and removed the bottle. I then aligned the small arrow point on the lid with the matching one on the bottle. Repeatedly, using all my thumb strength, my attempts were unsuccessful at popping the cap off the medicine bottle. With a near-bleeding thumb, I gave up in despair. I put the bottle of pills back in the cabinet, turned out the bathroom light and returned to my bed. Now I was too angry and frustrated to sleep. *Why is it that directions don't work for old people? What time is it?*

I again leaned toward the clock and squinted my eyes: *5:45.* I had been lying awake for two hours since the last urge to urinate had awakened me.

I crawled back into bed then suddenly remembered that I was supposed to call Dick last night…Something about playing golf today, I think…But I'll probably be too sleepy to play. Besides, I may not be able to walk very well with this swollen ankle.

I thought about my long-standing friendship with Dick Noble. If any two people have less in common than my two daughters, it is Dick Noble and I. In almost every way imaginable, we are direct opposites. In politics, my liberal leanings stand in direct contrast to his conservative views; also while I feel the need to plan every detail of my life, Dick is spontaneous. Despite our differences, our unlikely friendship has endured for more than fifty years.

Ever since I have known him, Dick has had an easy way with people. In high school he excelled in everything he attempted (except academics). He was great in basketball and baseball, but it was in football that his talents were unmatched.

"The greatest running back in the history of Northridge High School," said *The Northridge Banner.* "Northridge running back earns All-State honors," heralded *The Knoxville News-Sentinel.*

When young, Dick was handsome, gregarious, flamboyant and charismatic. Sporting wavy blonde hair, he was truly the "golden boy." He was six-feet two and weighed an even two hundred pounds. He was by far the most popular guy in school. Everyone loved Dick. He was elected senior class president, and to be among his circle of friends was to be a part of the elite in Northridge High. Unfortunately, he was also as dumb as a rock.

After high school he received an athletic scholarship from a small college where he excelled in football, and with the help of countless tutors, somehow graduated. After college he had made a ton of money as a sales manager for a large corporation in Knoxville that sold athletic equipment. He later retired at age sixty-five. His large salary in combination with the profitable investments he had made enabled him to retire with a small fortune. Dick had many influential friends and had always been lucky. Because of his fondness for the local people, he had retired in Northridge.

My initial relationship with Dick began when we were sophomores in high school. Although shy and not especially popular, I was a very bright student, keeping an "A" in most subjects. I didn't run in the same circle with Dick because he and his friends were the aristocracy of Northridge High School. Because failing grades meant ineligibility to participate in sports, he was struggling with his academics to the point of desperation.

At first, I didn't particularly like Dick because he was loud and sometimes overbearing. I also considered him to be shallow, pretentious, and stupid. Being quiet and reserved by nature, my personality was in direct contrast to his, and although I certainly had no desire to be like him or become a part of his band of cronies, I had a great admiration for his athletic ability. Also, his popularity with the girls ensured that he could date almost anyone of his choosing. I didn't consider myself his friend at the time, but I had a burning envy of him.

Because of his intellectual limitations, he was always on the threshold of failure in the classroom. It wasn't a case of his goofing off, for he really worked hard to make passing grades; but it became obvious to me that he was anything but a mental giant.

I began to help him with his studies. He moved to the desk beside me in class, and sometimes during exams I would turn my paper toward him to enable him to copy the answers. I even created cheat sheets for him.

Dick was an outgoing person, and because he appreciated my help and admired my intellect, we gradually became friends. Because of my close association with him, I accidentally became a fringe member of the elite group.

In our junior year, a true friendship had blossomed between us, and I began to be more popular by association. That's when Harriet Dawson came into our lives.

Harriet was a strikingly beautiful girl with a voluptuous figure and wavy auburn hair. She had transferred to Northridge High from a neighboring school and immediately became well-liked by the other classmates, particularly the boys. She became a cheerleader, and as expected, she was immediately attracted to Dick. However, she was very witty and exceptionally bright—qualities that gave her nature a closer similarity to mine than to Dick's. Since Dick and I, in spite of our dissimilar personalities had become almost inseparable, she began a close association with both of us. The three of us gradually evolved into our own separate threesome. We went together to movies, parties, hayrides, and school activities. Harriet liked to refer to us as *The Three Musketeers.* Both Dick and I took turns in dating her on occasions.

As time passed, because of the similarity of our interests and personalities, Harriet and I became infatuated with one another. It was the same old story: A love triangle in which Harriet and I felt that we were in love while Dick was left out in the cold. He was consumed by a burning jealously.

After graduation, Harriet and I talked of marriage…well, Harriet did most of the talking. She was ready for it to happen immediately, but I was not. First, I wanted us to attend college together, the same school where Dick was awarded his football scholarship. She agreed because she genuinely liked Dick, though not romantically, and wanted to keep *The Three Musketeers* together throughout college. In addition, Harriet craved glamour and attention, privileges that she could hang onto as long as she was a close friend of Dick, the football star.

But fate has a capricious habit of changing our best-laid plans. When I told Dick of my plan to marry Harriet, he became sufficiently enraged to beat the hell out of me. When I was released from the hospital, I learned that Harriet had eloped with a wealthy older man. Then, on the rebound, I got involved with Jenny and impregnated her, which, because I wanted to do the "right thing" resulted in our hasty marriage. Two children immediately followed.

The Three Musketeers were forever separated while Dick went on to college and became a football hero, but because of my mistake and new family responsibilities, I was denied the chance. I later learned that Harriet had moved to California with her wealthy husband. After college, Dick married and divorced a few times and ended up spending his career working in nearby

Knoxville, and living alone.

Actually, despite his cruel attack on me, Dick turned out to be a very gentle and compassionate man, but sometimes he still has the same explosive temper. After I healed from his beating, he was filled with remorse. He begged for my forgiveness and even offered to pay my hospital bill. I forgave him years ago, but in order to manipulate him, I never let him forget it.

Shortly after Harriet jilted both Dick and me, and after my discharge from the hospital, Dick made overtures to restore our close friendship. "Let's get out of this town for a few days," he suggested. "My dad owns a cabin in the Smokies. Let's head up there and maybe do a little trout fishing." So we retreated to the mountains to reclaim our friendship and lick our emotional wounds.

Over the years, Dick has laughed about the "Harriet episode," professing his gratitude to fate for not allowing either of us to fall into the clutches of the "wicked claws of Harriet."

Dick and I have grown even closer over the years. Ten years ago when Jenny died, he was my staunchest supporter, feeling my pain with me, and helping me through the rough times.

* * *

The sunrise in the east cast a banner of light across the room, enabling me to read the digits on the clock: *7:00 a.m.* Too late for sleep now. I might as well get up, get dressed and join the other old codgers for breakfast at the Cracker Barrel.

Chapter 2

I switched on the bedside lamp. Remembering my tendency to become dizzy when arising too rapidly, I slowly got up. As I stood erect, I spotted my glasses lying on the floor beside a book that I had been reading. It was sheer luck that I hadn't stepped on them.

My left ankle was beginning to swell and was now getting sore. I stared down at it, noticing the bluish tint that was beginning to spread to the inside anklebone, extending downward almost to the arch of my foot. I limped into the bathroom, flicked the light switch, and peered at my image in the mirror. My face made me appear to be older than I envisioned myself being. My meager strands of black hair were unruly, with a cowlick standing up on the back, the only part of my head that still retains hair in any abundance. A large crease was imbedded in my right unshaven cheek, a temporary blemish caused by the way I had positioned the side of my face on the pillow. I gazed into the mirror, saddened by the image of the old man staring back at me.

Where in the hell is my shaving cream?

I finally located the can, and as I shook it, I realized that it was almost empty. As a result, the sparse amount applied to my face was not sufficient enough to cover my whiskers, causing the sharp razor to nick my face in several places. To absorb the bleeding, I placed small patches of toilet tissue on the cuts.

As I peered at my image in the mirror, it seemed that I had become shorter; for I used to be five-eleven, but now I appear to be only about five-nine. *Who is this short man staring back at me?*

I wet my remaining hair and ran a comb through it, noticing with a touch of disgust that a large clump of my hair remained in the comb. However, I was pleased with the reflected image of how much younger I looked after grooming myself.

I skipped making coffee. Instead, I got dressed and prepared to leave for the Cracker Barrel. All at once I remembered that today was Saturday, the day that Melissa always comes by about noon to check on me to see what I need for the coming week. Since I had planned to play golf with Dick for most of the day, I would need to leave her a note telling her that I wouldn't be home until late afternoon. I always leave the door unlocked just in case she or Marsha decides to pay one of their unexpected visits. Maybe I should install a revolving door, considering the way that Marsha, Melissa, and their friends come and go with no warning and without even knocking. Even the widow Gertrude and my sister Jessica barge into my house whenever the mood strikes them. I have absolutely no privacy.

After leaving the note for Melissa, I limped out the door into the gray, cloudy morning. I then drove toward The Cracker Barrel to meet my friends.

There was a time in the not-too-distant past that I poked fun at old men who gather in local restaurants in the morning, gossiping and swapping stories while drinking up all the coffee in the place.

"Why don't those old men get a life?" I had presumptuously remarked to someone. But that was when I had a life…that was before I lost Jenny…before I really knew the meaning of what loneliness can do to a man's spirit. Since I no longer have Jenny, I now understand the need for fellowship with someone…Anyone. We all have the need to associate and communicate with our own kind, no matter that the only common bond we have is that we are all lonely old men. Sometimes I would rather begin my day by having breakfast with complete strangers than to experience the loneliness of gazing across the breakfast table at home…staring at the empty chair across from me that once cradled the warm and comforting essence of Jenny. Besides, a lifetime of being surrounded by female family members gave me a craving for male companionship. Since the death of Jenny, I had felt socially out of place in my efforts to 'fit in' with society.

It had begun to sprinkle rain when I entered the restaurant. I knew that my breakfast companions had already arrived because it was past 8:00 o'clock, and our morning meetings usually last from about 7:30 to nearly 10:00. I couldn't yet see them because our meeting place was in one of the secluded areas in the back of the restaurant.

Judy, the young hostess stepped in front of me. "Mornin,' Sweetie!" She popped her gum as she spoke, "Just go right in...Your buddies are all waitin' for you, Honey."

Although I smiled and thanked her, the "Honey" with which she addressed me made me wince, for I knew that the term meant that she saw me as an old "codger"...A harmless, childish old man who had long ago outlived his usefulness and who now posed no sexual threat to women. *Why do some young women see elderly men as child-like and "cute"?*

When I joined my buddies in the back room, they were eating breakfast and already engaged in an elaborate discussion. The men were all present; each in his usual chair, for it was viewed as almost a sacrilege for any of us to change the seating arrangement. They scarcely noticed my arrival, except for a grinning Dick Noble, who quickly stood and warmly shook my hand.

In his demeanor and manner of dress, Dick stood out from the others like a rose in a patch of ragweed. His cohorts were slouched in their usual chairs wearing nondescript clothing commonly worn by the typical retired man. But Dick had always refused to accept the fact that he is an old man. In his gaudy red and yellow Hawaiian shirt and white pants, his projected image suggested that he was a young, wealthy vacationer on Miami Beach instead of an old overweight has-been sitting in the Cracker Barrel in a hick town in Tennessee.

The lifts he wore in his glossy black shoes made

him appear taller. His handsome face had always reminded me of some celebrity, but I couldn't put a name to the likeness. Stylish sunglasses hid his eyes even in rainy weather; and the crowning touch was an obvious blonde toupee that didn't match his hair color resting somewhat precariously on top of his head.

Sometimes Dick's pretentiousness irritated me, but I had never mentioned it to him; for his affected demeanor and garish clothing were as much a part of him as his name.

The loud discussion in progress at our table indicated that our group members were oblivious to the fact that their voices could be heard by others at nearby tables.

Our daily gathering of retirees reflected a drastic difference in personality types. There were five people in our group: Sam Hedley presided over the group and sat in the center. Known as "Head" to the others, he was a widower, a retired contractor and the un-elected leader of the "panel." His toothless mouth caused him to lisp when he spoke.

Beside him sat Percival Pinkney, who to the group was "Pinky" or "P.P." Since he often dribbled in his pants, the latter nickname seemed more appropriate. A retired bookkeeper, his obsessive-compulsive personality had caused his wife to move out of their house. His obsession with cleanliness made it extremely difficult for him to cope with the urine spots that perpetually stained the front of his pants. Due to his queasy stomach, he was easily nauseated; sometimes the mere mention of human body excretions made him physically ill. Ironically, however, he had a fixation about his inability to have a satisfactory bowel movement.

Floyd Sutton was the group slob. Because of his impaired hearing he was known as "Dummy." In order to make sense of any conversation he found it necessary to read the lips of the speaker. A divorced, retired truck driver, he was the sloppiest member of our morning ritual. His bulging stomach hung over the front of his drooping pants, which sagged so low on his hips that when bending forward he exposed the top half of his butt crack. The contrast between his filthy, disgusting habits and the neurotic neatness of Pinky made them despise one another, which explains their seating assignment to opposite ends of the table.

Dick and I, of course, sat side-by-side and completed the unlikely brotherhood.

I tuned in during the middle of a rather heated discussion about the war in Iraq. Head was itemizing the indisputable facts, for residing in his bald head was the *wisdom of the ages*. Although he had never finished high school, something about his overbearing personality and arrogant self-confidence inspired his followers to believe that his word was law. His right-wing political views were mirrored in the attitudes of both Dick and Dummy, but stood in sharp contrast to those held by Pinky and me; however, I never argued politics with anyone but Dick, and sometimes not even with him.

"Tell you what they ort'a do," Head stated with authority."They ort'a get this Iraq War over with once and for all...They ort'a 'nuke' the whole damn country!"

Dick spoke up, "Well, I'm for winnin' the war, but nuking the whole country is a little drastic."

Pinky was outraged, "You'd destroy the whole country? What about all the women and children?"

Head slammed his fist to the table. "They're all foreigners! That's the biggest thing wrong with our country—foreigners! They're all takin' over! Niggers, Jews, Japs, Muslims, Mexicans…Hell, you name it! We need to ship them all back where they came from. I say, 'God Bless America'!"

Apparently, Head was still fighting not only today's War against Terrorism, but the Mexican War, World War II, and the Civil War as well.

Dummy spoke through the gigantic clump of sausage biscuit in his mouth, "Tell it like it is, Head!" Crumbs from his mouth fell to the table as Pinky glared at him in disgust.

The waitress, Marlene appeared with a pencil and order pad. She grinned at me.

"You came in kinda late this mornin' didn't you, Sweetheart? I'll bet your buddies here already have all the World's problems solved. What'll ya' have, honey?"

"Hi, Marlene. I'll have sausage and eggs—with biscuits and a cup of coffee," I answered. She jotted down my order and walked away.

Dummy removed the top half of his second sausage biscuit. "Pass the salt, Tom."

I passed the shaker to him and he proceeded to carelessly sprinkle salt on his sandwich. His vigorous application of the salt scattered grains around the tabletop.

Pinky glared at him with loathing. "Do you have to be so messy that you get salt all over the table?" Dummy sneered at him, for he delighted in agitating Pinky.

"Would you mind passing the salt back to me please?" asked Pinky politely, in his effeminate voice.

Dummy carelessly tossed the shaker back across the table on its side so that a handful of grains scattered on the tabletop as it slid. He again sneered at Pinky.

Pinky didn't use the salt, but placed it in the exact center of the table in precise alignment with the peppershaker, for he was obsessed with order and neatness. With his paper napkin he carefully wiped the scattered grains of salt to the edge of the tabletop and into his hand. With uncertainty about what to do with the salt grains and napkin, he dumped the grains into his shirt pocket. Then after meticulously folding the napkin into a small neat square, he carefully placed it beside his coffee cup, making sure that it was perfectly parallel to the edge of the table. He glanced at the ballpoint pen in his shirt pocket and fastidiously repositioned it in the center of the pocket. Dummy rolled his eyes and shook his head in revulsion.

"Pass the ketchup, Tom," said Dummy.

After I passed it to him, he repeated the same routine as he had with the salt, generously drenching his biscuit and the tabletop with a spattering of ketchup. He again smirked at Pinky.

"Why do you have to do that?" asked Pinky, in frustration.

"Knock it off guys, you're actin' like kids," Head commanded. "Now what was I talkin' about?" he continued.

"Foreigners," I said. The waitress brought my breakfast and I began to eat.

"Oh, yeah," he answered, "Hell, let's change the

subject…I get mad when I discuss foreigners."

"Let me ask you gentlemen something," interjected Pinky, being careful to correctly pronounce each syllable. "Do any of you gentlemen have a problem with regularity?"

"Huh? Speak up, I can't hear you! What was it about regularity?" asked Dummy.

Head interrupted in a booming voice, "He asked if any of us ever has trouble with taking a crap!" His thundering voice and the subject under discussion brought stares from nearby patrons.

"What's the matter, ain't your Metamucil workin'?" inquired Dick.

"Yes, most of the time, but I was talking to a gentleman the other day who said that there is some kind of herb tea that is more efficient," said Pinky, with perfect enunciation.

"Do we have to talk about this crap while we're eatin'?" asked Dummy, "Don't you guys have any respect for etiquette?" Ketchup dripped from his scraggly gray moustache that blended into the generous growth of hair protruding from his nostrils.

"You're a heck of an example to talk about etiquette," snapped Pinky, "I'll bet you haven't had a bath in ten years! And look at the way your shirt is buttoned in the wrong holes."

"Knock it off," said Head. "People are lookin' at us." He signaled to the waitress, Marlene for another round of coffee refills.

Dummy looked toward the people seated in a nearby table. Because of his impaired hearing he had developed the irritating habit of near shouting when he spoke.

"Hey, fellers," he boomed, "ain't that Homer Parker over there? I ain't seen him in twenty years I bet! Ain't he the guy that has that sister that used to bang half of the guys in town?"

Homer Parker glared back with an icy stare.

"You'd better tone it down a little, Dummy," I whispered, "Or that guy might just bang the hell out of *you.*"

"Huh?" Dummy stared at me in bewilderment. "You say his Aunt Belle has the flu?"

"Yeah, Dummy," I said. I turned to Dick. "Look Dick, I didn't sleep much last night, and I turned my ankle a couple of days ago...Can I beg off playing golf today? Maybe we can play when my ankle is better." I showed him my ankle.

He looked at it and whistled. "Man, I'll bet that's sore! Sure we can cancel out our golf today...It's gonna rain anyway."

I washed down the last bite of my biscuit with coffee. "I'll call you Dick, as soon as my ankle is better."

I stood and gestured to the group, "See you tomorrow, guys."

"I'm leaving, too," declared Pinky, as he stood I noticed that he had dribbled in the front of his pants.

* * *

The rain fell heavily during the drive to my home. I pulled into my driveway and parked behind Melissa's car. I figured that she would be surprised to see me after my note to her had implied that I wouldn't be home for most of the day. At the house next door, Silas Wooten eyed me from between the curtains of his living room window. Being the neighborhood gossip, he was always curious about any car other than mine that was parked in my driveway.

I felt under my seat for my umbrella, but it wasn't there.

I must have left it somewhere. *How many umbrellas have I lost?*

To avoid getting soaked I skipped along on my right foot as rapidly as I could to the side door and hurriedly stepped inside. The hectic activity caused my swollen left ankle to throb.

The lights were off when I entered the kitchen. The note that I had written was lying on the kitchen table.

"Melissa!" I called out. Silence. I walked through the dark dining room into the den, which was lit by a single small lamp.

"Melissa!" I yelled again. No answer. Room by room I searched the house, saving my bedroom until last. When I entered the room, the lamp was off, but the window offered sufficient light to reveal the rumpled bed. In the semi-darkness I could barely detect a careless distribution of discarded clothing on the floor.

"Melissa!"

The noise that came from behind my closed closet door sounded like giggling.

"Melissa—is that you in there?"

"Yes, Dad...(giggle) Is that you out there?"

"Yes, of course! Who else would it be? I live here, you know!"

"Daddy, go back out into the den...I'll be right out."

"Why should I go into the den? Come on out and stop acting silly!"

"I'm not dressed properly, Dad."

"What do you mean you're not dressed properly? Are you changing clothes? Why are you changing clothes in my closet?"

"Dad…I'm naked!"

"Naked?"

"Yeah, naked!"

"Melissa, what the hell is going on? Is there someone in there with you?"

"I'll explain it to you when I come out. Just go back into the den until I come out, okay? I'll be right out as soon as I dress."

I retreated to the den and paced the floor.

What the hell is going on? Is Melissa going nuts? Why would she be hiding in a dark closet, naked...?

...There must be a guy in there with her!

That would explain the rumpled bed and the clothes scattered on the floor. They had heard me coming in, and before I caught them in the act, they hid in the closet. *Why had I been so slow in recognizing the obvious?*

Maybe I ought to give her time to dress and then I can get one of my golf clubs and tee off on the guy! I realize that it is her life, but it is my house! She quickly appeared in the den wearing a pink bathrobe that had belonged to Jenny. Her bashful but naughty smile conjured up memories of the distant past when she was my mischievous little girl. Standing in front of me in Jenny's bathrobe, she was as breathtakingly beautiful as her mother.

"What's going on, Melissa? Who was in there with

you? Don't lie to me!"

"I won't lie to you, Daddy. Why should I? You and I have never lied to each other."

She stepped forward and hugged me tightly. She smelled like Jenny.

"Tell me who he is, Melissa!" I said, "No, hell, I don't care who he is, I just want him out of my house! You thought I'd be gone all day, so you use my house for your lovemaking." Melissa released me.

"Dad, don't get so worked up! I have an apartment of my own…It's just that we came by here…and well, it just happened. He's gonna leave as soon as he gets dressed…And his name is Steve."

"I want to talk to him…Maybe even knock the hell out of him. When's he coming out?" I wasn't sure how to handle the situation.

"Dad, listen to me! He's a very nice guy, so don't talk mean to him when he comes out, okay?"

"Melissa, I can't believe you let a guy make love to you right on your mother's bed. Don't you have any respect for her?"

"Yes Dad, I respect Mom…I still love her with all my heart…But she's dead! But I'm not dead, Daddy, and neither are you—we're alive! And unless you want to live like you're dead too, then it's time you live a little bit! Maybe you ought to marry again, so you'll have a companion. I mean, a woman with passion…but not someone like Gertrude."

"I could never marry another woman. I honor your mother too much for that. And you're not married. What are you doing having sex?"

"Daddy, life is short. I've been married twice, and I guess I screwed up both times. But does that mean that I'll have to marry again and maybe make another mistake before I can enjoy intimacy with the opposite sex? It's a basic need that we all have Dad! Even you! Mom's been dead now for ten years. How long has it been since you've enjoyed female companionship?"

"Well, I have sort of a relationship with Gertrude." I said, lamely.

Melissa winced when she heard the name. "Dad, Gertrude is not what you need. You need a real woman…a woman with spirit like Mom had."

"How did this conversation get turned around so that we're talking about me? I still want you to get that guy out of here! Where is he anyway…? How come he hasn't come out of the bedroom?"

I quickly strode toward the bedroom while Melissa tried to restrain me.

"Please Dad, give him time to come out!" she pleaded, "He's just shy and dreads facing you."

I pulled loose from her and opened the bedroom door. The room was empty. The window was open and the silky curtains adorning the window were floating gently in the morning breeze.

"Damn, just another loser!" Melissa walked away in disgust.

Chapter 3

Sunday morning has always been a depressing time for me. It brings back the sad feelings that I experienced when I was working full-time because it meant returning to work the following day. I had decided to stay home from church since I was not in the mood to be stalked by Gertrude Gossage, the widow who, with the full support of my sister Jessie and my daughter, Marsha, had designs on marrying me. Anyway, it was raining and my swollen ankle gave me a plausible excuse.

The fender-bender that I had last night when I went to McDonald's for my evening meal had left me anxious. It was just a matter of time until I got a lecture about my driving from Marsha and her Aunt Jessie…Maybe even from Melissa. I hoped that none of them had heard about it yet.

Gertrude would probably be calling me after church wondering why I wasn't there. "We missed you in church, Thomas," she would probably say, "Are you sick? Thomas, living there in that lonesome house all by yourself is not good for you. You need someone to help take care of you."

Yeah...Right. She intended for that "someone" to be her.

I dreaded calling the insurance company tomorrow to discuss my accident. Using the telephone used to be simple, but making a call to a large company was now a nightmare. The last time I called an insurance company I had to talk to a machine with an Asian accent. I became lost in a hopeless maze of numbers that the machine instructed me to punch. In frustration, I had finally hung up the phone and drove sixty miles to the insurance company where I could actually talk to a human being.

The purpose of advanced technology should be to simplify things; but with each new development it seems that the world gets more complicated. I realize that I don't belong in this high-tech world; I am an anachronism—Marsha has often called me a "dinosaur."

Worrying about my auto accident had given me a headache. I got up from the couch and walked to the kitchen where I selected a new bottle of aspirin from the cabinet.

"Press downward and turn," said the lettering on the cap. I soon discovered that it required the strength of a gorilla to push down with sufficient force to allow the cap to release so I could open the bottle. After several attempts I finally was able to push down hard enough to open it. But beneath the cap was a seal that required peeling back with my fingernail—which I had recently trimmed to a nub. I finally removed the seal only to discover a ball of cotton in the tiny neck of the bottle. The neck was too narrow for me to get my finger underneath the cotton ball in order to remove it. Each insertion of my finger only drove the cotton ball deeper into the bottle. When I continued probing, I got my little finger stuck in the bottle. I considered smashing the bottle with a hammer, but I feared cutting myself; also, I wasn't sure if I could find my hammer. After several attempts, I finally freed my finger from the bottle.

I began to search for a pair of tweezers. But who in the hell can ever find tweezers? After locating a toothpick, with several probing attempts at the illusive ball of cotton, I was finally able to remove it. By this time I really had a headache so I took four aspirin instead of my usual dosage of two. *When did opening a bottle of aspirin become such an enormous task?*

I returned to the den and began reading the Sunday morning *Northridge Banner.* From habit, I first turned to the obituaries, a routine that I had developed a few years ago—when I officially became old. I discovered that Frank Mercer, another of my old classmates had died at age sixty-eight. Not many of us are left now.

In the Local section of the paper, I noticed that my high school graduating class of 1954 was having a fiftieth reunion on the weekend of July 4th. Since so many of my classmates had died, the reunion committee had combined the classes of 1950 through 1954 in order to have enough people in attendance.

I hadn't gone to a class reunion in about twenty years, and I decided to be a "no-show" at this one too. Besides, there would be no way to attend without taking

Gertrude, who was in my graduating class.

I began to think of my reluctant relationship with Gertrude Gossage. She is a nice enough lady, but I have never felt the slightest bit of attraction to her; as a matter of fact, I have always felt somewhat repulsed by her. For starters, she is physically unattractive. She is taller than I and about thirty pounds overweight. Her thinning, shortly cropped gray hair in combination with her rugged facial features make her look like an elderly man. The determined set of her jaw is the result of an under-bite that gives her face a resemblance to that of a bulldog's. Actually, she could probably pass for a linebacker for the *Tennessee Titans.* She is also a gossiper and a hypochondriac, for she is always complaining of her aches and pains. In addition, she is an eternal pessimist, always predicting the worst. She is racially prejudiced, particularly against African-American men; as a result, she holds the perverted belief that their major passion in life is the seduction of white women. Her obsession with the subject makes me wonder if it is only wishful thinking on her part.

Gertrude is also an avid student of the obituaries. Having a morbid fascination with death, she probably attends more funerals than anyone in Northridge, even those of people she doesn't know.

She has three dogs and seven cats, which she seems to like more than people. She also exudes a peculiar smell; for her strong perfume appears to be mixed with some other chemical ingredient that gives off the pronounced odor of Pine-Sol. I figure it has something to do with some kind of deodorant or disinfectant she uses in some way in attending to her animals.

But Gertrude has always been good to me. Since Jenny's death, she has shown a concern for me, often preparing special meals that she usually delivers to my house with my sister Jessie, her best friend. I guess that could explain why Marsha and Jessie are always trying to play matchmaker between us. Even in high school, Gertrude had a crush on me, and I supposed that she hadn't yet given up on snagging me.

It was a rainy, dismal morning, so I decided to take a nap. I noticed that it was almost noon when I dropped the newspaper to the floor and lay down on the couch. Sometime this afternoon I would call Dick and see if he wanted to play golf tomorrow. Since I had not slept well for several nights, the sound of the wind and rain sweeping the window above the couch was like music to my ears, and soon it seduced me into a peaceful sleep.

*　　　　*　　　　*

"Thomas! Thomas! What's wrong—are you sick?" Jessie's high-pitched voice had ended my heavenly nap. I looked up to see her and Gertrude peering down at me. Again, they had barged into my house without knocking.

"We missed you in church, Dear…Are you sick?" Jessie seemed concerned.

"No, I'm not sick. I'm just taking a nap…or at least I *was* taking a nap!" I snarled.

"Well, Gertrude and I were worried about you," nagged Jessie, "You shouldn't be sleeping during the day, Thomas, because it will keep you awake at night. Why are you sleeping in the daytime?"

"Because I didn't get much sleep last night," I replied.

The look on Gertrude's face became even more tragic. "You poor man," she sighed.

Jessie looked sternly at me. "Well, like I just told you, the reason you didn't get much sleep last night is because you sleep during the day, like you were just doing," she lectured, "Sleeping during the day will keep you awake at night."

No Shit! I thought to myself. *What brilliant logic!*

"Thomas, you don't look well," moaned Gertrude, "I'm afraid you don't eat healthy foods."

"Don't worry about it, Gertrude," I said, "I eat what I like to eat."

"You look like you've lost some more weight," added Jessie, "You're getting skinny."

"My God, Jessie," I said, "Slimness runs in our family. Look at how slim you are…You could put on a few pounds yourself!"

Physically, Jessie's appearance is in direct contrast to that of Gertrude's. Jessie is small and slim, and her long jet-black hair is usually done up in a bun on the back of her head. Her facial features are attractive and smooth, making her appear younger than her age of seventy. Jessie had never married, and upon the death of Gertrude's husband twenty years ago, she had become her best friend. As soon as their friendship blossomed, they had joined in a unified effort to direct my life.

I rose to a sitting position on the couch. Jessie looked accusingly at me. "Are you taking your medicine regularly, Thomas?"

"Yes—don't worry about it."

"How about your Metamucil?" she asked.

"Of course. Do we have to talk about *that?"*

"You know how cranky you get when you forget to take your Metamucil." She shook her finger at me to emphasize the point.

Gertrude looked at me with sympathy. "I'll bring you some supper over here tonight," she said. "Thomas, I can tell by looking at you that you're not eating right."

"I'm eating fine Gertrude. Look, I really do appreciate your concern about my eating habits…And I appreciate your bringing food to me like you do. But please don't bring any food tonight because I'm having dinner with Dick Noble." I lied.

Jessie glared at me. "That Dick Noble is not a good influence on you, Thomas," she scolded, "I hear all kinds of stories about him."

"What kinds of stories?" I asked.

"Stories too awful to repeat! Stories about his wild carryings-on with younger women!" She was again wagging her finger at me.

"Well, I'd say that Dick is pretty well living up to his name," I commented dryly. Gertrude appeared to be in shock. I felt sorry for her.

"Look, Jessie…and Gertrude—I've gotta get dressed and meet somebody in a few minutes," I lied, "But I do appreciate your concerns about me, and the way you stopped to check on me." I began to gently usher them toward the door.

"Who do you have to see on Sunday that's so important? It's not that awful Dick Noble, is it?" Jessie looked concerned.

"No, Jessie, it's not Dick Noble," I said, "Why are you being so nosy?"

As they left by the side door, Jessie turned to me and said, "Oh, by the way Thomas...What caused that big dent in the side of your car?" She pointed at my vehicle.

"Jessie, are you just now noticing that? I did that weeks ago," I again lied.

I breathed a sigh of relief at their departure.

As I limped back to the couch on my swollen left ankle, I noticed that my arthritis was again flaring up in my right knee...*Oh great! Now I'll have to somehow limp on both legs.* From the pain in my knee I knew that I'd need a stronger painkiller than aspirin. I gingerly shuffled along to the medicine cabinet in the bathroom and took two hydrocodone tablets.

The instant that I reclaimed my seat on the couch, Marsha suddenly entered the door and walked into the den. I again thought about the convenience of installing a revolving door, or better yet, a dead-bolt lock.

The rigid stance that she assumed as she faced me indicated that she had already heard about my minor auto accident.

"Hi, Dad. Is everything going okay with you?" At least she had the courtesy to greet me properly before launching into her tirade.

"Hi, Marsha," I answered hesitantly, "Yeah, I'm getting along alright except for the fact that I turned my left ankle jogging and I have a touch of arthritis in my right knee."

"Why don't you go to see a doctor?" she asked.

"Well, even if I did I'd still have arthritis and a sprained ankle," I explained.

"But maybe he could prescribe more pain medication for you," she suggested.

"I already have some pain pills, Marsha. As a matter of fact, I just took two of them."

"You took two?" She seemed outraged. "You're just supposed to take one pill every four hours! You'll get high on two pills! You don't take those things when you drive, do you?"

Here it comes. A lecture about my driving.

"Yeah, Marsha, I do. Only sometimes before I drive, I take four pills so that when I have a collision I'll already be medicated when the ambulance picks me up." I answered sarcastically.

"Dad, get serious! Auto accidents are no laughing matter. I heard about your collision…I'm concerned about your driving!"

Marsha had always been lacking in a sense of humor.

"Well, it seems that news travels fast," I remarked, "How did you hear about it so quickly?"

"It's all over town, Dad! Everybody knows about it."

You'd think that I had committed the unpardonable sin. It serves me right for living in a small town.

"Marsha, calm down. It was no big deal. Just a little fender-bender. It could happen to anybody."

"How did it happen?" She queried.

"I ran a stop sign and this old lady rammed into the side of my car. She braked real quickly, so she only slightly bumped me."

"How come you ran a stop sign?" she asked.

"I didn't see it. Do you think I would run one on purpose?"

"Were you wearing your glasses, Dad?"

"No...As a matter of fact, I had lost them again before the little accident happened."

"Why didn't you call me when it happened?" she asked.

"I wasn't anywhere near a phone."

"Now, see? This is why I've told you repeatedly to get a cell phone!"

"I hate cell phones," I said.

"Yeah Dad, I know. You hate cell phones, computers, e-mail, and any other thing that can improve the quality of your life. I doubt if you can even use an old-fashioned adding machine. How do you add things—on your fingers? Dad, you need to join the rest of the world in the Twenty-First Century!"

"Marsha, I've done okay for more than sixty-eight years," I said, "I hate all those gadgets that you depend on. "

Marsha looked exasperated. "Dad, I'm worried about you living alone. You need someone to help take care of you."

"No, I don't need anyone to help take care of me! "I snapped, "And I want you and your Aunt Jessie to stop pushing that old widow Gertrude on me!"

"What's wrong with her, Dad? She's good to you, and she'd make good company for you. She's a good cook...also she loves you. Why don't you like her?"

"Because she looks like a bulldog and she smells like Pine-Sol," I answered, "And she is always complaining about her aches and pains. Besides, I still feel married to your mother."

"But Dad...Mom is not with us anymore," said Marsha,

"You're lonely here by yourself...You need a mate."

"Well, that may be true, but don't I have the right to choose my mate? A woman that appeals to me?"

"Dad, be realistic. A man your age can't expect to attract a woman who has the beauty of a movie star. Simple companionship should be enough...and somebody who can cook your meals. Aunt Jessie and I both feel that Gertrude is the right woman for you."

"You can forget about that, Marsha!" I said.

"Well, then I think its time for you to sell the house and move into an assisted living facility because both Aunt Jessie and I continually worry about you."

"What about Jessie? She's two years older than I am! You don't hound her about marrying someone or moving into assisted living," I said.

"Yeah, Dad, but Aunt Jessie has been living alone all her life. Also, she's a good cook and she seldom ever drives a car."

"Marsha, if it will make you feel better, I'll cut down on my driving...And I promise I'll try to eat better. But I don't know if I can ever warm up to Gertrude."

Marsha looked at her Rolex watch. "I've gotta go, Dad. Listen, I don't mean to nag you. I only try to give you advice because I love you, and I want the best for you."

"I know, Marsha," I said.

"Bye Dad," she said. I stood in silence as I watched her leave through the side door. I was glad the lecture was over. I wondered how bad it would be when Melissa confronted me.

Chapter 4

"Good Mornin,' sweetie," purred Judy, as she handed me the breakfast menu. "Your buddies are waitin' for you in your usual meetin' place, honey."

I thanked her and proceeded to walk toward my table.

With the exception of Head, who always presided over the group, the others were all assembled in their usual places eating their breakfast. Because of Head's absence, both Pinky and Dummy seemed somehow disoriented, and without Head's leadership, they seemed at a loss to bring up a subject for discussion.

I greeted the group and shook hands with Dick, and then ordered breakfast from Marlene, who had followed me to the table.

"I'm glad you called me last night, Tom," said Dick, "I got us a tee-time for ten o'clock. Do you think your ankle is well enough to play golf?"

"Well, actually no…but since we're getting a cart, I guess I can suffer through it."

Dick smiled and looked at his watch. "Well, we can't hang around here too long because we tee off in an hour."

My plate of bacon and eggs arrived and I began to eat. Dummy got up and headed for the restroom. His sagging blue jeans offered a generous view of the upper half of his butt crack as he walked away.

Head walked in and claimed his center seat at the table. When I looked at him, I hardly recognized him. He was wearing a new pair of horn-rimmed glasses with lens so thick that his magnified eyeballs appeared to be as big as golf balls. He flashed a proud smile, revealing a brand new ultra-white set of false teeth that appeared to be too large for his mouth. The bulbous size of his eyes combined with his gleaming, menacing dentures gave me the uneasy feeling that he was glaring at me just prior to sinking his fangs into me. The saliva dripping from the corners of his mouth confirmed the fact that he was not yet accustomed to his new teeth.

"Well, guys, how do you like the new *me*?" His ill-fitting teeth caused his speech to be almost unintelligible.

We all stared at him in amazement.

Pinky spoke up. "Well, your teeth are certainly white."

"Ain't they purty?" asked Head, "I got 'em fer $150.00 dollars down at the new Economy Dental Clinic!"

"And your eyes are a lot easier to see," continued Pinky.

Dummy returned from the restroom. Before he reclaimed his seat, I noticed that his drooping pants were unzipped. I started to point it out to him, but then I decided against it because I figured that he probably didn't care anyway.

Head smiled at him. "What do you think of my new teeth, Dummy?" Dummy's mouth fell open as he stared at Head in disbelief.

"Son of a bitch!" he exclaimed, "I hardly recognized you, Head!" His arched, bushy eyebrows bore a resemblance to those of Andy Rooney's.

Pinky spoke up. "By the way, fellows, that herb tea I tried *does* work better than Metamucil." He removed his spectacles and cleaned them before carefully replacing them on the bridge of his nose. He neatly folded the napkin and placed it in his shirt pocket.

"Huh? What'd ye say?" asked Dummy.

"I really don't like to repeat myself, Dummy," said Pinky, in a louder voice.

"The hell you don't!" said Dummy, "Every time you mispronounce a word in a sentence, you say the whole damned sentence over again!"

"Knock it off, fellas!" warned Head.

Pinky began to slowly nibble on his eggs while ignoring the strips of bacon on his plate. Dummy curiously watched him eat.

"You know, Pinky, I've been noticin' how peculiar you eat your food. You only eat one thing at a time...You ate your toast, now you're eatin' your eggs, and when you finish them, you'll eat your bacon. Why do you eat like that, Pinky? It seems to me that you'd alternate between things on your plate...Take a bite of eggs, then while you're chewin' on that, take a bite of bacon...kind of mix the taste of the two together while you're chewin' it up."

Pinky became more frustrated. "Yeah, that sounds

like the way a slob like you would eat. Just mix it all up in your mouth like a bunch of slop! If you're going to do that, why not just stir it all up in your plate like a bunch of garbage before you eat it? I'll just be neat with my eating style, if you don't mind!"

Head became angry. "Damn it, guys, can't we talk about something else? Why do you care how Pinky eats his food, Dummy?"

Dick peered over the top of his sunglasses and laughed. "Yeah, we've got the economy to fix, the war in Iraq to win, and health care issues to solve."

I smiled. "And you and I have a round of golf to play, Dick." I had always been a stickler for punctuality.

My remark prompted Dick to again look at his watch. "We've got plenty of time, Tom."

Dummy was not yet ready to end his goading of Pinky. "And another thing, Pinky," he sneered as he spoke, "I've noticed that every morning you eat the same thing for breakfast…bacon and eggs. You never order anything else. Don't you ever get curious about how something else might taste?"

Pinky glared at him. "I'm becoming very annoyed with you, Dummy."

"Knock it off, Dummy!" ordered Head.

After a brief period of pouting, Dummy gradually changed his mood. He looked at Dick.

"How about them Vols, Dick?"

"Well, they're a good team, but their offense is not consistent. They need a good runnin' back. Damn! I wish I was young enough to play football for Tennessee. Hell, I could put them into the national championship game!"

There was a momentary lapse in conversation as we continued to munch on our breakfast. Finally, Head looked up at an elderly man who waved at him as he entered the room. With a puzzled expression, Head waved back as the man claimed a seat with some of his friends.

"That guy who's sittin' down over there that just waved at me," commented Head, "I think I know him, but I can't seem to place him in my mind…who is he? Where do I know him from?"

Dick glanced at the man. "I think he went to high school with us. He wasn't very popular, as I remember."

Dummy turned his head and pointed at the man. Speaking in his usual loud voice he said, "You mean that guy in the red shirt?"

"Yeah," answered Head. He curiously eyed the man. "There's something about him that makes him stand out in my mind, but I can't seem to remember what it is."

Dummy announced in a booming voice, "Oh, you remember him…His name's Oscar…something. Don't you remember? He's the guy that sneezed and let that tremendous fart in economics class when we were seniors. Damn near shook the rafters!"

Apparently having heard the remark, the man in the red shirt and several of his cronies looked in our direction.

"Oh yeah," said Head, "Now I remember him. I knew there was something about him that stood out in my mind."

Pinky looked peeved. "Can't we discuss something more pleasant while we're eating?"

I also remembered the incident. It seems sad that the most enduring remembrance of every person is defined by his worst moment. The guy might have been an honor student, a star on the debating team, or a talented band member; but he would not be remembered for any such accomplishment. Sadly, the deed for which he was most remembered was confined to that one isolated incident: The unfortunate moment when he had released that spectacular, thunderous expulsion of gas. The vivid memory of that single, ill-timed event had endured for more than fifty years, to be forever enshrined in the annals of Northridge High School folklore. Yet, we laughed at the memory of it.

Pinky changed the subject. "I saw in the paper where our graduating class is having a reunion over the fourth of July weekend."

"Yeah, I noticed that," said Dick. He turned to face me. "Are you goin' Tom?"

"I don't think so, Dick," I said, "I haven't been to one of those things in twenty years. Where are they having it, anyway?"

"In the high school gym," replied Head, "I think they're combinin' two or three graduating classes so there'll be enough people to have it. Reckon there'll be any of the old football team attendin,' Dick?"

"I don't know," answered Dick, "Not many of us are left. Man, we had a powerhouse team back in fifty-four…went undefeated for three years in a row!"

"Yeah, we had a great team," said Dummy, "Remember when you ran two kickoffs back for touch-downs in the same game? What game was that, anyhow, Dick?"

"That was the game with Springwater," replied

Dick, "Remember that time I took that pitch-out from the quarterback in the East Hampton game and ran ninety-nine yards for a touchdown?"

Dick loved to relive his football heroics, and I realized that if he really got cranked up, I'd never get him out of the restaurant and onto the golf course. I peered at my watch. "We've gotta go, Dick, or we'll miss our tee time."

"Oh, we've got a few more minutes," said Dick. He continued to ramble on about his miraculous feats in football, embellishing his achievements as he recounted them.

Dummy pulled out his handkerchief and vigorously blew his nose with a resounding honk that caused several nearby patrons to stare at us.

"Damn it, Dummy," complained Pinky, "Can't you see that I'm trying to eat?"

"I gotta do something about my sinus problem," complained Dummy, "I blew my nose when I got up this mornin' and all that came out was pure pus. I gotta go to the doctor and get a check-up. My hemorrhoids have been actin' up, too. I may have to eventually have surgery."

Dick looked at him. "You'd better tell the doctor about those hemorrhoids for sure, before they get worse. You know that old sayin'...*A stitch in time saves nine."* Dick had always had an irritating fondness for uttering hackneyed adages.

"That's enough, damn it!" griped Pinky, "I'm leaving! A guy can't even enjoy his breakfast around you guys!" After carefully aligning his silverware beside his plate, he left his remaining breakfast and, in robotic fashion, marched out of the room.

"Now see, Dummy, you've run him off!" said Head. "Why do you pick on him so much?"

Dummy looked agitated. "I can't stand his little 'picky' ways. He drives me crazy with the little lists he keeps, the way he corrects people, the way he itemizes everything he's gonna do every day, his compulsive neatness… Even the way he eats pisses me off!" To a lesser extent, Dummy's description of Pinky's odd personality traits resembled those of mine.

"Hell, get over it, Dummy," said Head.

I again looked at my watch. Oblivious to the time, Dick launched into another exaggerated story about his football glory days.

"Damn it, Dick, let's go!" I got up from my chair. "We're supposed to be playing golf! Unless we leave now, I'm going home! We're already late for our tee time!"

"Okay, pal…Keep your shirt on!" Dick rose from his chair. "See you, guys…I'll tell you the rest of the story tomorrow." He smiled and put his beefy arm around my shoulders. "Come on, Tom, let's go have some fun!"

I slowly limped toward the door as Dick followed closely behind.

Chapter 5

Dick removed his driver from his golf bag and teed up his ball.

"How about we play for about two dollars a hole, Tom?"

"You're on!" I answered. It was our tradition—to bet on each hole, but neither of us ever paid off—another part of the tradition. Had we even bothered to keep a record over the years, I probably would have owed Dick hundreds of dollars.

He hit a beautiful drive down the center of the fairway, and I followed his shot with a severe slice that sailed deep into the rough on the right. Our first shots more or less established the pattern for the day, for by the end of the round, Dick had beaten me by at least twelve strokes. However, my arthritis was better, and the use of the golf cart spared my swollen left ankle from further aggravation.

In the clubhouse after the match, Dick and I ordered

beers and relaxed in the comfort of the air conditioning that felt cold on our sweating bodies.

"Your golf game's a little rusty, pal," said Dick.

"Yeah, for some reason I had a hard time getting my mind on golf," I answered.

"What's wrong, Tom? You worried about something?"

"Well, not exactly *worried*..I'm more frustrated and aggravated than worried."

With a puzzled expression, Dick eyed me closely. I noticed that his toupee was lopsided.

"Dick, you need to straighten your hairpiece," I informed him, "It kinda looks like all your hair is growing out of the left side of your head."

He laughed and gazed into the wall mirror that hung above our booth and realigned his toupee.

"Okay, so what are you frustrated about?" he queried.

"Several things. Sometimes I feel like a damned wimp. For instance, the other day I went home and caught Melissa in bed with some bastard!"

Dick looked shocked. "What did you do?"

"That's just it...I didn't do anything. Before I had a chance he went out the bedroom window."

Dick exploded with laughter. "Hell, Tom, don't sweat it! Melissa's a pretty woman and has the same needs and desires that you and I have. Is that all that's botherin' you?" He again chuckled.

"No, there's this other situation that's aggravating me. Marsha and Jessie are always trying to push that Gertrude on me...And they'd really like to see me marry her so she can *take care* of me. I'm such a wimp that I've given in to their wishes to a certain extent, but it'll be a cold day in hell when I marry that woman!"

"You can lead a horse to water but you can't make him drink!" He said, profoundly. (Another of Dick's adages). He again laughed. "I'd disown you as a friend if you ever married that old bag. Why's your sister so hell-bent on you marrying her?"

"She thinks that Gertrude is a good influence on me," I said.

"Good God, man! If I ever went to bed with that woman, I'd have to put a sack over her head! What's that funny smell she always seems to have?"

"I don't know…Pine-Sol maybe?"

"Yeah—that's what it smells like. Why does your sister think she's a good influence on you?"

"I don't know. Maybe for the same reason that she thinks you are a *bad* influence on me," I replied.

Dick laughed uproariously. "Man, your sister Jessie never did like me…I wonder why?"

"She thinks that you engage in sex marathons with young women."

Dick again laughed, then became quiet. He finally spoke. "Tom, I'm worried about you."

"You too, huh? Melissa, Marsha, Jessie, Gertrude, and now you. Everybody's worried about poor old Tom!" I hung my head.

"Well Tom…You know that you've always been my best friend—ever since high school. You know what you need to do? Get away from here for awhile…Escape some of Marsha and Jessie's naggin' and get away from that dog-faced Gertrude. Why don't you and I breeze down to New Orleans for a week or so?"

"I've got my business to think of," I alibied.

"Close it for a few days."

"No, that's not the real reason, Dick," I said, "You know damn well that I don't have the money to go away for a week."

"Money's no problem, Tom. I'll foot the bill. You know that money has never been an issue between us."

"I know, Dick…and I appreciate the offer. I'd love to go to New Orleans with you, but only if I could pay my own way. I was never able to make money like you."

"You know Tom, to be so smart in books, you've always been as dumb a hell when it comes to makin' money."

I snapped back at him. "You're a hell of an example to accuse anyone of being dumb! You couldn't have even made a living if your influential, jock-sniffing college buddies hadn't worshiped the great Dick Noble's football heroics. Luckily for you, they set you up with that cushy job in Knoxville—even before you finished college."

"Tom, in this dog-eat-dog world you have to take all the help you can get. You know, you should have listened to your daughter Marsha. You should have taken a job with a big corporation years ago. Look at all the fringe benefits they give: Vacations, sick leave, paid insurance."

"Without a college education? What kind of job could I have gotten? Working on an assembly line somewhere?" I was getting frustrated.

"Well, you should have gone to college. With your brains you could have called your own shots in the corporate world."

I glared at him. "How could I have gone to college? I had a family to support!"

"Tom, I loved Jenny. She was like a sister to me. You could never have found a better wife...But you married too young. How old were you, anyway...eighteen?"

"You know damn well why I married so early. Jenny was pregnant."

Dick looked at me sadly. "That's life pal. We reap what we sow...No pun intended. Let's face it Tom. You shouldn't have knocked her up."

I became more irritated. "You've got a lot of gall to give lectures about not knocking up women. Look at the hundreds of woman you've laid in your lifetime. You're *still* taking women to bed. You're just lucky you never got a woman pregnant, because I can't see you ever using a condom. As a matter of fact, there's no telling how many little 'Dick Nobles' you've spawned. How can you stand not knowing how many children you have?"

"I know exactly how many kids I have. Nada, zero, zilch. There is only one Dick Noble, and here I am in the flesh."

I rolled my eyes. "Yeah, and I know you well...spontaneous, always living on the edge, and never planning ahead for anything in your life..............." My words suddenly uncovered a stark truth. For the first time in my life, it shockingly occurred to me that Dick was sterile. During his promiscuous years, it was a lucky break for him. Nothing got in the way. But as I looked at him now, I wondered if he ever wished that he could change the terrible finality of it. We sat silently, staring into each other's eyes. Then, I blurted out the words…"I'll be damned! You've been shooting blanks all this time!"

"Shhh…you don't have to tell the whole world! Yeah, I've known it for years. But I tell you what, if I hadn't been sterile, I would have used a condom. I wouldn't be stupid enough to knock some woman up and screw up my life."

"Well, maybe I was that stupid," I confessed.

"Tom, I'm not blamin' you…Hell, it could happen to anybody. You shouldn't still be kickin' yourself in the ass over it. I shouldn't have brought it up. I hope you're not mad at me." Dick looked sad.

I smiled at him. "Forget it, Dick."

Dick instantly returned my smile. "I'll tell you what we should do, buddy. You're down in the dumps. We need to go to Knoxville together for a fun weekend. Remember that hot little gal I lined up for you last year? Well, she liked you and she's still available." His eyes lit up with the suggestion.

"I don't know, Dick. When I went to bed with that woman I felt somehow that I was cheating on Jenny. I felt guilty for a long time afterward."

Dick's face displayed a pained expression. "Tom, you were always faithful to Jenny, and she was a wonderful wife to you…But she's *dead,* Tom, and you're alive. I'll tell you what. Forget that little chick in Knoxville that made you feel so guilty. Come down to Florida with me for a week…We'll meet some new women. I know some real pretty women who live in Miami Beach. If you feel guilty so easy, just take it slow. You don't have to rush into anything. A day or two around some of the women I know will get rid of some of your guilt real quick."

"I don't know, Dick. I'd still feel guilty."

Dick thought for a moment. "Yeah, I kinda know how you feel. When I bedded down with that young thing in Knoxville last week, I felt guilty for a long time…probably for about ten minutes."

I laughed. "Dick, just being with you has raised my spirits. Let me think about that Florida trip for a few days. Maybe I'll talk it over with my sister Jessie…or maybe with Gertrude."

Dick winced. "Oh hell! If you mention it to them they'll probably have the Klan burn a cross in my yard."

I slowly stood, favoring my sore left ankle. I was beginning to feel stiff. "Got to get home Dick," I said, "If I don't get home by dinner time Marsha, Jessie, and Gertrude will have the police our looking for me!"

Dick laughed and rose from his chair. "I gotta go too, pal. I got a hot date tonight!"

We both shared a laugh and walked toward our cars. As we separated, Dick called to me, "Well, you lost to me again in golf. You owe me another twenty-four dollars."

I smiled and waved to him. "Put it on my tab."

Chapter 6

I parked my car in the usual space in front of my shop and killed the motor. It was only after I stepped out of my vehicle that I realized that I was again having another "senior moment." *Why did I drive here, to my shop? I had intended to drive to the post office!* Once again, I was frustrated by my absent-mindedness. When I left my house, I apparently had become so engrossed in thought that unconscious habit had replaced my conscious thought. *Oh well, since I'm already here, I might as well check my messages. I can go to the post office later.*

I tore the note from the clipboard that hangs in its usual manner on the front door of my shop. It displays a notepad so that potential customers can jot down messages whenever I am not there—which lately is most of the time.

I squinted at the blurred letters on the note while at the same time patted my empty pockets in search of my forgotten eyeglasses.

Shit! These bleary old eyes are worse than my hand - icapped mind! In anger, I crammed the crumpled note deep into my pants' pocket and finally unlocked the front door. I stepped inside the shop, and from across the room the large illuminated numerals on the phone receiver told me that I had five new messages.

Damn! More business. More of doing something that I have no enthusiasm for doing.

I located a magnifying glass and saw that the note from the clipboard turned out to be a reminder from Dick about the upcoming class reunion. Four of the phone messages were from people with foreign accents…all trying to sell me something. Only the fifth message held the promise of potential business.

I called the number and talked to the owner of a local business who was fishing for the lowest quote he could get for a small real estate sign. He gave me the specifications for the sign and I gave him an inflated estimate. He declared that my quote was ridiculously high and hung up on me. Since I didn't feel that compelled to work, I was immensely relieved. I deleted the messages from the phone, re-hung the clipboard on the front door, locked up, and drove away toward home.

I realized that in order to pay the bills I would eventually have to knuckle down and do some work in my shop, but lately I was becoming increasingly more apathetic about my business. In the old days—the time before signs were produced by a computer, I loved my work; for signs of the past were rendered by hand, requiring a certain amount of artistic skill from the craftsman. In addition, I was one of the few people in the area who possessed the required skills, which mostly gave me a corner on the market.

But with the introduction of computer graphics, I had begun to dislike my profession. Artistic skill had been replaced with expertise in technology. Vinyl lettering, produced by a machine, made hand-painted lettering obsolete, which enabled the experienced computer nerds with absolutely no artistic skill to open small sign businesses, sometimes in the basements of their homes. Prices came down as more small businesses sprang up. Although I had installed expensive computerized equipment in my shop and had become somewhat proficient in their use, I no longer enjoyed the work. Modern technology had left me behind. (Actually, it hadn't left me behind…I just wasn't interested).

From the time that I had married Jenny, I had always operated my own small business. I never accumulated much money, and since my semi-retirement three years ago, my small IRA account and Social Security benefits have kept me fairly solvent, although there has been little extra money for pleasure.

I pulled into the driveway, noticing Jessie's car parked at the curb in front of my house.

What's she doing here at 10:00 in the morning? Is something wrong?

The improved condition of my left ankle enabled me to walk briskly into the house, half-expecting to hear some tragic news. I hurriedly entered the side door to the den and quickly detected the distinct odor of Pine-Sol. Jessie and Gertrude stared up at me from their seats on the couch, both displaying elaborate smiles.

"Jessie!" I said, "What are you doing here this early in the morning? You never visit me until the afternoon. Is something wrong?"

"No, Thomas, nothing's wrong. Gertrude came to my house to visit me and to bring some lunch that she had prepared for you. She wanted me to bring it to you. Wasn't that sweet of her? And I just thought it would be nice if I brought her with me so that she could give it to you herself." She turned to face Gertrude, "That's so sweet of you Gertrude…Isn't that sweet of her, Thomas?"

My heart sank. "Why yes, Gertrude…that was sure nice of you…Thank you."

Gertrude's pronounced underbite gave her smiling face the appearance of a growling bulldog.

"Good morning, Thomas," she greeted, in her sexiest tone. She picked up a large paper bag from the floor and placed it on the coffee table. It obviously contained my lunch.

"Yeah…Good morning, Gertrude," I replied.

Jessie again smiled at me, "I figured that you wouldn't be working this morning with that terrible ankle of yours, and with your arthritis, so I just brought Gertrude over here. I was surprised when we drove all the way over here to see you, only to find you gone. By the way, where were you, Thomas? Where have you been?"

"I drove over to my shop to check for phone messages," I explained.

"Well, I'm somewhat relieved," said Jessie, "At first, when I didn't see your car here, I thought you might have been out all night. But then I thought, how silly of me, because I quickly realized that you would never do anything to worry us like that."

"No, Jessie, I'd certainly never do anything like *that,"* I said resentfully.

Jessie eyed me curiously. "Thomas, have you heard about the class reunion your graduating class is having?"

"Yes, I heard about it. Dick Noble has told me about it a couple of times."

Jessie wagged her index finger at me. "Thomas, you need to stay away from that terrible man…Oh, the awful things I've heard about him…"

"You were talking about the reunion," I reminded her.

"Oh, yes, the reunion. Are you going? Of course you are. I'm sure you wouldn't miss that! And I was telling Gertrude that I bet you'd just love to take her!"

I panicked. "Wait a minute, Jessie! I'm not going! I hate class reunions…! I'm sorry, Gertrude—it's not because of you," I lied, "But I am definitely not going!" I suddenly felt sorry for Gertrude.

Jessie looked shocked. "Now, Thomas, you don't mean that. It's still a few days away, and I'm certain you'll change your mind…He doesn't mean that, Gertrude…I'm sure he'll go when he has time to think about it."

I quickly changed the subject, "Well, thanks for the lunch, Gertrude…I really appreciate it. But if you ladies will excuse me, I've got a lot of things to do today. By the way, that's a mighty big sack you've put my lunch in…I doubt if I can eat that much food."

"Oh, it's not all for you, Thomas," said Jessie, "Gertrude is going to have lunch with you. She wants to prepare it for you."

"But Jessie, I…"

Jessie interrupted, "Now, I've got to run along because I have to go home and do some cleaning. I'll just leave you two lovebirds alone, because three's a crowd! And don't you two get into any trouble!" She grinned mischievously and winked.

I looked at my watch. *10:12 a.m. I've got to spend almost two hours with her before we eat lunch!*

"Wait a minute, Jessie, How's Gertrude going to get home?"

"Oh, Thomas, you can take her home. It will be a nice drive for the two of you, and it will be a chance for the two of you to get better acquainted."

"But Jessie, Wait! Jessie, I…"

But she had already made her exit.

In despair I stared at the closing door. *How am I going to stand three or four hours of Gertrude? And then I have to take her home!*

I turned around and saw her smiling at me from the couch. She patted the cushion beside her.

"Sit down, Thomas, and let's have a nice little visit together."

I picked up the bag that contained our lunch. "I better put this food in the refrigerator, Gertrude."

I walked into the kitchen and slowly put our food away. I stood in front of the refrigerator for as long as possible in an attempt to stall for time before beginning my ordeal.

"What are you doing in there, Thomas?" Her voice was loud as she shouted from the den.

"I'm just putting away the food, Gertrude."

"Well, come on back in here, Thomas, I have so much to talk to you about!"

The aggressive tone of her voice made me wince, then curse under my breath. I gritted my teeth and rejoined her in the den, sitting beside her in obedience to her command.

"Now, we can have a nice little visit together, Thomas." Her smile melted to an expression of sadness as she carefully inspected me.

"Thomas, you're not looking well," she said, "Have you been worrying about something? You must be because you look just terrible, you poor man."

"No, I'm not worrying, Gertrude, and I feel just fine…How are you feeling?"

"Well, actually, I haven't been feeling so well. You know all the bad things that are wrong with me don't you?"

Oh hell! Why did I have to ask that?

"Well, as you probably know, I have very painful arthritis, and oh, those terrible headaches! Also, I asked my doctor what caused my dizzy spells and do you know what he had the gall to say? He said he couldn't find anything wrong with me that would make me dizzy! My stomach's been bothering me too…And worrying about you makes me so anxious that I could just cry!"

"You shouldn't worry about me, Gertrude," I replied, for the lack of anything else to say.

"Oh, but I do, Thomas. Even when we were in high school together I worried about you. Do you remember how we had such a crush on each other?"

Is this woman crazy? I practically had to run from her in high school!

I felt a pang of pity for her. Like me, she too had lost her mate and probably had experienced the same loneliness that I had felt over the years.

In an effort to stop her monologue about her aches and pains, I changed the subject. "By the way, Gertrude, I saw in the paper where another one of our old classmates died...Frank Mercer—remember him? He used to play trumpet in the marching band."

"Oh, yes! I went to his funeral...It was so beautiful. Charlene Stapleton sang 'Amazing Grace'. I just cried my eyes out when I heard that. I looked at poor Frank lying there in the casket, and his poor wife crying...But you know I watched the family closely, and I didn't see either his son or daughter shed a tear! Speaking of his daughter, I've heard some terrible stories about her. And I think Frank's son is an awful drinker. It seemed to me that neither of them cared."

"People grieve differently, Gertrude. I'm sure Frank's son and daughter took it hard."

Her face reflected sadness, "Speaking of funerals, I've got to go to Walter Bailey's funeral tomorrow."

"Walter Bailey? I can't place him. Should I know him?" I asked.

"I doubt it. He was a young fellow—not more than twenty or twenty-one. I didn't know him either. Got killed in a car wreck." She leaned toward me and whispered, as if revealing a secret, "There's talk among some people that he was drinking when he had that wreck! And it's rumored that he'd been out all night with that trashy Wilson girl."

"You attend quite a few funerals, don't you?" I asked.

"Well, yes, whenever I can. I just want to help comfort those poor people."

Damn! How did we ever get onto this morbid subject?

I changed the direction of our conversation. "What time do you want to eat?" I was hoping she would want to have an early lunch.

"Oh, it's not even 11:00 o'clock. We can talk a lot more before we eat." She again looked me over carefully, inspecting me.

"Thomas, you just look so sad. Something is worrying you, isn't it?"

"No…Nothing, Gertrude."

"Dear, is Melissa worrying you?"

Dear? Now she's calling me "dear!"

"No, Melissa's not worrying me. Why do you ask that?"

She looked at me skeptically, then leaned toward me and patted me on the shoulder. "Thomas, now don't take this wrong, but I've heard some talk about Melissa."

"What kind of talk?" I asked.

"Some people have whispered to me that she's been seen driving around at two or three in the morning."

"Well, whoever saw her must have been out at two or three themselves," I said.

"But there's some talk that sometimes she has a man with her."

"So? I guess she dates men. After all, she's a single woman."

"Now don't you tell that I told you this, but you

know Myrtle Bevins? She lives right across the alley from Melissa's apartment. Well, she told me that she just happened to see through her window into Melissa's living room last Saturday night." Gertrude again leaned toward me and lowered her voice as if embarrassed to utter such words. "Myrtle said she saw Melissa and some man kissing and wallowing around on the couch!"

She sensed my anger as I glared at her, then she quickly added, "But now, don't you get riled up about it, Thomas. You know that getting upset is not good for you. Anyway, if I were you I wouldn't believe a word of it because you know how some people gossip and try to see the worst in people!"

"Yeah, you can sure see through those tongue-wagging gossipers, can't you, Gertrude?"

"I sure can! And I only told you these things because I felt that you might have heard some of this gossip, and it might be worrying you!"

I looked at my watch: *11:15*. "Look, Gertrude…I'm hungry!" I lied, "Let's go ahead and eat."

"Oh, dear!" she said, "Here I have been ranting on and on, and you've been sitting here hungry!"

"Come on into the kitchen, let's eat." I said.

I wasn't hungry at all, only desperate to finish lunch so that I could take her home and be rid of her.

In the kitchen I told Gertrude to take a seat at the table. "I'll get our lunch ready and set the table, Gertrude. After all, I'm supposed to be the host…And you've done more than necessary in preparing the food for us." I displayed a phony smile.

I took the sack from the refrigerator and removed the

plastic container from it. I had planned on using the microwave, but when I removed the container's lid, I saw that the bowl was filled with only a large, tossed salad. And that was lunch. Nothing else but salad. However, I did place three kinds of salad dressing on the table.

She smiled. "I made us a nice salad that we can share, dear," she said. "Jessie tells me that sometimes you're not regular, so I decided that you should eat more roughage."

Between bites, she continued to ramble on about her ailments, her animals, funerals, and of course, dirty stories she had heard about other people. I occasionally nodded and ate my salad in silence.

After lunch, we retreated to the den. A glance at my watch told me that the time was 11:45.

"I guess I should drive you home now," I said, eager to rid myself of her.

The side door opened and Melissa walked into the room. When she saw Gertrude, she stopped in her tracks.

"Oh, excuse me, Dad," she said, "I didn't know you had company. I hope I'm not disturbing you! Hi, Gertrude!"

Gertrude nodded.

I was relieved to see Melissa. "Come on in, Melissa!" I smiled at her. "What brings you here?"

"Not anything special. I just wanted to touch base with you and see how you're doin'. What happened to your car? How'd you get that dent?"

I didn't answer. "Have a seat, Melissa." I gestured to the space on the couch beside Gertrude. Melissa remained standing.

"Did somebody run into your car?" Melissa persisted.

I hung my head and sighed. "I wondered how long it would be until you gave me a lecture about my driving."

"I'm not giving you a lecture, Dad. I was just asking a question. I was just curious. The same thing happened to me about a week ago…Heck, it can happen to anybody."

Gertrude spoke up. "Aren't you concerned about your father's driving? Your Aunt Jessie and I feel that he is much too careless. And he very seldom wears his glasses. Why, if it wasn't for Marsha, Jessie, and me, I don't know how poor Thomas would get by."

"You worry too much Gertrude," said Melissa, "Dad's a good driver. And he only needs glasses for reading."

Gertrude glared at her.

"Is that the only reason you came by…to comment on my driving?" I was thankful that Melissa was not censuring me.

She claimed a seat in the rocking chair before answering.

"Well, Dad, it was that...but it was also to tell you that I am going to be out of town for a few days."

"Oh?" I said, "And where are you going?"

"I'm going to Daytona Beach for about five days. I'll be staying in a quaint little house right on the beach!" She flashed an excited smile.

Gertrude was curious. "Are you going alone, dear?"

"No, actually I'm going with a friend."

"Oh, really? How nice! Who is she? Do I know her? What's your friend's name?" Gertrude leaned forward for the answer.

"My friend's name is Aaron Hathaway. And no, I

don't think you know him."

Gertrude recoiled in shock.

I smiled at Melissa, "It'll be good for you to get away for a few days, Melissa."

"I was thinking the same about you, Dad. You know, you need to consider going somewhere for a week or so, too. After all, you lead a pretty boring life sometimes, Dad." She looked straight at Gertrude.

Gertrude's face expressed extreme anger. "I believe I can speak for your father on such matters, Melissa. I believe that he would tell you that he is perfectly content with his life just as it is."

The anger within me began to escalate. I felt sympathy for Gertrude, but lately I had grown disgusted with the way that she, Jessie, and Marsha were trying to control my life.

"No, Gertrude, that's not correct. I'm not *perfectly content* with my life just as it is," I said, bluntly. I became even bolder as I continued, "As a matter of fact, Dick Noble has invited me to go on a trip with him for a few days, and I might just take him up on it!"

Gertrude's eyes widened. "Dick Noble? Oh no, Thomas...Surely you wouldn't go anywhere with that awful man. You just wouldn't believe the stories I've heard about him!"

"Dick's a good man, Gertrude. He's kind and generous, and not only that, he's my best friend. I may just go to Miami Beach with him after all!"

"Cool, Dad!" Melissa flashed a mischievous smile, "I hear that Dick Noble has some very special friends. Maybe he can introduce you to some interesting people." Her smile broadened as she winked at me.

The determined set of Gertrude's lower jaw reflected her anger.

I turned to Melissa. "You said you were going to Daytona Beach with this guy named Aaron Hathaway. I thought the guy you brought over here that day—'Steve'—was your boyfriend."

Melissa rolled her brown eyes. "Oh, gosh no! His actions proved him to be the loser-type, Dad. Can you believe he was so gutless that he escaped out the bedroom window? And I actually thought he would come out and meet you that morning...Apparently, the guy has no balls!"

Gertrude's face turned a pale-shade of gray as she covered her ears in disbelief.

I was curious in regard to Melissa's new boyfriend. "So, who is this Aaron Hathaway? What kind of guy is he?"

"He's a great guy, Dad. You've met him. Remember that man I introduced you to at the mall last weekend?"

"You mean that black guy?"

"Yeah! Don't you think he's nice?"

Gertrude was now sick. "Oh, my Word! Thomas, I've got to lie down! I'm having another one of those dizzy spells." She lay back on the couch.

"Are you okay, Gertrude?" I asked.

She groaned, "Would you please call Jessie and tell her to come over here and get me? Tell her that I want her to take me to my doctor."

"I'll call Aunt Jessie, Dad," said Melissa. As she picked up the phone, she made an unsuccessful attempt to hide her devilish smile.

Chapter 7

Today is going to be a scorcher, I thought. I wiped the sweat from my face and squinted at the shimmering mirage reflected by the heated asphalt. I was in a somber mood as I sat on the bottom row of the bleachers. Dick was supposed to meet me here at 10:00 for a three-mile jog on the Northridge High School track, but it was now 10:15 and he still had not arrived.

My bleak frame of mind was brought on not solely from Dick's tardiness, but mostly from other recent negative aspects of my life. I again wasn't sleeping well, I was becoming more forgetful, and I had recently had the traffic accident that had Marsha up-in-arms about my driving. Also, there was the matter of Gertrude. What was I to do about her?

But weighing heavier on my mind was the unfortunate event of earlier this morning. I had gone shopping at Kroger's, and while unloading the groceries from the cart to the back seat of my vehicle, the cart had gotten away from me, rolling into the side of a young man's BMW.

Remembering his castigating words still angered me: "Damn! Look what you've done to my car!"

"I'm sorry," I had said, "The cart just got away from me."

"You're *sorry?* Look at that dent! You old fart! They oughta round up all you old geezers and put you in nursing homes!"

After hearing his stinging rebuke, I was no longer sorry, but *glad* the cart had rolled into his car. Immediately after his verbal assault I had strongly considered slapping the hell out of him.

There were, however, some positive things that had recently taken place in my life: My ankle no longer bothered me, Melissa hadn't censured me about my fender-bender, and it had been quite a while since Gertrude had aggravated me. The "dizzy spell" that she had experienced at my house had confined her to her bed for nearly a week, and Jessie was terribly worried about her. My secret wish that her dizzy spell would last indefinitely caused me to feel a bit guilty. I should go t o visit her; but if I did, that would start the whole damned thing over again.

I looked to the other side of the track and spotted Dick walking toward me. As I stood for my stretching exercise, the empty back pocket of my jogging shorts indicated that I had forgotten my wallet.

Oh, great! Not only am I broke, but after jogging I'll have to drive my car back home without my license.

Dick was wearing Nike running shoes and was

dressed in an expensive white workout suit when he joined me. On his head, a beige Tennessee Titans cap had replaced his toupee. The cap was an improvement over his hairpiece. He was breathing hard from his rapid walk to meet me, and his face was sprinkled with great beads of sweat.

Displaying a pleasant smile, he shook my hand and then wrapped his beefy left arm around my shoulders.

"Sorry I'm late, Tom." His smile evolved into an expansive grin. Except on rare occasions when he was angry, Dick was always in a good mood.

"You're twenty minutes late," I commented.

"Sorry ol' buddy," he said, "I couldn't find my car keys. Must've looked for them for half an hour before I finally found them."

"Where did you finally find them?"

"In the ignition of my car, where I forgot to take them out last night."

Since the same thing had happened to me before, I let him off the hook.

"You're gonna get hot in that thick outfit you're wearing," I told him. "It must be nearly a hundred degrees. Why didn't you wear shorts and a light tee-shirt, like I did?"

"Got to think of the old 'image,' pardner." He grinned. "Can't tell when you might run into a good lookin' dame."

"Out here on the high school track? Not a chance, Dick."

"I guess you're right. Maybe I ought to pull off this jacket. I'm wearin' a tee-shirt under it." He removed his jacket and carelessly tossed it on the grass beside the track.

"Look, Dick…I've been jogging for years but it's probably a new thing for you. If my usual pace is too fast for you, just tell me, and I'll slow it down."

"Are you kiddin'?" He looked outraged. "You're looking at the old 'Gallopin' Ghost' of Northridge High School. I'll bet I can still outrun you!"

"We're not in a race, Dick," I said. "Anyway, let's get started!"

I established my usual pace as we began jogging, but Dick was soon five yards ahead of me.

"What's keeping ya' Tom?" He asked, with a broad grin.

"You go on ahead of me, Dick. Remember, we're gonna go three miles…That's twelve times around this quarter-mile track."

Halfway through the first lap I had already caught up with him. Although he often lied about his weight (as well as his golf scores), he appeared to be about thirty pounds heavier than when he had played football in high school. His flabby stomach bounced with each of his pounding steps, and his sweaty face was as red as a beet.

I slowed my pace, but still edged ahead of him as he finally slowed to a walk.

"Wait up, Tom," he rasped, "I've got a pain in my side."

I stopped, waiting for him to catch up to me, but he came to a standstill, bending over with his hands on his knees and wheezing for air.

I walked back to him. "Are you okay?"

"Yeah (gasp), I'm okay...Let's walk for a little bit (gasp) until my side stops hurtin.' (gasp) Must be somethin' I ate."

Walking slowly, we continued around the track in silence as Dick caught his breath.

"Hell, let's take a breather," I said. "To tell you the truth, I'm not sure that my ankle's ready for this yet. We may finish our run after your side quits hurtin'." I could see that he wasn't up to it.

We left the track and took a seat at the end of the bottom row in the bleachers. The shade of the massive oak tree that hovered over us protected us from the blistering sun.

"Man, it's hot!" said Dick. With his handkerchief he wiped away the accumulating sweat from his face. "Tom, I'm really not in as bad a shape as it appears," he lied. "I must be comin' down with somethin'."

"You gotta remember," I reminded him, "we're not eighteen years old anymore. Besides, it's not important that we jog today, anyway."

For a while we sat in silence. When his breathing returned to normal, Dick finally spoke.

"Tom, the real reason I asked to jog with you today was so we could get away from everybody and talk privately."

I was curious. "What's on your mind?"

"Guess who called me last night!" His expression suggested that he was about to reveal to me the answer to the mystery of life.

"I have no idea, since there are so many people in the world. How many thousand guesses do I get?"

"Harriet!" He said, as if the name would astound me.

"Harriet? Harriet who?"

"Come on, Tom... How many Harriets do you know?"

"Well, there's Harriet Billings? Was it her?"

"Who the hell is Harriet Billings?" asked Dick.

"She was the librarian when we went to high school."

"Damn, Tom! I haven't thought of her in years. She must be nearly a hundred years old by now. That old bag hated me...Why on earth would *she* call me? Get serious, Tom! Stop actin' like you don't know who I'm talkin' about. It was Harriet Dawson, our old *lost love* that called me."

Although the mere mention of her name still excited me and stirred my curiosity, I faked an attitude of disinterest.

"Oh? And what was on her mind? I wonder why she would be calling?"

"Why are you so unconcerned, Tom? Aren't you even interested in what she had to say?"

"Not particularly."

"Sorry, Tom...But I'm gonna tell you anyway. She says that she might come back to Northridge for the class reunion."

"Am I supposed to be excited?"

"Well, maybe you're not, but *I* am," said Dick. "Man, the three of us had some great times together, didn't we? You haven't forgotten those times, have you?"

"I wonder why she called *you*, Dick...Why didn't she call *me* instead? Or at least, why didn't she call both of us?"

"She explained that to me, Tom."

"What was her explanation?" I was curious.

"She said...well, she wasn't so sure about how you'd feel toward her, after..."

"After *what?*"

"After she...Come on, Tom! After all, she more or less jilted you at the altar. But in a way, she also jilted *me*...and *I'm* not mad at her anymore."

"I'm not really mad at her either, Dick. As a matter of fact, I don't feel any emotions about her at all. If she comes to the reunion—is she bringin' her husband? Or is she married to a different guy now?"

"She's not married at all. She told me that she had been divorced for over twenty years. If you go to the reunion, the three of us could hook up again and have a great time!"

"Just like old times, huh? You and Harriet can 'hook up,' but you can count me out. By the way, where does she live now? She used to live in California."

"She said that she was livin' in Dallas, Texas."

"How long is she going to stay when she comes in?" I asked.

"I'm not sure. As a matter of fact, she is not sure she's comin' in at all. I got the impression that she was just feelin' me out to see if you and I were receptive to her coming back to Northridge."

"That's up to her, Dick. I don't have any opinion about it."

"Oh, come on Tom! So she jilted you...! You lost your *true love!* But that was fifty years ago. You know the old saying, 'It's better to have loved and lost than to never have loved at all'!"

I was growing tired of Dick's corny adages. "But I didn't love and lose. I loved and *won!* I won the heart of Jenny! You remember Jenny, don't you Dick?" I asked sarcastically.

"Don't insult me, Tom. Of course I remember Jenny. I loved her too, like she was my sister. But I also remember how you felt about your first love, Harriet. You must still be carrying the torch for her if you're so unforgiving of her after fifty years."

I thought about what Dick had just said. Why *was* I still so mad at Harriet?

"You know something Dick? We might not even recognize Harriet if we saw her. A lot can happen to a person's looks in fifty years."

"Yeah…that's true," said Dick, "But man, she was some good-looker when you and I knew her, right pal?"

"But everybody changes, Dick. Just look what the last fifty years has done to *our* looks…to you and me!"

"Speak for yourself, Tom! I don't think I've changed that much!" Dick's outrage made me feel sorry for him. In order to lessen his pain, I made a feeble attempt to say something humorous.

"Well, for instance, look at how time has changed Gertrude," I said, "Remember how sexy she was in high school?"

Dick exploded with laughter. "Yeah, if you see a bulldog as being sexy. The only way she has changed is that she looks like an older bulldog."

I began to feel sympathy for Gertrude.

Dick's face became serious. "I wonder what Harriet does look like, Tom. Do you reckon she has gotten fat and ugly?"

"God only knows, Dick. Everybody changes with time."

Dick smiled. "You know…for some reason I got excited when I heard her voice on the phone last night. She sounds the same—she has the same sense of humor. I can't wait to see her again!"

"Yeah, but like you said, she may not even come to the reunion." I said.

"She would if she knew that both you and I would be there…She practically told me that. You're going, aren't you?"

"I don't think so, Dick. Besides, Jessie has her mind made up that if I go, I'm expected to take Gertrude. That's enough to keep me from going."

Dick looked angry. "Damn it, Tom! Where's your balls? When are you going to stop letting other people direct your life?"

Dick's words stung me, probably because I knew they were so true. At some point during that hazy milestone that introduces us to old age, I had gradually relinquished my independence, turning my life over to others.

"Is it that obvious, Dick?" I asked.

"I don't want to hurt your feelings, Tom, but you don't run your own life anymore! Your two daughters—and your sister control almost everything you do! You know, you used to rule your family with an iron hand. What happened to that assertive guy I used to know?"

"You don't know what it's like, Dick. You never had any kids. When they grow up—and we get old, their judgment is better than ours."

"The hell it is!" he retorted, "And what gives you that ridiculous idea? You're smarter than your sister and either of your kids. You've had a hell of a lot more experience, too…so that makes you *wiser* than they are! Step up to the plate, Tom, and reclaim your manhood!"

"What you say may be true, Dick…but I hate to hurt other people. For instance, I can hardly stomach Gertrude, but I hate to hurt her feelings."

"Screw her feelings, man! What about *your* feelings? Where is that gutsy guy who stood up to me in that fight years ago?"

I began to get angry.

"You're beginning to get on my nerves, Dick," I said, "I don't like the shitty way you're talking to me!" I knew that he was right about me, but his blunt analysis of my shortcomings made me feel like even less of a man.

"If the shoe fits, wear it!" he snapped.

I glared at him. "You're good at pointing out other people's faults! What about some of yours? You strut around wearing that ridiculous looking wig, wearing your gaudy, outlandish outfits, bragging about your 'glory days' in football! You go around pretending that you are twenty-five years old! Face reality, Dick! You're an old, used-up has-been, just like me!"

Dick looked hurt. "Tom, you're the only man on God's earth that I'd let talk to me like that. If it was anybody else but you, those would be fightin' words!"

"Don't threaten me, Dick. You beat the hell out of me once a long time ago, but I'm warning you! Don't even try it again!"

"So you're still carrying around that old grudge are you? I knew you had never forgiven me…and the same is true about the way you feel about Harriet! After fifty years you're still holding a grudge against her too!"

"You don't know my innermost feelings," I said, "I don't consider Harriet important enough for me to hold a grudge against her."

"Bullshit!" he said. He abruptly stood and walked across the track. After picking up his jacket from the grass, he turned and gazed sadly at me. Then, without uttering a word he strode briskly away.

I remained sitting on my seat in the bleachers, immobile, as he walked away from me. For a long while, I stared after him as his figure grew smaller, widening the expanse of grass between us until he finally disappeared from sight.

I gradually began to feel physically ill, as if I might throw up. I was suddenly so terribly tired that I wondered if I had the strength to walk to my car. Sadness filled my mind to the point that I felt like crying. My emotions were in turmoil. I didn't know which was more painful to me: The hurtful things that Dick had said, or the painful knowledge that the things he had said were true. And if they *were* true, why had I so cruelly crushed his sensitive ego? To get even? To get even for *what?* For telling me the truth?

I began to deeply regret my retaliation against him. Dick was my best friend…I had no doubt that he truly loved me like a brother. I thought that I had long ago forgiven him for his attack on me fifty years ago…But if I had, then why did I bring it up? Also, why had I acted so flippant about his excitement over Harriet?

I was so absorbed in thought that I scarcely remembered walking to my car. On the way home, I drove through a red light and a cop pulled me over, resulting in my being ticketed for both the traffic light and driving without a license. Now I not only would catch hell from Marsha, Jessie, and maybe even Melissa, but I had also probably lost my best friend.

Chapter 8

The drizzling rain that engulfed my world on the blue Monday morning coincided with my dark mood. It was the kind of relentless, misty rain that permeates every blade of grass and every leaf on the trees; not even the smallest crevice escaped its drenching, persistent penetration. It saturated my soul.

The rhythmic flap of the windshield wipers and the sound of my tires sloshing through the standing water on the street underscored the wetness of the bleak morning.

I turned left on Locust Avenue, the street where Dick lived in his modest ranch-style home. His house was probably the only unpretentious thing in his life. A small, two bedroom dwelling, it reflected the vintage of the fifties. With his small fortune, he could have afforded a luxurious home, but the house was completely devoid of luxuries. Without a deck, den, or recreation room, the inexpensive house contained only the bare rudiments for living. Although it seemed a contradiction to his lavish nature, it actually was quite fitting for him; for he was not given to entertaining guests in his home. The only kind of diversion that Dick savored was his enjoyment of women, which usually took place in bars and motel rooms.

I parked in front of his house and killed the motor. I had been eager to arrive at his place, but now that I was here, I was hesitant to approach him. *Will he be up yet? Is he still angry? What time is it, anyway?* I looked at my watch: *7:35*, I noted.

I gazed down the misty, gray avenue as I listlessly sat in my car. I dreaded facing Dick. From habit, I reached under my seat for the umbrella that I already knew wasn't there. Since I had misplaced it somewhere last week, I had forgotten to search for it.

For a while longer I remained in the car, dreading the unpleasant task that lay before me. Most of the previous night had been sleepless and worrisome, and the payoff for my insomnia was the fatigue that now consumed my aching body.

I got out of my car, locked it, and to escape getting wet, I hurriedly walked to the small front porch, briefly hesitating before ringing the doorbell. Assuming that his preceding night had been as restless as mine, I worried that I might be awakening him. To my surprise, he immediately opened the door. Fully dressed and reeking of strong cologne, he eyed me with a puzzled stare.

"Well, can I come in?" I asked, meekly.

"Door's open." He gestured toward the interior of his house.

We were quiet as I took a seat on his living room couch. Dick remained standing. In search of a way to break the ice, I muttered, “Sorry I came so early. I had trouble sleeping.”

He studied me for a long while before claiming the recliner that faced me. His silence unnerved me.

Finally he spoke. “You look like hell.”

“I feel like hell,” I responded. An awkward silence followed. *Well, I’d better get on with it,* I thought.

“Dick, I came over here this morning to apologize to you. I had no cause to be so critical of your habits and ways. You were only being honest with me. I guess I got so sensitive because what you said was true.”

For a brief period he didn’t speak. He sat quietly, thinking, weighing his words. He looked me directly in the eye.

“Tom, I did a little pondering about the way you reacted toward me. At first I was pissed. But then, after I thought on it for awhile, I realize that I am really kind of proud of you.”

“Proud of me? What for? I lost my head.”

“Because when I thought about it later, I realized that it’s the first time in a long while that you’ve shown some backbone. I’m beginnin’ to see some hints of that assertive Tom I used to know.”

“Well, thanks Dick, I…”

He interrupted, “There’s only one part of our little argument that I’m still kinda pissed about…It’s when you brought up that fight we had fifty years ago.”

“You mean the time that you beat the shit out of me?”

"See? There you go again! Ain't you ever goin' to forget that?"

"I'm trying."

"Did I ever apologize to you after I clobbered you?"

"Not more than a million times," I said.

"Well, did you ever forgive me?"

"I don't know."

"Damn it, man! Can you ever forgive me?"

"I don't know…I'll have to think about it for awhile."

"For how long? Hell, You've been thinkin' about it for fifty years!" He seemed frustrated. I felt sorry for him, but for some reason I was hesitant to set him free from his guilt.

He gave me an accusing look. "Tom, do you know what the biggest difference there is between you and me?"

I could think of so many big differences between us that I was puzzled in regard to what he considered the biggest.

"The biggest difference between us," he said, "is that you hold grudges, and I never held a grudge in my life!"

For a man with so much empty space between his ears, he was amazingly perceptive; for he was right on target with his appraisal.

I smiled at him. "Dick, you're right about me again…And you were right about most of the things you said about me yesterday."

He returned my smile. "Well, as bad as I hate to admit it, you were right about some of the things you said about me, too." He seemed embarrassed.

"What things?" I asked.

"The things you said about my pretentious ways, and the way I try to act younger than my age...But I'm not sorry I'm that way, Tom. I'm not sorry that I'm not givin' in to old age. My pretentiousness is the only thing that keeps me from bein' like you! And God forbid that!"

"What do you mean? What's wrong with me?"

"Tom, I don't want you to get mad at me again, so I ain't sayin'."

"Go ahead and say it. I promise I won't get mad." I wasn't so sure I meant it.

"Tom, you're only an old geezer because you feel like an old geezer! Sure, we all have some physical limitations when we get older, but you've begun to place limitations on your spirit...On your soul! You've let growing old make you feel inferior. Well, not me! Even if it means bein' a little fake and acting half my age, I'm not goin' to consign myself to a life of bein' outdated and worthless! When I die of old age you can bet I'll go down fightin'."

I considered what he had said. "The trouble is, Dick, is that we *are* outdated. We're slower, and sometimes we can't remember things."

"Bullshit!" He said, "Do you know why we can't remember things? It's because we've stored so much information and knowledge in our brains. Our brain is like a computer, Tom. It's so full of data that it takes longer for us to locate the information. Younger people's brains are a lot more empty than ours, so they can find what little they know pretty quick. That's another reason you shouldn't hold grudges… they're just negative thoughts that crowd out the good memories."

I was amazed at Dick's analogy. I had always considered him to be dumb, but his insight was surprisingly astute. Since I was in a forgiving mood, I pressed him further.

"Okay, Dick…I buy part of what you're saying. Maybe I have given in to old age a little bit. But short of dressing like you and wearing a hairpiece, what else do you suggest I do? Go ahead, buddy, give me both barrels…I can take it!"

"Well, for starters, you can stop lettin' Marsha and Jessie push that fat pig, Gertrude on you…And you might try makin' your own decisions about who your friends are! Also, you could stop takin' crap about the way you drive…And another thing: You need to take a trip occasionally… Maybe get out and mix with some good lookin' women!" His eyes lit up with his last suggestion.

"Speaking of mixing with women, Dick…How do you keep up your exhausting pace? As you've pointed out, growing old is no crime, but it does somewhat limit our sexual stamina."

"Hey Man! Modern science helps us to stay young! Haven't you heard of the blue pill?"

"Yeah, but I've never taken one."

"Why would *you* need to take one? Hell, you haven't had a date in years. That is, unless you consider Gertrude a date. But in her case, before you could get it up, you'd need a blue pill the size of a *watermelon!"*

We both broke into laughter.

Dick suddenly stood. "What do you say we have a drink, pardner?"

"A drink? This early? It's only a little after eight."

"So? What difference does it make what time it is? Is there some kind of law that says that two retired buddies can't take a drink whenever they please? What's your pleasure, Scotch, or Bourbon? It'll have to be one of those because that's all I've got."

"How about a beer?"

"Hell, a beer ain't even drinkin'. You ain't getting' nothin' unless it's Scotch or Bourbon."

"Okay, Bourbon then."

"I'll take Scotch…Hell, we ain't alike in nothing, are we Tom?"

He retreated to the kitchen for the liquor as I waited for him on the couch. Emotionally, I was feeling much better since we had mended our friendship.

He came back carrying a tray containing a bowl of ice, two glasses, a two-liter Coke, and two fifths of booze. My eyes widened.

"I thought you said a drink, Dick. You didn't have to bring the whole liquor store!"

"Hell, one drink ain't even drinkin'. Live a little, man. I won't tell Jessie or Gertrude on you." He mixed both of us a drink and handed my Bourbon to me.

Because early morning drinking, particularly of hard liquor was unusual for me, I was tentative, taking only a small sip; however, after exclaiming "Cheers", Dick drained his glass in a single drink.

"Drink up, pardner," he said, "Get out of that sad mood you've been carryin' lately!"

What the hell! I thought, *Why not?* Following his lead, I tossed down the entire contents of my glass. He quickly refilled both glasses with pure liquor, without bothering to mix in the Coke.

"Look, Dick…I'm going to limit myself to only a couple of drinks. There's no way I could keep up with you. Besides, I have no intention of getting drunk."

"Why not? Gettin' drunk occasionally is good for you. Clears up the old noggin. I do some of my best thinkin' when I'm drunk. Some of my best lovin', too." He grinned mischievously and downed his second drink.

I slowed my pace, taking only a moderate drink. The straight, unadulterated Bourbon burned my throat.

Dick appeared to be in deep thought. "Hey, Tom…What was it that started that argument we had, anyway? Do you remember?"

"We were discussing Harriet, and how she might come in for the reunion," I said. I took another drink.

He cast a worried glance toward me. "She won't come to it unless both you and I go. Come on, Tom…Go to the reunion." He refilled his glass with pure Scotch.

"No, I don't think so, Dick. I'm really not that crazy about seeing Harriet."

"Well, if you don't go she probably won't be there, so I won't get to see her either." Dick hung his head.

"Too bad, pal". I finished my second drink. "By the way, Dick…That was my second drink. No more booze for me today." He ignored my comment and refilled my glass.

"Why don't you want to see Harriet?" he asked.

"She's bad news, Dick…At least for me."

"See? There you go again! Can't you finally get over it? Hell, it's been fifty years!" Dick contributed another of his countless adages, "Time heals all wounds, you know."

"But meeting her fifty years ago changed my life forever...Especially after she jilted me. It messed up my life." I was beginning to feel the Bourbon.

"You haven't had a bad life, Tom. What's been so bad about it?"

"You know what's been so bad about it. Because of her, I rushed into marriage, and that deprived me of a chance to go to college." I started my third drink.

"Are you sayin' you're sorry you married Jenny? She's the best thing that ever happened to you, pal! Harriet's not worthy of standin' in Jenny's shadow! As far as that goes, neither are you and I!"

"No, of course I'm not sorry I married Jenny. I just wished I'd waited instead of rushing into it. But after she got pregnant, waiting was not an option."

For a long while we sat without speaking, enjoying the glow that the liquor had roused in us. I finished my drink, then poured myself another. Dick did likewise. I began to feel mellow and longed for Dick's understanding.

"Dick, I'm not exactly *mad* at Harriet. It's just that the pain that she caused me after toying with my life set me off on the wrong path. People like Harriet play with other people's lives. I guess that you could say that I'm more afraid of her than angry at her. You know, you should understand how I feel, because she screwed you up, too. You cared for her just as I did.

She even came between us…Two best friends! Because of that, we ended up in a fight!"

"Yeah, I know…And I beat the shit out of you, right? When are you gonna forget that?"

"I'm workin' on it. Anyway, you're the one that brought it up." I was beginning to slur my words. We again sat silently as I poured myself another drink.

Dick polished off another glass of Scotch. "Listen, ol' pal. I'm sorry I hit you, but you gotta remember that she jilted me."

"You mean she jilted *me!"* I drained my glass of bourbon. "And after that, you proceeded to beat the shit out of me," I again reminded him.

I was now officially drunk. Dick poured himself another Scotch and stared stupidly at me. The glaze in his eyes reflected the mentality of a stunned ox. It was obvious to me that he was feeling no pain. In spite of his idiotic expression, he made an attempt to offer words of wisdom in regard to the fairer sex.

"Tom, I've been married twice, an' I've hadda lotta women in my time. So I think I prob'ly know a little more 'bout women than you do," he mumbled, "Way back then, I kinda lost my head over Harriet, jus' like you did. But with all my 'sperience since then, I learned somethin'. I learned that you don't marry women like Harriet…You marry women like Jenny. You jus' have fun with gals like Harriet."

As my state of drunkenness increased, so did my bravado. I began to feel like asserting my manhood. "Dick, I been thinkin' 'bout that li'l lecture you gave me,"

"What lecture, pal?" Dick stammered. His fifth of

Scotch was half empty. His toupee had slid forward, the front edge of it barely clearing his eyebrows. His stupid expression in combination with the misalignment of his hairpiece gave him the appearance of a moron. He repeated his question. "What lecture?"

"You know, that lecture where you said that I'm a wimp, an' had given in to ol' age, an' let ever'body boss me 'round, an' stuff like that..."

He eyed me with a blank stare. "Oh...*That* lecture. You ain't gonna try to start a fight with me again, are you?" He leaned back in his chair and placed his crossed feet on the coffee table.

"No, Dick...I don' wanna fight you. Hell, I wanna thank you for puttin' some starch in my backbone. From now on, I'm takin' charge of my life!" I sat up erectly on the couch and thrust out my chest. "Pour me another drink, Dick!" I commanded

He smiled. "Careful, ol' buddy," he slurred, "I might jus' tell Gertrude on you."

"Screw Gertrude!" I shouted.

He smiled stupidly. "Not me, pal. Not in a million years."

Chapter 9

I watched intently as Pinky meticulously aligned his silverware beside his plate as he sat erectly in his chair. He carefully repositioned the salt and pepper shakers in the exact center of the table; then, with his napkin he fastidiously wiped any accumulation of imaginary dust from around his plate before neatly folding the napkin into a perfect square and placing it in his shirt pocket. *No wonder Dummy can't stand this obsessive-compulsive idiot!*

I turned my attention to Dummy, who sat sloppily slumped in his chair. After picking his nose, he eyed his finger, inspecting the results of his probing activity. He wiped his finger on the leg of his pants, then continued to eat. A speck of runny egg yolk stained his chin. His recent haircut was a disaster. Since no licensed barber would dare commit such an atrocity, I figured that Dummy unseemly haircut must have been self-inflicted. Its ragged appearance made it look as if someone had beaten the hair off his head with a stick.

What a disgusting slob!

Head was having difficulty chewing with his new teeth, the laborious activity causing him to drool. His enormous, magnified eyeballs glared at me through his thick lens when he caught me staring at him. *What a ridiculous looking man!*

Between bites, Dick rambled on endlessly about his grandiose exploits on the gridiron a half century ago. I was so tired of listening to his rehashed fables that I felt like screaming.

Yeah Dick! We've all heard that story before!

They were all getting on my nerves. How am I able to stand these people every morning? Maybe they feel the same way about me.

I've gotta get out of this funky mood! But shifting moods in not as easy as shifting gears, especially when you're suffering with raw nerves and the granddaddy of all hangovers.

Yesterday had been a nightmare. After getting drunk at Dick's house, I had passed out on his couch. Then, late in the afternoon after he sobered me up and helped me out of his house, I discovered that after parking my car in front of his home that morning I had locked my car keys in the vehicle. This oversight required the expertise of a locksmith who charged me a hundred dollars for his services.

When I had finally arrived at home, I was too sick to eat. After deleting phone messages from Marsha, Melissa, and Jessie, I went to bed, only to awaken early, causing me to spend the last half of the night submerged in morbid brooding. Depressed by loneliness and with nothing better to do in the early morning, I had again ended up here in the Cracker Barrel with my cronies. I was sorry that I had joined them, for with my terrible hangover I was bad company this morning.

Dick finally finished his endless monologue about single-handedly winning the high school state championship in football. He turned toward me.

"How do you feel this morning,' ol' buddy?"

"Don't ask. Talking makes my head hurt."

"Why do you feel so bad?" Dick's gregarious mood was proof that he felt fine.

"Can't you guess? Hell, I feel like a train ran over me. My arthritis is bothering me again, too."

He grinned and placed his muscular arm around my shoulders. "You'll feel better later, pal."

I had noticed in the past, with some resentment, that he seemed impervious to hangovers…Or perhaps, like the usual pattern of behavior in his life, it was only an act.

Dick turned his attention to Pinky. "Pinky, how is that new herb tea workin' for you?" Is it keepin' you regular?"

"Well, actually I've switched back to Metamucil." He realigned his silverware beside his plate.

"Huh?" asked Dummy, "Ye say ye went back to usin' Metamucil?"

"Yes, Dummy," replied Pinky, courteously.

"Hell, I never fool with that stuff," said Dummy.

"Then how do you manage to stay regular without it?" Pinky was curious.

Dummy sneered. "A couple of six-packs of

Budweiser every night does the trick for me. Why, every mornin' when I get up I'm so regular that I can shit through a keyhole! I bet my poop is as thin and runny as that coffee you're drinkin', Pinky! About the same color, too!" People seated in nearby tables stared at us in revulsion.

Pinky gagged, then spat coffee into his plate. He cast a menacing glance at Dummy. I am not usually easily nauseated, but with my queasy stomach and terrible hangover, Dummy's analogy caused me to share the sentiments of Pinky.

"Dummy, you've absolutely ruined my breakfast!" screamed Pinky.

Head threw a disapproving look at Dummy. "Knock it off, Dummy! Hell, you're even makin' me sick!" His voice was loud and commanding.

"I'm tired of you orderin' me around!" answered Dummy. It was one of the few times that he had ever dared question Head's authority.

Head glared at him; then speaking in a soft voice, said, "Dummy, don't give me any back-sass!"

"Who are you callin' a jackass?" yelled Dummy.

"Damn it, Dummy, get you a hearing aid!" Head screamed at him, "You can't hear yourself fart!"

Dick's boisterous laughter stood in sharp contrast to my stony silence. For me, laughing was far too painful to my throbbing head.

I began to wish that I had stayed at home. Our breakfast discussions had never reflected the enlightened thinking of learned scholars, but this morning's idiotic prattle was even more ridiculous than usual. I closed my eyes and made a fruitless effort to tune it out.

Head seemed to share my cranky mood, for he appeared to be exceptionally grumpy. He lectured both Pinky and Dummy.

"Look, you guys, I've had it up to here." He pointed to his neck. "You two guys are direct opposites…You're always jawin' at each other! If you despise one another so much, why don't you move away from each other? I don't believe it's possible for you to get along!"

Dick chimed in with an adage: "Water and oil don't mix," he profoundly uttered.

"Very original, Dick," I said. The vibration of my voice made my head hurt.

Head looked at Dummy. "Why do you always pick on Pinky?"

"Because he's so damned peculiar!" Dummy protested. "For instance, just look at the way he wears his pants!" He glared at Pinky. "Pinky, why do you wear your pants so that your belt is up around your armpits? Another thing…I know that you're extra careful in everything you do…but do you have to wear both a belt and suspenders? Are you that scared that your pants will fall down?"

"That is none of your business, Dummy!" declared Pinky.

"Knock it off, Dummy!" ordered Head, "You and Pinky are just extreme opposites! He wears his pants around his armpits, and you wear yours just above your nuts! There ought to be a middle-ground on where a man wears his pants!"

What a profound discussion, I thought. *I'm sitting*

here with a throbbing head, in utter misery listening to a discussion about whether or not a man's trousers should be supported by his nuts.

"Dick, I've got to get out of here!" I abruptly announced.

"Where are you goin', pal?" he asked.

"Hell, I don't know…Anywhere! Want to come with me?"

"Sure, Tom."

We said goodbye to the others, paid our bills, and slowly sauntered out of the restaurant. When we stepped outside, the intense heat that enveloped us made me feel even more nauseated.

"Why are you in such a big hurry?" asked Dick.

"I'm sick, buddy. My head's splitting. That bunch of dumb-asses was driving me nuts. I may just quit meeting with those guys. They're all idiots…I don't believe any of them is capable of ever changing."

"A leopard can't change its spots," said Dick.

The interjection of his adage made me feel even worse.

"What do you say to shootin' some pool, Tom?"

"Are you kidding?" I asked. "I'm gonna go home and go back to bed."

"Do you feel that bad?"

"I'm dying, man!" I complained.

"I got a little somethin' that'll bring you back to life, ol' friend! Follow me!"

"Where are we going?" I asked. He led the way to his car and opened the passenger door for me. "Step into my office, pal!" he invited.

I got into his car. “Where are we going, Dick?” I again asked. Wordlessly, he walked around the car, entered the driver’s side and took a seat.

“We ain’t goin’ nowhere, just yet. Not ‘til we get ol’ Dr. Seagram’s to fix what ails us.” He reached under the seat and pulled out a nearly full pint of whiskey.

“You first, kiddo,” he said.

“I’m not drinking any of that stuff, Dick.”

“Really? Come on, Tom. I thought you wanted to feel better.”

“Well, drinking that crap is what made me feel like hell in the first place.”

“Listen, Tom…I know what I’m talkin’ about. I know you’ve never been much of a drinker, so listen to the voice of experience. Ain’t you ever tried a little bit of the ‘hair of the dog’? I promise it will fix you right up.”

“What about a chaser? You expect me to drink that stuff straight? On a sick stomach?”

“Hell, it’s better that way. Besides, Cokes are bad for you. Don’t take a drink yet…not until that guy walkin’ by passes the car. We could get arrested if somebody complained.”

I watched as the pedestrian walked past the car. *What the heck! I can’t possibly feel any worse…I might as well have a drink.* After carefully scanning the area I tilted the bottle and swallowed a generous portion of liquor, which I had extreme difficulty in keeping down. I held my hand over my mouth as I retched a couple of times.

“Good, huh?” he asked, smiling. I handed him the

bottle from which he took a lengthy drink. "Now let's go shoot some pool!" he said, enthusiastically.

"I don't feel like it, man!" I moaned. Ignoring my comment, he started the car and drove away.

"Take me to my car, Dick…I'm sick!"

"You won't be sick for long, ol' pal. That big drink you took will revive you in a hurry."

He turned out to be right, because by the time he pulled his car into the parking lot behind Capitol Billiard Parlor under the cooling shade of a large elm tree, I was feeling much better.

The seclusion of the back lot afforded us the necessary privacy for another drink…then another, until we had ultimately consumed the entire pint. By now I was feeling great, but both of us remained mostly sober. We left the car and strolled through the back door into the poolroom.

The air-conditioned interior felt almost too cold on our sweating bodies. A mixture of teens and middle-age men were shooting pool, while a few older men loafed in seats that aligned one of the walls. The odor of stale beer saturated the room. Dick walked up to the nearest vacant pool table.

"Why don't we play some Nine Ball…is that okay with you?" He racked the balls in preparation for our game.

"Fine. I'll break," I said.

"How much are we playin' for?" he asked.

"How about a dollar a game?" I responded. If I had suggested that we play for a thousand dollars a game, the ultimate payoff would have been the same..*nothing*.

After breaking the balls, I came up empty, only the nine ball came close to falling, hanging up on the edge of the corner pocket.

"Your shot," I said. Dick's first shot won the game for him, for he made an easy combination shot on the nine ball. Our first game had lasted less than thirty seconds.

"You owe me a buck," he declared.

In the second game Dick sank two balls on the break, then proceeded to run the table. I never even got a shot.

"Two bucks!" he gloated.

Our continued play was sprinkled with casual conversation, as Dick easily won nearly every game.

"Tom, please tell me that you're goin' to our class reunion…Six ball in the side pocket."

"I'll think about it, Dick."

"Seven ball in the corner…the main reason I want you to go so bad is because I've got a little part in the program…eight ball, one rail across the side."

"What kind of part?" I asked, "Why didn't you tell me about it before?"

"I wanted to surprise you…nine ball in the corner…YES! Rack 'em!"

For a long while we continued to discuss the reunion. Because the effects of the alcohol that I had earlier consumed had begun to subside, my headache was returning. We had been playing pool for at least two hours, spending most of our time in a discussion of our class reunion. Since I only had an occasional opportunity to shoot, I was beginning to tire of playing.

"Dick, let's rest for awhile. I'm tired and the arthritis in my right knee is flaring up again."

"Why didn't you tell me, buddy?" he asked, "Do you still have a hangover?"

"A little. The effects of that booze we drank has kinda worn off."

"We'll fix that. Grab that booth over there and we'll have a beer."

We retreated to the booth, facing each other and ordered two beers.

He grinned cheerfully. "Well, I beat you again, pal. I just put another ten bucks on your tab. Your bill is gettin' astronomical."

I smiled. "You were telling me about having a part in the reunion entertainment. What kind of part?"

"I can't tell you what the part is because it's a secret. That's the main reason I want you to go," he said, "If you don't go you won't get to see me do my act, and then I'd be disappointed. Will you attend?"

We both ordered another beer. After taking a hefty drink, I answered him.

"I don't know. But I'll have to admit, you having a part in it makes me lean toward going. Let me think about it, okay?"

"Okay, great! We'll have a wonderful time! You, me…and Harriet!"

"Now wait a minute! I didn't say I'd go for sure." I emphasized.

He ignored me and grinned broadly. "After the reunion, I want you and me to take us a trip together. Just the two of us…that is, unless we happen to meet a couple of women who might like to go with us. Remember how much fun we had on that trip to the Smoky Mountains fifty years ago, just after our fight…right after Harriet jilted us? I really think that was when you and I became life-long friends."

"Yeah, I remember. I had a great time."

"I think that trip we took together is what made you forgive me for attacking you." He eyed me closely, as if inviting a response.

"Dick, I'd like to take another trip with you, but as I've already told you, I can't afford it."

"But I don't mind payin' for it, Tom," he said, "If you'll remember, I paid for that trip fifty years ago."

"Dick, thanks anyway, but I don't want your charity!"

"Is that what you consider my offer of friendship to be? *Charity?* Tom, that's what makes me know that you've never forgiven me. When the day comes that you trust me enough to let me pay for it, then that will be the day that I know that you've forgiven me."

"Hell, Dick…What kind of crazy logic is that? Let's forget this talk about forgiveness, pal. We're good friends. Leave it at that. Look, I've gotta go home. You need to drive me back to my car." I grinned at him. "Jessie will chew me out if I don't get home soon!"

He laughed. "Oh, I think Jessie is probably a pretty good ol' gal, at heart. Her bark is worse than her bite." His adage caused me to smile.

We drank our final beer together before he drove me back to my car. When he dropped me off, I asked him, "Want to get together tomorrow night?"

"I can't, Tom. I gotta get with the reunion committee and practice my routine. The reunion is in ten days, you know. By the way, I didn't want to tell you this yet because I was afraid it would keep you away from the reunion. Harriet called me last night. She's comin' to the reunion for sure!" He grinned. "See ya' pal."

I waved to him as he pulled away. I thought about what he had just said about Harriet. I wasn't sure whether her attendance at the reunion would inspire me to attend, or scare me away.

Chapter 10

I opened my mailbox and pulled out the usual handful of bills, noting that at the bottom of the stack was a letter that someone had written to me. Since I wasn't wearing my glasses at the moment, I was only able to read my name and address on the envelope, for the return address had been written in smaller print. The letter surprised me. I rarely received mail from anyone other than from my grandson, Pat, who was now a senior at L.S.U. Even then, his letters were usually mailed to his mother, Marsha, who would personally deliver them to me.

With curiosity, I hurriedly limped into the house, favoring my right arthritic knee. I pitched the bills and letter onto the coffee table and then retreated to my bedroom where I usually keep my glasses.

I walked into the bedroom, then suddenly stopped in my tracks. My mind seemed to have gone blank. *What did I come in here for?* Realizing that the only way to recall the purpose of my trip to the bedroom was to retrace my steps, I limped back into the den. When I spotted the mail on the coffee table my memory immediately returned. I headed back to the bedroom, and with each step I mentally repeated, "Glasses, glasses, glasses".

But once in the bedroom, I discovered that my glasses weren't in their usual place on the small table beside my bed. I scoured the room, then the entire house looking for them, but with no luck. Refusing to leave a stone unturned, I explored several shirt pockets in my closet and even the interior of my car; but the whereabouts of my misplaced eyeglasses still eluded me. In my kitchen drawer I looked for my magnifying glass, but finally gave up the search in despair. Apparently, I had misplaced it as well.

Maybe I left my glasses in the bathroom. A quick glance in the bathroom mirror solved my dilemma: my bifocals rested precariously on top of my head where I had positioned them after reading the morning newspaper. *Maybe I do need someone to take care of me.* However, I remembered that even when I was young I used to frequently lose things. But youthful forgetfulness is easily forgiven by society. It is the stigma of old age that makes it unacceptable.

I put on my glasses and carefully inspected the unopened letter. Harriet Dawson was the name on the return address...Dawson. So Harriet had gone back to using her maiden name.

With curiosity, I hurriedly opened the letter. It was so brief that it could more accurately have been called a note. Beginning with the traditional greeting, "Dear

Tom," the tone of the letter was friendly but vague, mostly confining itself to such trivia as asking how I had been, stating that she had been doing okay, and relating her plans to attend the class reunion. There was no reference to the past, no apology or explanation for jilting me, nor any indication that anything special had ever existed between us. The letter had the general tone of a cordial greeting between casual friends. She ended the letter by saying that she hoped to see me at the reunion and then signed it, "Your special friend, Harriet." *Special? What's special about our friendship? I hadn't even seen her in fifty years*!

I folded the letter as I reflected on its contents. I had opened it with great curiosity, in excited anticipation; but after reading her brief message I felt a stab of disappointment...even dejection. Her letter had depressed me.

I wondered about her reason for writing to me. I figured that it was a peace offering, or maybe a compromise; for after contacting Dick by phone, not once, but twice...maybe even numerous times, she probably considered that it would be a slap in my face if she completely avoided any contact with me. Also, a letter instead of a phone call would enable her to say that at least she had contacted me; and a letter is more impersonal than a phone call, during which she might have felt an obligation to explain her former behavior.

I began to have ambivalent feelings about attending the reunion. On the one hand I was burning with curiosity about Harriet. *What does she look like now? What happened with her marriage? How does she feel about the way she jilted me? Does she still have her sense of humor and the same vibrant personality?* In addition, I was curious in regard to whatever part Dick would play in providing entertainment for the reunion.

On the other hand, I was strongly tempted to avoid the reunion. *If Harriet could be so casual about our relationship, then so could I!* Her letter displayed a subtle lack of concern in regard to my attendance. She certainly hadn't insisted or pleaded with me to attend, as Dick had done. *Well, two can play that game!*

Then another thought occurred to me: If I stayed away, she also might assume (correctly) that I'm doing so in order to avoid her, which carries the implication that I am placing too much importance on my feelings about her. The answer, I concluded, was to ignore her letter, attend the reunion (without Gertrude) and to casually relate to Harriet in the same way that I would with my other former classmates.

Why am I so concerned about what Harriet thinks? For that matter, why do I give a damn what anybody thinks? Dick had been right when he called me a wimp! I had let everyone else in my life dictate my feelings and reactions. It became clearer that I needed to take charge of my life.

I decided that I was more angry than depressed. I walked into the kitchen and removed a fifth of Old Crow from my cabinet. Dick had given the bottle to me several years ago at one of my birthday get-togethers. After removing a two-liter bottle of Coke from my refrigerator, I carried it along with the booze into the den and took a seat on the couch.

I opened the bottle and took a generous drink, gagging at the biting sting of the liquor; then I quickly chased it with a long swallow from the Coke bottle. Gradually a warm glow began to develop in the pit of my stomach, offering me the tingling relief that I sought, as my anger began to subside.

Why am I so angry? Should I be mad at Marsha and Jessie for assuming that they could control my life? At Gertrude, for trying to smother me? Or Dick, who pointed out my wimpish ways? How about Harriet, who had dumped me long ago? I began to realize that directing my anger at others was merely a smoke screen, a diversion to sidetrack any reproach to the real culprit: *Me.* I was to blame, and any anger that I felt should be directed toward myself. Because it had seemed the easy way, I had let it happen when I became old and stopped being a man.

I took another swallow of the liquor. Normally, I am not a drinking man, but because of the negative aspects of my life, I found that the booze helped me to cope…or escape.

The alcohol was beginning to relax me, causing me to be less cynical in regard to my circumstances. I became more reflective as I made a mental assessment of my life: It was time to face the fact that I suffered some of the ravages of old age. I was rapidly balding, plagued by occasional spells of arthritis and an enlarged prostate; also, I was becoming more forgetful, often misplacing things and becoming cranky when I was unable to find them. Lately, it was becoming more difficult to sleep at night. But worst of all, I had allowed myself to become more dependent on others…both physically and emotionally. Surrendering my independence had robbed me of my confidence.

On the other hand, I still had a lot of things going for me: In spite of my symptoms of old age, my health was generally good, better than that of most people my age; also, my financial status was not terrible, even if my two-bedroom house still retained the knotty pine walls of the fifties in the small den. *What the hell! I'm comfortable with it!* The only shortcoming in my life that was really bugging me was the one thing that was fixable; and that was my submission to the domination of others.

I took another hefty drink from the bottle…this time without a chaser. Since I again hadn't slept well last night the alcohol was making me sleepy. I could hardly hold my eyes open.

I thought about what Dick had said to me: "Step up to the plate and reclaim your manhood." Although he was sometimes shallow and pretentious, he had refused to allow old age to reduce him to submissiveness and dependence. Dick was still a functional, independent man.

Damn, I'm sleepy…

I yawned and removed my glasses. When I placed them on the coffee table the right arm of the pair of glasses came off. The tiny screw that had attached it to the lens was lost somewhere on the carpet. Scouring the floor with my hand failed to locate it. I gave up the search and set the glasses aside; anyway, even if I found the screw I couldn't re-attach the arm without my glasses, which I couldn't use because they were broken. Besides, I was becoming too drowsy for such tedious work. I decided that I would deal with it later.

I determined that I'd had enough whiskey so I replaced the cap on the bottle.

Why am I so sleepy? A nap would be nice, but it would mean that tonight would be another sleepless ordeal, so I decided against it.

I lay back on the couch, reflecting on my recent assessment of my life. My anger was gone and I felt much better. I had decided to reclaim my manhood!

I can't figure out ...why I'm so...sleepy...it must be ...the...boozzzzzzzzzz...

* * *

A vigorous shake awakened me. I looked up into the angry eyes of Marsha. The obvious aroma of her expensive perfume would probably have awakened me without the shake.

"When did you start getting drunk?" she asked.

For a moment I lay silently on the couch trying to comprehend my surroundings. Gradually, my awareness of reality returned.

"I'm not drunk, Marsha," I said, casually.

I rose to a sitting position, cradling my aching head between my hands. Three feet behind Marsha stood Jessie, her arms crossed, eyeing me with a disapproving stare.

Marsha continued, "Well, you've got more than a half bottle of liquor setting there…when did you take up the habit of getting drunk? I've never known you to drink!" She was becoming impatient with me.

Ignoring her question, I asked her, "What time is it?"

"Six o'clock...I just got off work," she replied, "How long have you been asleep?" her demanding tone irritated me.

"Hell, I don't know, and I also don't give a shit!" My disrespectful reply surprised her and caused Jessie to gasp.

"When did you start talking 'trash talk'?" Marsha asked, "Hanging around with Dick Noble is having a bad effect on you!"

Jessie also reprimanded me. "Thomas, I'm shocked that you would use such language. You're just not yourself lately...and it's all because of that awful Dick Noble. You know, from what I've heard, he's a terrible man!"

I didn't bother to reply.

"What's going on with you, Dad?" asked Marsha, "You're acting weird lately."

"Weird?" I smiled at her.

"Yeah, Weird!" she said, "Want me to itemize some of your weird behaviors?"

"Yeah, sure. I'm kinda curious about some of my weirdness."

"Aunt Jessie and I came over here because we're worried about some of the peculiar things you've been doing lately." She placed her hands on her hips in a determined stance while Jessie claimed a seat in the recliner. Her face displayed a tragic expression.

"What am I doing that's so weird?"

"Are you kidding? First of all, Gertrude has been sick for more than a week because she overheard that terrible conversation between you and Melissa. Before that, you had that auto accident. Also I heard about you locking your keys up in the car when it was parked over at Dick Noble's house."

"How'd you hear about that?" I asked.

"Dad, this is a small town. I hear things. I also know about you and Dick Noble drinking beer in that low-brow pool room. In addition to that, you've almost broken Gertrude's heart!"

"How'd I do that?"

"You told her and Aunt Jessie that you weren't going to the class reunion. It's only five days away, you know. Of course you realize that Gertrude has been counting on you taking her. Also, we've called you several times and left a message. For some reason, you're never at home lately."

The side door opened and Melissa walked into the den. The room was getting like Grand Central Station. She grinned and spoke to all of us, then walked to the couch and took a seat beside me. When she hugged me she smelled like some kind of fertilizer, an indication that she had been working with her flowers.

"How have you been doin', Dad? I've tried to call you but you're never at home lately," she said.

"I'm a busy man," I answered. I wondered why she had dropped by.

"Yeah, Melissa," said Marsha, "Aunt Jessie and I have been calling him too." She looked at me. "Where have you been going, Dad?"

I ignored the question. "Who called this family conference?" I asked, "Are you a part of this inquisition, Melissa?"

"No, Dad...I didn't even know that Marsha and Aunt Jessie were coming here." She looked at the bottle. "Whose booze?"

"Mine," I said.

"What are you doin' with liquor?" Melissa asked.

"I was just putting some alcohol on my sore toe," I answered, sarcastically.

"When did you take up drinkin', Dad?" she asked.

Again ignoring the question, I asked, "Melissa, why did you come here?"

"Oh Dad, don't get paranoid," she said, "I just came over to check on you."

"You mean, *check up* on me."

"No, Dad, I..."

Marsha interrupted, "Dad, we hate to jump on you like this, but we're all worried about you."

"Speak for yourself!" said Melissa.

Marsha glared at her, then turned to me. "Dad, I know that you feel defensive when we all start questioning you, but it's just because we love you. We're worried about you."

I smiled at her. "Marsha, why don't you sit down, like Jessie and Melissa? You kinda make me nervous, standing over me like that while I'm sitting on the couch...Sorta makes me feel like you're about to behead me."

Marsha took a seat in the rocker. Jessie immediately spoke. "Thomas, I've got something else on my mind that concerns me. I was talking to Kathy Plemons from your graduating class and she told me that she had gotten a letter from her old friend, Harriet. She said that

Harriet is coming to your class reunion. Did you know that, Thomas? Is that why you don't want to go?"

"Harriet who?" I asked, innocently.

"You know who I mean! *Harriet Dawson!* The woman who made a fool of you years ago! Maybe you shouldn't attend the reunion if you have to be around that hussy!"

"No…that's not why I'm not going. But since she's going, maybe I ought to go and see if she still has the hots for me." I was again being sarcastic.

"Thomas, I wouldn't joke about such things," said Jessie.

Melissa laughed.

Marsha stood and stared at me. "Maybe we ought to go, Jessie. Dad's in one of his contemptuous moods. When he gets like this you can't talk to him. I'm sorry we came here. I guess Dad's sorry, too."

I smiled at her. "No, Marsha, I'm not sorry you came…as a matter of fact, I'm kinda glad. I'm glad Melissa's here, too, because I've got a few things I want to say to all of you. Sit down, Marsha."

She remained standing.

"I said, SIT DOWN, Marsha!" I spoke in a commanding voice. She looked surprised, then reclaimed her seat.

"First of all, I want to tell you that I really appreciate your concern for me. I love all of you, and I know that you love me; also, I realize that I'm getting old, and sometimes I need help from you, but when I do, I'll ask for it. However, I'm not a child. I have some physical limitations, but as far as I know, I'm still sound of mind.

I appreciate your love, but damn it, you're smothering me to death! You've been running my life and it's more my fault than yours because I've permitted you to do it. I want you to know I'm reclaiming my life!"

Jessie appeared to be stunned, while Marsha's face reflected anger. Melissa only smiled.

"That was quite a speech, Dad," said Marsha, "But the simple fact is that you need someone to take care of you."

"Someone like Gertrude?" I asked. "That's another thing I want you to stop doing...pushing Gertrude on me!"

"Well, you need someone to help you," she said.

I looked her in the eye. "Marsha, maybe I didn't make myself clear, so I'm going to lay down some ground rules for all of you: First, I want you to lay off of me about Gertrude; second, I want you to stop choosing my friends; third; stop barging in here without knocking; fourth, stop bringing food over here that you think is good for me...I'll eat whatever I please! Also, I'm tired of you always criticizing my driving. When it's time for me to stop driving, I'll know it. I would enjoy your visits a lot more if you didn't nag at me every time you come to see me. Starting now, I'm taking charge of my life!"

Except for Melissa, who only smiled at me, my declaration of independence had fallen on deaf ears.

"What are we going to do with him, Jessie?" Marsha appeared to be frustrated.

Jessie looked at me with a pitiful, pleading gaze. "Thomas, why don't you close the house up...maybe sell it and come and live with me?"

"You know that wouldn't work, Jessie," I said.

Marsha stood and looked at Melissa. "Maybe Melissa could move in here with him. She could cook for him and drive him to wherever he needs to go."

Melissa smiled. "I don't think that's a good idea. With Dad's wild, swingin' ways I might cramp his style." She got up and walked into the kitchen.

Again, I started to feel depressed. Establishing my freedom was going to be a tougher job than I had thought.

Melissa walked back into the room carrying two glasses and a bowl of ice cubes. She placed them beside the liquor on the coffee table and reclaimed her seat beside me on the couch.

"What's that for?" asked Marsha.

Melissa dropped ice into the two glasses and poured two generous drinks. She grinned at Marsha and her Aunt Jessie. "I feel like having a drink…and anyway, if Dad's gonna start drinkin,' he might as well learn to do it right!"

Jessie was astounded. Marsha glared at Melissa. "I must have been out of my mind to suggest that you move in with Dad! You're just trying to make me madder! Ever since we were little girls you've always tried to irritate me. Rather than having you move in with him, Dad would be better off living by himself!"

"Amen!" I said, and lifted my glass. Melissa did likewise. "Cheers, Dad!" In unison, we downed our drinks.

"Let's get out of here, Aunt Jessie!" said Marsha. As they walked through the door Jessie gave me a tragic look.

I looked at Melissa. "Why do you like to irritate Marsha like that?"

“I don’t know, Dad.” She poured herself another drink. Questioning me with her eyes, she held the bottle toward me.

“No thanks, Melissa. I’m really not much of a drinker.”

“That’s not what I’ve heard, Dad.” She smiled, mischievously.

“Well, I probably couldn’t keep up with you,” I said.

“Dad, I really don’t drink that much.”

We sat for a while without talking as she sipped on her drink. Finally she smiled and spoke. “Dad, what Marsha said about me movin’ in with you…it’s occasionally crossed my mind, but I wouldn’t want you to feel like I was doin’ it so I could take care of you. Someday you may need someone to help you, but that day’s not here yet.”

“Thanks for understanding, Melissa,” I said. I smiled at her. “It’s not that I wouldn’t enjoy your company here, Melissa, but I want to live my own life.”

She returned my smile. “You’re a good man, Daddy, but sometimes I’m not so good…and I want to live my own life, too. Maybe when I’m about eighty years old I’ll move in with you and we can take care of each other.”

She set her glass down on the coffee table. “I gotta go, Dad.” She again hugged me and was soon quickly out the door. Melissa was never one to dally around for very long.

I carried the remaining whiskey, ice cubes and glasses into the kitchen, and then pulled a roll of duct tape from the cabinet. I returned to the den and using the duct tape, re-attached the arm to my pair of glasses. To test them, I put them on and noticed that the tape worked fine; however, about a half inch of the right lens was covered by the tape. Even while wearing my glasses I was unable to find the tiny missing screw. *Oh, well...I'll get them repaired in a day or so.*

For the remainder of the evening I watched television. Because of my alcohol-induced afternoon nap, I dreaded bedtime, for it probably meant another sleepless night.

At midnight before retiring to bed, I went into the bathroom for a sleeping pill. I opened the bottle, noticing that there was only one remaining capsule. When I extracted it from the bottle, it somehow slipped from my hand and fell into the damp sink, promptly dissolving.

Reluctantly, I crawled into bed. If I could only relax and not allow my mind to relive any disturbing episodes from my past, I might be able to sleep. The instant that I placed my head on my pillow, the phone rang. It was Dick, and he sounded excited.

"Tom...Harriet just got into town!"

Chapter 11

It was 4:30 a.m. when the urge to urinate again awakened me following a near-sleepless night. I had previously gotten up at 2:00, then after a trip to the bathroom I had briefly drifted off to sleep. Now that I was fully awake, I knew that going back to sleep would be difficult for me.

Physically exhausted and with sleepy eyes, I crawled out of bed. I walked into the bathroom, and while relieving myself, gazed into the mirror. The mole on my right sideburn appeared to be larger. I promised myself to schedule an appointment with my dermatologist about removing it, along with several other moles on my back. I badly needed a shave and my nostrils appeared to have sprouted a new crop of hair; in fact, it seemed that even the hair in my eyebrows and ears had grown thicker. *Why is it that when a man becomes old, hair seems to spring up everywhere except where he wants it...on top of his head?*

Since I still felt sleepy, I crawled back into bed; however, my attempt to doze off was thwarted by the snarling mating calls of a chorus of amorous cats in my yard. Particularly irritating was the siren-like mournful wail of a horny tomcat near my bedroom window. His amplified groans were louder than all of the moans of the other cats combined. This feline family was the cherished collection of my disgusting next-door neighbor, Silas Wooten. He and I shared a mutual loathing for each other that stemmed from the many confrontations between us caused by the intrusion of his unattended gang of cats. His seven cats spent most of their time on my property. When not depositing generous amounts of cat manure in my yard, they were often draped across the hood or the roof of my car. I realized that I should park my car in the garage, but there wasn't room; for it was filled with discarded items that mostly belong to Melissa and Marsha.

Silas Wooten was a peculiar man who was disliked by almost everyone who knew him...particularly by me. A retired county deputy who was now in his seventies, he had remained a bachelor during the entire span of his life, probably because no woman in her right mind could tolerate him. He was a grouchy old hermit who divided most of his time between accumulating cats and spreading malicious gossip about his neighbors. Because of their common interests, I figured that it would be a fitting twist of fate if somehow he could hook up with Gertrude. Actually, however, she was too good for him.

In frustration, I lay awake as the desperate howling

of the cats grew louder. With a sigh of resignation, I realized that it would be necessary to go outside and chase away the horny little pests.

My arthritic right knee throbbed with pain as I rose from the bed. I quickly put on my robe, and in my bare feet I walked into the hallway and switched on the outside light. I hurriedly limped out the side door into the yard beside the driveway. Before I had a chance to chase away the pesky cats I stepped on some sharp object beside my car with the arch of my right foot. *Damn, that hurts!* Instantly, I almost jumped out of my skin when an unending series of ear-piercing reverberations from my car horn disrupted the early morning silence. *How did this happen?* My mind was in turmoil as I desperately tried to find a way to stop the repetitive blasts from my horn. I quickly realized that only pressing the alarm button on my car keys would stop the irritating pandemonium.

The outside light of my next-door neighbor came on and Silas Wooten stepped onto his front porch. With his hands on his hips, he assumed a defiant stance.

"Damn it, Spencer, shut off that car alarm!" he shouted, "You're waking up the whole damned neighborhood!"

Instead of answering him, I quickly turned to go back inside my house, with the full intention of finding my car keys in order to shut off the horn. At that moment, I stepped into something soft and wet with my left foot. The sickening odor that followed clearly identified the substance: It was cat manure. Three steps later, my right foot suffered the same fate. I almost fell on my face as my foot slid in the wet feces. I now had a gob of cat poop between my toes and on the balls of both of my bare feet.

Angrily, I turned to my repugnant neighbor. I shouted in order to be heard above the blasting blare of the horn, "Wooten, I just stepped into another pile of cat shit! Gather up your damned cats and get them off my property!"

"Screw you, Spencer! Just shut off that damned alarm!" he screamed.

When I turned away from him to go back into my house I again stepped on the sharp object. *How could I be so unlucky? Not only did I step in cat crap with both feet, but I also stepped on the same gravel twice!* With my next step, I again felt the sharp thing dig into the same foot. I instantly realized that the spiny object had become lodged in the cat poop on the ball of my foot.

As the horn continued its repetitive blasts, I took a seat on my front steps and inspected the bottom of my right foot. Embedded in the blob of cat manure that was caked between my toes was my set of car keys. I dug them from the gob of feces and shut off the car horn, realizing that I now had cat manure on my right hand and car keys as well as on both feet. Apparently, after parking my car last night I had accidentally dropped my car keys beside my vehicle. Stepping on them after walking into my yard to chase away the cats had activated my car alarm.

Silas Wooten laughed as he watched my unsuccessful attempts to clean my feet in the grass; then he re-entered his house and turned off the porch light. I casually walked over to his front porch and wiped away most of the cat dung from my feet on his welcome mat.

Walking awkwardly on my heels in order to keep the cat manure off my carpet, I re-entered the door to my den. I wobbled like a drunken sailor as I stumbled through the house toward my bathroom. Although I was finally able to cleanse my feet of the cat manure, I wasn't nearly as successful in ridding myself of the sickening odor. *What a frustrating way to begin the day!* Not only was I absent-minded, but I was accident-prone and plagued with bad luck as well.

Since I was now too agitated to go back to bed, I decided to stay up. Dick's midnight phone call about Harriet had kept me awake for most of the night, anyway. Her arrival in Northridge filled me with both excitement and worry. I wanted to confront her at some point; yet, I dreaded the confrontation.

I cringed at the burdensome task of shaving and getting dressed, so I compromised: I dressed myself and decided to forego shaving; after all, who would see me except my old cronies at the Cracker Barrel? I brushed my teeth and then ran a comb through my thinning hair. When I inspected the image of my head in the mirror, I noticed that the part in my hair had continued to gradually inch toward the left side of my head, for I was now parting it just above my left ear.

Before leaving, I decided to check my phone messages. The only call on my answering machine was from my doctor's office reminding me of my appointment for June twenty-seventh at 9:30 a.m., which was yesterday's date. *Oh my God! I was scheduled to have a colonoscopy yesterday and I completely forgot it!* I realized that I would have to pay for the missed appointment and then reschedule it.

I arrived at the restaurant later than usual and claimed my customary seat beside Dick. I greeted both him and Head, noticing that neither Pinky nor Dummy had yet arrived. Both Dick and Head had finished eating. I ordered breakfast and began sipping on my coffee.

Dick's dark sunglasses hid his eyes. "You look like hell, pal."

"Thanks, Dick," I said sarcastically, "I feel like hell. I didn't get a much sleep."

Head spoke up, "What's the matter…are you still gettin' up several times durin' the night to pee in little dribbles? I got some stuff from my doctor that cures that problem. Since I been takin' it I don't get up but once durin' the night. No more dribblin' for me! Now I'm pissin' a stream that's like squirtin' a garden hose!" He grinned at me menacingly with his oversized dentures.

"What's the name of the medicine your doctor prescribed?" I asked.

"It's…uh…hell, I forget. I'll bring it tomorrow so you can ask your doctor about prescribin' it for you."

I looked at my watch. "It's almost nine o'clock," I said, "Where are Pinky and Dummy? They're usually the first to arrive."

"Oh, that's right, you weren't here yesterday," replied Head, "Haven't you heard the news about Pinky? He fell down an escalator at J.C.Penney's and broke his hip. He's over at Park View Hospital. They had to do surgery on him…it took several hours."

"Oh, no! When did it happen?" I asked.

Dick answered, "Day before yesterday…wasn't it Head?"

"Yeah, it was late in the afternoon," replied Head.

"Well, where's Dummy?" I asked.

Head took a sip of coffee. "He's been at the hospital with Pinky most of the time since it happened."

I was puzzled. "I thought they hated each other."

Head smiled. "Yeah, well, you can't tell about them two guys. I think they're just blowin' off steam when they jaw at each other. They're probably just gettin' rid of some of their frustrations."

Marlene arrived with my breakfast. "Here you are, sweetheart," she cooed, as she placed my plate of sausage and eggs in front of me. Before leaving, she winked and patted me on the shoulder as if I were a cute puppy.

I began nibbling on my breakfast. Dick took a sip of coffee and then turned toward me. "What did you do yesterday?"

"Nothing much. I was supposed to have a colonoscopy at 9:30, but it slipped my mind."

Head grimaced. "Damn! I hate those things. I had one last month and they found polyps. Had to have 'em cut out. I'm scheduled for an upper G.I. next month." His thick lens magnified his bulbous eyes as he looked at me.

"How are your new glasses?" I asked. "Can you see a lot better with them?"

"Yeah, so-so. I'll be able to see much better when they remove my cataracts." He looked at Dick. "Dick, you never complain about your ailments. Don't you have anything wrong with you?"

"Well, other than this bad knee I got from playin' football years ago, and a toenail fungus, there's nothin' else wrong with me," he proudly announced.

I had known for years that Dick had arthritis in one of his knees, but his pride kept him from admitting it.

Head slowly stood. "I gotta go over to the hospital and see how Pinky's doin'. By the way, Dick, it was sure nice of you to stand good for Pinky's hospital bill. He never did carry enough insurance."

Dick seemed embarrassed. "Hell, it was nothin'." Dick's generosity didn't surprise me, for he had always had a soft spot in his heart for those less fortunate than he.

"Tom, try to get over to the hospital and visit Pinky if you have time. Dick, he'd probably like to see you again, too," said Head.

"Sure thing, Head…What room is he in?" I asked.

"Room 304…He'd appreciate seein' both of you."

We told Head goodbye and he strolled out of the restaurant.

"I guess I ought to go see Pinky sometime today." I looked at Dick. "Do you plan to go see him?"

"Yeah, I guess so. If you want, we can go together."

We sat for a while sipping our coffee. Now that Dick and I were alone, we both seemed reluctant to initiate a conversation about Harriet.

"Why didn't you call me yesterday?" Dick suddenly asked.

"Well, I meant to, but I had a couple of drinks and then slept away most of the afternoon."

Dick laughed. "In other words, you got drunk and passed out!"

"No, I didn't get drunk at all. But I suppose you could say that I passed out. I hadn't had much sleep the night before, and I guess the booze just relaxed me."

He again laughed. "Man, you've been hittin' the booze a lot lately. I must be a bad influence on you. Where'd you get the liquor?"

"It was a bottle that you gave me years ago for my birthday."

"See? I told you I was a bad influence on you." He smiled mischievously. "Is that all you did yesterday…pass out?"

"No, not really. Remember how you told me that I ought to start showing some spunk? Well, yesterday, I had a little talk with Marsha, Jessie, and Melissa. We had a family meeting. I reclaimed my manhood, Dick."

"Good for you, Tom! But I ought to warn you, it ain't gonna be easy. It's hard to break people out of an established pattern."

"Yeah, I quickly found that out," I said, "They're already resisting me."

"Well, at least you made a start. Just stick with it and don't back down. I'm proud of you, buddy…and you should be proud of yourself!"

"To a certain extent I am proud. But I'm not too proud of not going to see Gertrude when she was sick for a week. She's unattractive to me, but I should have gone to see her and at least checked on her. Hell, I'd even go visit a dog if it was sick."

Dick stuck a toothpick in his mouth and signaled to Marlene for more coffee. He pointed his finger at me. "Tom, you know as well as I do that Gertrude was just fakin.' You need to hold the line with her," he emphasized, "You give Gertrude an inch and she'll take a mile."

Another Dick Noble adage.

"Dick, why would anybody in his right mind want to give Gertrude an inch?" I asked.

"An excellent question, Tom. I must be a complete idiot to have made such a statement." We both laughed and then sat for a long while without speaking.

Marlene arrived with the coffee and refilled our cups.

"Thanks, Marlene," Dick smiled at her.

"Sure thing, honey," She returned Dick's smile and walked away. He lowered his sunglasses and lustfully eyed her bouncing bottom.

"You know, Tom, I bet she wouldn't be half bad in the sack. I believe she probably feels the same about me. Did you notice how she always calls me 'honey'?" Dick's enormous ego had thrust his mind into a deep delusion in regard to Marlene's perception of him.

For a brief period we remained quiet, sipping our coffee. Finally I smiled at him. "Dick, I know that you're just dying to tell me about Harriet, so go ahead and tell me. Why are you being so reluctant to bring up the subject? Last night when you called me you seemed excited."

He looked embarrassed. "It's just that every time I bring up her name you start acting weird. You even acted weird last night when I called you and told you that she had arrived in town."

"I was just about to doze off to sleep when you called, Dick. And why does everybody keep calling me weird?"

"If the shoe fits, wear it, buddy," He peered at me over the top of his sunglasses.

"How did you learn that she's back in town?" I asked.

"She called me, of course."

"Of course? Why do you say *'of course?'* Why is it such a foregone conclusion that she'd automatically call you? Why not *me?"*

"I guess that she figured that you'd act weird…or maybe she feels a little guilty about jilting you. Hell, I don't know." He seemed confused.

"Well, she didn't call me, but I did get a letter from her," I said.

"Oh? When?"

"Yesterday."

"What'd she say?"

"Getting a little personal, aren't you? I didn't ask you what she said in her phone call to you."

"Okay, then don't tell me."

I looked at him and smiled. "I don't mind telling you, Dick. She wrote, 'Dear Tom', then asked how I was doing, then she said that she was doing okay, and that she was coming to the reunion. End of story."

"And that's all?" He removed his sunglasses.

"That's all." I inspected his face for a reaction, but I only received a blank stare. "How long is she going to stay, Dick?"

"She didn't say."

"Where is she staying while she's in town?"

"At the Mountain View Inn on Highway 321. She has the room for a week or so but I don't know if she'll stay longer. Why do you ask?"

"Well, I might just drive over there and crawl in the sack with her tonight, if that's okay with you."

"Get serious, Tom! Anyway, if you can pull it off, I'd say it'd be worth the drive, and it's perfectly okay with me." He grinned. "I'd do the same thing if I thought she'd let me."

"Really? Why does that not surprise me?" I asked. He laughed.

Marlene came back and refilled our coffee.

"Thanks, honey," Dick said, with a wink.

"You're welcome, sweetheart." She flashed her sexiest grin at him and walked away, while Dick again ogled her rear end.

"Don't you ever think about anything else?" I asked him.

"Yeah...occasionally."

I went back to the subject of Harriet. "Dick, do you think she'll call me?"

"I don't know, Tom," he replied, "Anyway, you'll see her at the class reunion."

"Unless she calls me, I'm not going," I declared.

"Don't say that, ol' buddy! I want the three of us to get together, just like old times!"

"If she wants to include me in the relationship she'll have to invite me."

Dick signaled Marlene for our checks. "Let's get outta here, Tom," he said, "Why don't we go to the hospital and see Pinky?"

Marlene arrived with our checks as we stood to leave.

"You two cutie-pies come back to see me, y'hear?"

After leaving the restaurant, Dick and I drove

directly to visit with Pinky. We stayed with Pinky for about a half hour before Dick drove me back to my vehicle. When I got out of his car, I said, "Dick, don't be surprised if I don't attend the reunion."

He only shook his head. "Man, you're weird."

After watching television until about 11:00 p.m., I showered and prepared to retire to bed. I picked up the ringing telephone. "Hello?"

The sound of her voice rendered me almost speechless.

"Hello…Tom? This is Harriet."

I knew that I was facing another sleepless night.

Chapter 12

Her voice sounded the same as the memory that was embedded in my mind…throaty, melodious, and sweet, yet witty and mischievous; it transported me a half century backward in time. Upon hearing her name, my heart skipped a beat, and I sat without speaking for a moment.

"Tom…can you hear me? Are you there? This is Harriet!"

"Yes, I'm here…I can hear you…this is Tom…" I was almost tongue-tied.

She laughed wildly. "I know who you are, Tom. Don't you think I know who I called?"

"Oh yeah. How are you, Harriet?"

"I'm fine, Tom. Gee, it's good to hear your voice!"

"You sound the same," I said.

"In some ways I am the same, but not entirely. A lot of water has passed over the dam since we last saw each other."

At a loss for words, my mind struggled for something to say.

"How have you been doing, Harriet? How's your health?" What a dumb question, I thought.

"My health is fine, Tom. I have a touch of arthritis in my hips and an occasional hot flash. Other than that, I'm doing okay. How about you?"

"The same as you," I said.

"You have hot flashes, too?" She again laughed.

"No, but I do have a little bit of arthritis."

"You sound the same, too, Tom. And I can see that you're still bashful when you're talking on the phone."

"It's just that your phone call surprised me," I explained, "I wasn't expecting a call from you."

The sound of her voice stirred the mixed emotions of excitement and guilt within me; for I felt that in some obscure way I was betraying Jenny.

"Did you get my letter?" she asked.

"Yeah, I got it yesterday. You didn't say much in it."

"I was kinda in a hurry when I wrote it, Tom. I knew I'd be calling you anyway."

"Well, it's been a long time, Harriet. You probably didn't have that much to say, anyhow," I said. "Unless we just talk about high school days, we don't know enough about each other to carry on much of a conversation anymore."

"Oh, but that's not true, Tom. You don't know much about me, but I know a lot about you."

"Such as?"

"Such as ...I know that you stayed here in Northridge and operated your own small business. And

I know that you married Jennifer Clinton and had two daughters…Let's see, wasn't it Melissa and, uh…"

"Marsha," I reminded her.

"Tom, I know that Jenny was a wonderful wife to you. I'm so glad."

"Yes, she was wonderful. She was the love of my life. I lost her ten years ago." I felt a tinge of sadness.

"I'm so sorry, Tom. But I'm glad that you had a wonderful marriage. You deserved it."

"How do you know so much about me? And Why?"

"Kathy Plemons writes to me occasionally. She graduated with us. Do you remember her? The reason I kept up with you is because I've never forgotten you, Tom….and the good times we had together in high school. Remember?"

"Yeah, I remember. But you knowing so much about me kinda puts me at a disadvantage because I know very little about your life after you left here. Dick tells me that you're not married anymore."

"That's true. I've been divorced for several years. It's a long story, Tom."

I didn't press her for the details. "So what brings you back to Northridge? And how long will you be staying?"

"Oh, I don't know. I wanted to attend the reunion and I guess the memories of this place, and the memories of my good times with you and Dick just drew me back. I'll probably stay for at least a week."

"Where are you staying?"

"At the Mountain View Inn, for now. I can't wait to see you, Tom!"

"Yeah, maybe our paths will cross while you're

here," I was still wary of her.

"Maybe our paths will cross? Tom, the main reason I came back to Northridge was to see you...and Dick!"

"I'm flattered," I said. sarcastically. I somehow hoped that my sarcasm would hurt her. She ignored my cutting remark.

"Tom, I want us to get together before we go to the reunion."

"I'm not sure I'm going to the reunion, Harriet."

"You're not sure you're going? How could you miss it? It's special! It's our fiftieth reunion!"

"I was never much of a social creature, Harriet. Besides, all it amounts to is a bunch of has-beens acting half their age, and three or four successful people bragging about how rich and important they've become compared to the other nobodies like me."

"Tom, you're far from being a nobody! You've had a successful and happy life! I envy you. I only wish that my life had been as rewarding as yours. And you had a wonderful wife who really loved you, and two fine children."

"Yes...and I'm very thankful for that," I said.

"You know, Tom, I think I'm a little jealous of Jenny."

"Get serious, Harriet!" I said, with some resentment.

"I truly am jealous of her, Tom. I'm jealous of both her and you because you've both had a life of happiness that I never experienced."

Although I was tempted to tell her, 'You asked for it,' I somehow felt sympathy for her. "Fate sometimes plays some cruel tricks on us, Harriet," I said.

I changed the subject. "Have you talked with Dick yet?"

"Yes, and that's another reason I called you," she explained, "We have so much to talk about. Dick and I would like for you to join us for dinner tomorrow night at Ruby Tuesday's. Can you come?"

"You've already talked to Dick? And you have a dinner date with him? How gracious of you to have an after-thought of your old friend! And you both even had the generosity to ask me to join you!" I said, caustically.

"No, Tom, you've got it all wrong. I used an unfortunate choice of words. What I meant was that I called Dick and asked him if the three of us could get together. I don't have a date with him! If you want to call it a date, then I guess you could say it would be a date with both of you."

"You've been calling Dick a lot lately, haven't you?" I asked, "It's nice that you finally got around to calling me!"

"Tom, you know how Dick is. He's easy to talk with. Everybody feels comfortable talking to Dick," she explained.

"And you don't feel comfortable talking with me?" I asked.

"I've wanted to call you many times, Tom. When I heard that Jenny had died, my heart just ached for you. But I was afraid you wouldn't want to talk to me, after…"

"After what?"

"After the way we…parted, years ago."

"Why don't we change the subject?" I asked.

"Yes, why don't we? Anyway, will you join Dick and me for dinner tomorrow night? We planned it for seven o'clock."

"I don't know if I can, Harriet. I'll have to look at

my calendar to see what I have scheduled." My calendar? That's a joke. I have one somewhere, but I don't even know where it is. Anyway, I hadn't scheduled anything in weeks.

"Are you that busy?" she asked.

"Well, I still have a small business, you know. Sometimes I have dinner with a customer."

Her tone became softer. "Tom, do you remember homecoming night when we were seniors? I've often dreamed of that night over the years. The big harvest moon overhead, and you and I and Dick got together after the big football game? Then we took Dick to join his friends, and it was just you and me, remember?"

"Yeah, I remember that night. You weren't able to be a cheerleader because you were on the homecoming court. Too bad you didn't win the homecoming queen crown. Who was it that won, anyway. Do you remember?"

"Patsy Armstrong." Harriet laughed. "I'm still mad at her!"

"Yeah, well, like you said, a lot of water has passed over the dam since then. I've about forgotten most of those days."

"Yes, it was a long time ago." She sounded sad.

"Fifty years," I reminded her.

There was a moment of silence.

"Tom, will you please try to come? To dinner tomorrow night, as well as the reunion?"

"I'll let you know, Harriet. What's your phone number there at the motel?"

She gave me the number and we said our goodbyes. I hung up, and for a long time I stared at the phone.

Chapter 13

In utter frustration, I meticulously stuck the tip of the thread in my mouth to wet it; then, with my fore-finger and thumb I twisted the end to a sharp point. With my magnifying glass I peered intently at the eye of the needle. Once again, my attempt to insert the thread into the tiny eye had resulted in failure. *Damn! Missed it again!*

In disgust, I put away the button, needle, and spool of thread; then I tossed the shirt with the missing button into the corner. I decided to give up replacing the button and take the shirt to a seamstress. *When did the simple task of threading a needle become so difficult?*

My failure at the tedious task had been partially caused by my trembling fingers, the result of a near-sleepless night brought on by Harriet's late phone call.

The ringing doorbell gave me a start; however, when I opened the front door no one was there. I closed the door, but I again heard the ring. This time I discovered the source: The chime was coming from the soap opera on my television set. I was glad that no one had witnessed my senility.

I began to feel guilty about neglecting my business, so I decided to drive to my sign shop. I wasn't in the mood to work, but at least I could check my telephone messages. Before climbing into my car I noticed the muddy cat tracks on the hood. *Silas Wooten's cats again,* I thought. As I drove toward my shop I held the fervent hope that no one had called. Maybe I would be lucky enough to escape the responsibility of work for a while longer.

I pulled the car into the parking area in front of my small business. A quick glance at the sign on the building depressed me. "Spencer Sign Service, Established 1960." It had probably been at least ten years since I had repainted it. The paint on the hand-lettered sign had faded terribly. I badly needed to replace the painted sign with a modern, more durable vinyl sign. The sign reflected the most typical characteristic of its owner: *Outdated.*

My answering machine contained at least a dozen messages. *Damn it, business is booming, I see!* Several calls were from people trying to sell me something, one was from Dick, a couple had left no message at all, and I was relieved to see that only three were from potential customers. Two of them wanted an estimate, which I gave them by phone to ponder over, and the final message was about a legitimate job that I had already promised. With a quick phone call I managed to stall the customer until after July 4th…after the class reunion. I decided to return Dick's call later.

I locked the front door and drove away. While driving home I reflected on last night's phone call from Harriet. I was in a quandary about making the right decisions in regard to having dinner with Dick and Harriet as well as attending the class reunion. The recent conversation with Harriet had reawakened old emotions that I had long ago buried, causing an ambivalence in me.

I had some quick decisions to make; also if I decided to attend the reunion, it would be necessary to call Gertrude, informing her of the fact that I wouldn't be taking her. I owed her that much, and after all, I had finally taken control of my life, hadn't I?

Since it was impossible for me to think objectively, I needed another perspective on my whole situation. I decided that I needed to talk to someone about my dilemma. For obvious reasons I couldn't talk to either Marsha or Jessie; neither could I get an objective nor intelligent opinion from Dick, for he was involved in the situation. I decided my most viable option was to seek the advice of Melissa. Since she had cancelled her vacation trip with her boyfriend, she would more than likely be working in her shop today. She would hear me out without making a snap judgment about me; but it would require my telling her about my former romantic relationship with Harriet. *Would she see Harriet as a rival, or an enemy to Jenny...her mother?*

It was 7:30 a.m. when I pulled my car to the curb in front of Melissa's shop, MISSY'S FLOWERS. The sign identifying her small business was simple and direct. By comparison, its contemporary style made the sign on my building appear as outdated as the hula-hoop. I thought it ironic, indeed, that I, as a sign shop owner would have an outdated sign on my business.

The small bell that jingled as I entered the front door captured her attention. From her stooped position she looked up at me as she swept fallen flower petals into a dust pan. Smiling, she set aside her broom and walked to me, greeting me with a hug.

"Why, hello Dad, what brings you here? Are you shopping for some flowers for Gertrude?" She laughed.

The pained expression etched on my face drew a hearty laugh from her. I quickly replaced my sour look with a grin.

"Hi, Melissa. I just dropped by to see you, and see how your business is going. Do you still have Becky working for you?"

"Yeah, but she doesn't get here 'til nine."

Melissa resumed her sweeping as I glanced around the interior of her small shop. It was a modest business, at best, and I figured that other than the satisfaction she derived from creating flower arrangements, Melissa probably profited very little from it. Her shop was tiny and sparsely furnished, but neat. In spite of her haphazard personal life, in business matters she was very well organized. In the front area of her shop, a variety of potted flowers and plants were neatly arranged in evenly-spaced rows on plastic shelves. In the back was the large cooler where she kept her freshly-cut roses, carnations, and gladiolas. Hanging baskets containing a variety of plants and flowers adorned the opposite wall. A large table resting in the center provided the necessary space for creating flower arrangements, while a small cubicle to the right of the table served as her office.

She stopped sweeping and began to pluck some withered petals from one of her potted plants. Without looking up from her task, she asked, "And what brings you here so early, Dad? You're not usually up and about this early."

"Am I keeping you from your work, Melissa?"

She stopped working and grinned. "No, Dad. I'm just piddlin' around, tidyin' up a bit. I don't open 'til 8:30. Don't have much business right now anyway. Had a funeral last week, and I've got a wedding this week…that's about it."

I was hesitant to begin. I took a seat on a nearby stool and smiled at her.

"Melissa, can we talk?"

She looked at me curiously and then slowly claimed a seat facing me on a vacant end of a low shelf. "What's up, Dad? Are you worried about something?"

"Well, I'm not exactly worried, but I'm just pondering over some things. I need to make some decisions. I realize that you can't make them for me, but I just felt like talking to somebody."

She laughed. "I'm not so sure you can trust the judgment of your scatter-brained daughter, but I'll give it my best shot." Then her expression grew serious. "Dad, you know you can always talk to me."

"Melissa, my life has been getting kinda weird lately," I stated hesitantly, "I feel like my life is in limbo."

"In what way, Dad?"

"Well, since Marsha and your Aunt Jessie have

been nagging at me so much lately, I decided to regain my independence from them. But maybe they're right about me, because I keep goofing up. Maybe I *am* slipping."

"Everybody goofs up, Dad. Join the club!"

"But I seem to be goofing up more than usual lately. Maybe I shouldn't be living by myself. Marsha and Jessie seem to be genuinely worried about me. Maybe their worry is justified."

She leaned toward me, crossing her arms, then looked into my eyes.

"Dad, I'm worried about you, too."

"You too, huh?" I asked.

"Yeah, but I'm worried about you for the opposite reasons than those of Marsha and Aunt Jessie."

"What do you mean? Why are you worried about me? What opposite reasons?"

"Dad, I'm worried that if you give up your independence, you'll just wither away and die. I'm scared that you'll start feeling useless and worthless. And when a person feels that way he might as well be dead. You're still an intelligent, productive man. You can still have some rewarding years ahead of you."

"But Marsha and Jessie don't seem to feel that way," I explained.

Her expression became more serious. "Dad, I don't doubt that Marsha and Aunt Jessie have your best interests at heart. But I think they're wrong. I think you ought to regain your independence. Don't drop out of the world, but rejoin it! What else is worryin' you?"

My mind drifted back across a half century as I

hesitantly related the story of my past involvement with Harriet: Our steamy love affair, her abandonment of me, Dick Noble's involvement and my fight with him, and the emotional pain that had afterward consumed me. I bared my soul to her, with the exception of one detail: I spared her the information about her mother's unexpected pregnancy…the unplanned event that had brought Melissa into the world.

After I finished the story, we sat for awhile in silence. Melissa's expression was a mixture of sympathy and puzzlement. Finally, she spoke.

"I don't understand, Dad. Why is this worrying you now? Fifty years later?"

"Harriet is back in town. She came back for our class reunion," I explained.

"Yeah, I heard Aunt Jessie say something about that the other day, but I didn't attach much importance to it. What's the problem? You're not still carrying the torch for her, are you?"

"No, Melissa, I'm not! And I want you to know that I loved your mother with all of my heart! This was before I met your mom."

"So what's the problem?" She looked puzzled.

"I don't know exactly. She hurt me so deeply that maybe I have never forgiven her. Also, Dick seems to feel that I've never forgiven him. For some reason, I don't want to see Harriet. She took away my self-esteem. I don't want to face her. I just want to hide from her until the reunion is over…until she leaves Northridge. But at the same time, I'm curious about her."

"Is she still married?"

"No, she's been divorced for several years."

"Did she have any kids?"

"No."

"Dad, you seem to be trying to reach a decision about something. What is it?"

"Well, she called me last night and asked me to join her and Dick for dinner tonight. Also, she wants me to go to the reunion. I have mixed feelings about both events."

"Are you asking me whether you should do either, or both?" She was curious.

"No...but I'd kinda like to hear your comments about it."

She slowly stood and faced me, crossing her arms. "Dad, I'm going to give you the same advice that you used to give Marsha and me when we were growing up. *You don't solve any problem by hiding from it.* Remember telling us that?"

"Yeah, I remember."

"Dad, you're at a crucial point in your life. You can either stiffen your backbone and face the world and be a part of it, or you can hide from it...and wither up and die! I don't know whether or not you should join Harriet and Dick for dinner, but I think you ought to attend your class reunion. That's the only way you're going to get back your self-esteem and resolve your feelings about Harriet."

"Melissa, even if I choose to stay away from the reunion, that doesn't mean I'm hiding from the world." I protested.

She displayed a look of impatience. "It means that maybe you're afraid to discover your true feelings, and that you don't trust your own judgment enough to deal with it! Besides, this 'Harriet' person may not be such a bad woman after all. We all make mistakes, you know."

"Maybe I don't trust my own judgment," I said, "I don't seem to have the confidence that I once had. For instance, Dick Noble has been trying to get me to go on a trip with him, but I don't have the confidence or the enthusiasm to leave Northridge for a week."

"Maybe you should take him up on it."

"I can't afford it. He insists on paying for it, but I don't want Dick's charity."

"Why not? I'm sure he doesn't consider it *charity.* He has plenty of money. He wants to show you what a good friend he is to you. Maybe you haven't forgiven him, either."

"I've forgiven him. At least, I think I have."

She reclaimed her seat on the edge of the lower shelf and looked directly into my eyes. "Dad, I feel that I really need to say this to you. We all get old eventually, but you've let getting old rob you of your confidence. Lately, you've crawled into a shell. Break out of that shell! Re-establish your independence. Trust your judgment…go to the reunion. Get involved in your business again; also, take that trip with Dick Noble, and above all, dump Gertrude! You should get back into circulation…maybe even meet some women friends. You know, it's possible that you may even want to get married again. And another thing, Dad, you need to stop feeling guilty about getting involved with a woman. I know you loved Mom, but she's gone.

She'd want you to be happy."

I smiled at her. "You seem to have more confidence in me than I have in myself," I said, "What about my forgetfulness, and my blunders?"

"We all make blunders, Dad, and I forget something every day!"

I was feeling much better. We both stood as she smiled and again hugged me.

"Melissa, I've gotta go and let you get some work done. Thanks for your advice. By the way, why did you cancel your little trip with your boyfriend?"

"Oh, I've got a new boyfriend now. The other relationship didn't work out. MEN!" she exclaimed.

"You can't live with 'em, and you can't live without 'em, right girl?"

"Right, Dad. Did my comments help you any? What have you decided to do?"

"Your comments gave me food for thought," I said, "I'll have to think about it."

I again hugged her. I then turned to leave when she suddenly called to me with additional advice. "Dad, after you think about it and make a decision, then trust your judgment." She grinned impishly, "And lay off that booze."

I pondered over my conversation with Melissa as I slowly drove homeward. She seemed to be non-judgmental in regard to my former involvement with Harriet. She had even said that it was possible that Harriet might not really be a bad person. She had strongly suggested that I once again get involved with life.

It was 8:15 when I pulled my car into the driveway

and entered my house through the side door. The early hour of the day afforded me ample time to accomplish the many tasks that lay before me.

First I needed to make several phone calls. I picked up the telephone book near the phone, took a seat on the couch and turned to the yellow pages. It suddenly occurred to me that I wasn't wearing my glasses. I once again performed the familiar ritual of searching for them in every nook and cranny in the house. *What was I doing the last time I wore them?* Oh yeah…I was attempting to sew a button onto one of my shirts earlier this morning. I finally located them where I had tucked them into the sewing kit beside the needle and thread before putting away the kit. *Why did I put them there?*

I concluded that I am continually losing my glasses because they are so inconspicuous. Being clear and encased in thin wire frames makes them so unnoticeable that they are almost invisible to a person who isn't wearing glasses; and if one is wearing glasses, then obviously there would be no need to search for them. I decided that I needed to establish the habit of always keeping my glasses in a case, so that when I looked for them they would be easier to find. Luckily, I easily found the case for the glasses and then stuck it into my shirt pocket. After locating a writing pad and pencil, I claimed a chair by the telephone and picked up the phone book.

In my first call I made an appointment to have my glasses repaired and to buy an additional pair. I made a note of the appointment on the writing pad.

My second call was to Gertrude. When she answered the phone her tone was despairing.

"Hello?" The sound of her weak voice made me wonder if she might be having another of her dizzy spells.

"Hello, Gertrude? This is Tom. Look, I don't know exactly how to say this, but..."

She interrupted, "Oh, Thomas, I'm so glad you called. I was just about to call you. It just about breaks my heart to disappoint you, but I'm not going to be able to go to the reunion with you, dear. My youngest second cousin, Eunice, in Chattanooga has gone into early labor, and I have to go there to help her. I'll probably be gone for a week or more. I've got to catch a bus to Chattanooga tonight. Jessie has agreed to take care of my animals for me while I'm gone. I'm terribly sorry, Thomas. I just know how disappointed you must be!"

"Well, Gertrude...that's too bad. Is your second cousin doing okay?"

"Yes, but she really needs me, Thomas. I'm so sorry."

With a sigh of relief, I cut the conversation short. By a stroke of luck, fate had spared me the unpleasant task of dumping Gertrude. If I had only waited, she was on the verge of calling me with the liberating news. However, I was glad that I had called her first with the full intention of freeing myself of her; for if I was to rehabilitate myself, it was necessary for me to have the courage to address my problems.

Dick was not at home when I called him. Probably at the Cracker Barrel with the other retirees, I figured. I left a message on his answering machine:

"Dick, this is Tom. Look, pal, I've made some decisions. I won't be able to have dinner with you and Harriet tonight because I'll be working late at my shop. Give Harriet my apologies, okay? But I'm definitely going to the reunion. You can count on me for sure. I can hardly wait to find out about your part in the entertainment program. If you need to call me back, I'll be at the shop. I'll talk to you later, pal."

I toyed with the idea of calling Harriet but quickly decided against it. Although she had given me her phone number, I hadn't actually promised to call her for sure; after all, I had called Dick. He could tell her that I wasn't going to meet them for dinner.

Since I had decided to take charge of my life, I called a carpenter friend and got an estimate on doing away with the outdated knotty pine walls in my den.

My recent life style had been dictated by sheer impulse; also, I had become lazy. In order to regain my self-discipline, I called the customer whose job I had postponed until after the class reunion, telling him that I would do his job today.

To re-establish my self-reliance, I made a vow to myself that I was going to stop losing things, particularly my glasses. I removed them and tucked them into the empty case in my shirt pocket. Then I placed the note pad on my clipboard and headed for my shop.

It was past 7:00 p.m. when I completed the customer's sign. I locked up, drove home and prepared myself a simple dinner. I ate alone in my small kitchen, realizing that at that very moment, Dick and Harriet were having dinner together at Ruby Tuesday's. I figured that maybe they were discussing my absence.

When I retired to bed that evening I was weary from my long day's work. However, I was proud of my accomplishments, for I had taken the initial steps toward living the independent life that Melissa had prescribed. I switched off the bedside lamp and quickly drifted into a peaceful sleep.

Chapter 14

We were parked in our secret haven. It was *our place.* The crisp October evening was highlighted by a brilliant harvest moon. The lush, glowing sphere suspended in the eastern sky appeared to be swollen, larger than its usual size. The autumn atmosphere carried the blended aroma of burning leaves and the musty dampness of the surrounding forest, and the chill of the night forewarned the inevitable approach of winter. As we sat together in my car on the dead end country road, the moonlit environment created a perfect ambience for our evening rendezvous.

It was homecoming night for Northridge High School. Harriet had been named runner-up to the homecoming queen, and as usual, Dick Noble had won the big football game for us in the last minute of play. Dick had joined Harriet and me after the game for a brief celebration but was soon lured away from us by his entourage of adoring fans. At last, Harriet and I were alone together.

The romantic, luminous moon rose higher in the star-studded sky as we sat silently for a long while, spellbound by the magic of our intimacy in the soft moonlight. Turning toward her, I took her hand, slowly pulling her toward me so that her head was nestled on my shoulder. She turned her head toward me, facing me, and I gently kissed her waiting lips. Our kiss was long and sensual, causing me to become keenly aroused.

When I kissed her graceful neck, its scented aroma excited me. She gently snuggled her head to my chest, captivating me with the intoxicating fragrance of her hair. Our conversation was soft and intimate. For a time we remained silent, cuddling together, enjoying our shared closeness as we gazed at the soft, luminescent panorama of the moonlit forest that stretched in front of us.

With tenderness and patience, I slowly showered her with playful kisses. I tenderly kissed her face, her neck, and her full, moist lips. When my kisses gradually became more passionate, they were greeted with an enthusiastic response from her. I pulled her closer, pressing her voluptuous body against mine. With a hungry mouth, I kissed her sensuously, almost desperately as I lifted her skirt and fondled her. Her exploring tongue sent blissful shivers throughout my body. When I slid my right hand behind her shoulders in an attempt to unfasten her bra, she suddenly pushed me away from her.

"Please don't, honey!" she pleaded.

"Don't you love me?" I asked.

"Oh yes, sweetheart, I'm crazy about you!" Her rapid breathing made her voice tremble.

Suddenly she hugged me and lustfully kissed me.

Then she again pulled away from me. "It's because I love you that I want you to stop. I want to save myself for you!"

I slowly untangled myself from her embrace and scooted away from her, sitting erectly in my seat. My entire being was consumed by an unsatisfied lust. My heart was palpitating so wildly that I became short of breath, and my mood was a mixture of anger and frustration as I became aware of the terrible ache in my genitals.

My bladder discomfort and my pounding heart awakened me. The perceived reality of the dream had been so vivid that for a short while I believed that I was sitting in my car in that autumn of 1954 with Harriet beside me. When reality finally returned, I was saddened by the fact that I had never been able to succeed in making love to her…not even in my dreams. She had said that she was 'saving herself for me'…what a joke! Saving herself *from* me would have been more accurate! I felt like an idiot for honoring such a false claim. For a long while I lay in bed, haunted by my imagined reality of the nocturnal fantasy.

My bedside clock revealed that it was 7:30 a.m. Amazingly, this was the only time during this imaginary amorous night that the need to urinate had awakened me.

I switched on the bedside lamp. To avoid becoming dizzy, I rose very slowly from my bed. As soon as I stood erect I knew that the arthritis in my knee was back again. I limped to the bathroom where, after relieving my bladder, I leisurely showered and shaved. In my kitchen I made some coffee and took a pain pill for my arthritis; then I retreated to the den and turned on the television set.

Since I had made a decision to no longer lead a haphazard life, I retrieved my clipboard in order to continue making a list of necessary chores for the current day. Already listed as number one on the agenda was a reminder of today's appointment to have my eyeglasses repaired. I continued the list: (2) Meet customer at shop, (3) Call carpenter with go-ahead on refurbishing den, (4) Call Dick…

The doorbell rang. After making sure that the sound of the doorbell wasn't coming from the television set, I limped to the front door and opened it. Before I recognized his face, the distinctive aroma of his expensive cologne identified my visitor: It was Dick Noble.

He flashed a broad grin. "Well, don't just stand there starin' at me. Invite me in!"

"Oh yeah, come in Dick. I just wrote your name on my list. I'm supposed to call you."

"When did you start makin' lists?" he asked, as he limped toward my couch. I ignored his question.

"Why are you limping?" I asked.

"I've got an ingrown toenail," he explained. I suspected that his arthritis had returned.

He took a seat on the couch. "Ain't you goin' to ask me about last night?"

I claimed a seat in the easy chair facing him. "Ask you *what* about last night?" I asked, innocently.

"About how it went with Harriet and me," he said.

"Okay. How did it go with Harriet and you? By the way, what are you doing here this early?"

"Oh, I just woke up early. Couldn't sleep. I would have been here even earlier but my car ran out of gas."

"How come you ran out of gas? I thought you always kept a full tank."

"Well, I usually do, but lately it's been slippin' my mind." He appeared to be embarrassed. "Tom, guess what happened to me on my way over here."

"I'm not very good at guessing, Dick," I said, "Can't you give me a clue?"

"I stopped at the Exxon station to fill up. You know you have to *pre-pay* for your gasoline there? Well, I paid for it and then drove off without pumping it! Can you believe that? When I left there I hadn't driven over two blocks when my tank ran out. I had to walk back and get some gas in a can. When I finally drove back to the station, they remembered me and let me pump in the gas. What a nightmare!"

I laughed. "Yeah, the forgetfulness of old age is sometimes a pain in the ass, Dick." I slowly stood. "Why don't we have some coffee?"

"I thought you'd never ask." He followed me into the kitchen where he sat down in a chair at the small dinette. I poured our coffee and took a seat facing him. He took a sip of the brew.

"Sugar's on the table and the cream's in the 'fridge," I said.

"You know that I don't use either, Tom. I like for my coffee to be like my women...*black!"* He laughed.

"I didn't know you had a preference about your women, Dick. I didn't think it mattered."

"Well, actually it doesn't, as long as they're pretty."

We both laughed and then sat silently for a while, sipping our coffee. I knew that he was desperate to tell me about his dinner date with Harriet so I finally asked him.

"Okay, tell me about it. How did it go?"

"Tom, it's too bad that you couldn't join us. I wish you could have seen her! You won't believe this, but Harriet is gorgeous! She looks as pretty as she did in high school!"

"Really?" I asked. I knew that Dick wasn't very discerning in his evaluation of the beauty of women, so I took his appraisal with a grain of salt; for I knew that almost any living creature endowed with female plumbing was beautiful to him.

"Tom, she looks twenty years younger than her age! I couldn't believe it!"

"So how did dinner go? Did you keep her out late?"

He grinned. "Why? Are you jealous?"

"Don't be silly, Dick. Why should I be jealous?"

"Just kiddin,' pal. To answer your question, I left her about midnight. We sat in the restaurant 'til about 9:30. Then do you know what we did for the rest of the evenin'?"

"You took her to bed?" I asked.

"No way, pal. I know I'm a fast mover, but not even the great Dick Noble is that fast! We walked! For more than two hours, we walked! Then we sat for a while in the old stadium at the football field…just for old times' sake."

"Didn't you take her home?"

"No, she drove her own car and met me at the restaurant, so I just walked her back to her car and said goodnight."

"So what was so exciting about the evening? Is that all you did?"

"Yeah, that's about it. Ain't you goin' to ask me if I kissed her goodnight?"

"No."

"Well, I didn't. She was mostly in the mood to just be pals. Know what I mean?"

"Did she ask about me?" I was curious.

"Yeah, we talked a lot about you. She really is dyin' to see you, buddy. Are you sure that you're goin' to the reunion tomorrow night?"

"Sure, I'm going. I told you I was going, didn't I?"

"Great, Tom! Harriet is just dyin' for *The Three Musketeers* to get back together again!"

Before commenting, I thought for a while. Finally I spoke.

"Dick, I'll join you and Harriet tomorrow night, and I'll do my best to bring back the spirit of *The Three Musketeers*, but just for one night. You know, maybe the combination of the three of us as a group is not a healthy relationship. Maybe it wasn't healthy fifty years ago."

"What do you mean? How can you say that? Don't you remember the good times we had?"

"Yeah, but they weren't all good times. We also had some bad times."

Dick's expression became sad. "So you're still poutin' over that fight we had."

"No, I'm not pouting, Dick. But I'm just remembering that our abnormal relationship is the thing that caused the fight."

"Abnormal? What was abnormal about it?"

"Dick, two guys and one girl is not a normal relationship. If you remember, it sort of ended up in a love triangle. Have you forgotten? We both wanted Harriet for our own. We both wanted to marry her."

"Marry her? I didn't want to *marry her!"*

"Then why did you beat the hell out of me when I told you that I was marrying her?" I asked.

"Because you hit me first! Have you forgotten that? But we never talk about that, do we?"

"That's because you said she was a bitch. You called the girl I was going to marry a bitch! Why did you do that?"

Dick stared at me. "Because she was a bitch! I sorta fell for her the same as you did, but I would never have *married* her! Like I told you before, Harriet is not the kind of woman that a man marries. Harriet is the kind of gal that a man just pals around with."

"Then why did you get so mad when I told you that I was intending to marry her?"

"Well, like I said, the main reason I got so mad is because you hit me first. The other reason is because you were my best friend, and you were about to make a damned fool of yourself! And it all turned out for the best, because you ended up marryin' Jenny, the best little gal that I've ever met!"

I was puzzled. "Well, if you considered Harriet to be a bitch, why did you want to hang out with her?"

"Hell, Tom, I've hung out with bitches for most of my life. Some bitches are a lot more fun than non-bitches. I didn't know it when I married them, but both of my wives turned out to be bitches. Of course, they were the kind of bitches that weren't fun to be with."

I felt a pang of pity for him. "You were with Harriet last night. Does she still seem like a bitch to you?"

He reflected on my question before he spoke.

"You know what, Tom? Come to think about it, last night, Harriet didn't seem like a bitch at all. She's still as bossy as hell and likes to have her way, and she's still a little flirty, but there's a kind of gentleness about her now. She seems somehow different…more settled, less materialistic."

"I wonder why she divorced. Did she say?" I asked.

"No. There's a kind of mystery about her. She doesn't elaborate about her past. Maybe life has given her some hard knocks."

"Well, she couldn't have had too rough a life, if she looks as good as you say," I said.

His face reflected a look of sheer ecstasy. "Man, I'm tellin' you she's a livin' doll, Wait 'til you see her."

"How's her sense of humor?"

"That side of her hasn't changed a bit, Tom," he said, "She has that same appetite for havin' fun. She also still has that headstrong nature. A leopard can't change its spots, you know."

He finished his coffee and slowly stood. "I gotta be goin,' pal. I just wanted to tell you about Harriet, and make sure you're goin' to the reunion tomorrow night."

"I'll be there," I promised, "Say, Dick, can't you tell me what you'll be doing to entertain us tomorrow night?"

He laughed. "Nope. You'll just have to wait and see, ol' buddy."

With a firm grip, he clasped my hand and then walked to the door. “See ya’ tomorrow night, Tom.”

We said our goodbyes and he strode out into the early morning sunlight. After limping a couple of paces, he stopped and turned to face me.

“Tom, you’re not still mad about that fight we had, are you?”

“No… I’m not still mad.”

“Do you forgive me for hitting you?”

“I’ll have to think about it,” I said.

“Shit!” he muttered. Then he turned and walked away.

I closed the door and returned to the couch. I picked up my list and crossed out the written reminder to call Dick.

Noting that the first item on my list was to have my glasses repaired, I got up from the couch to get them. Suddenly, I stopped in my tracks. *Where did I put them? Well, they should be easy to find since I had placed them in their carrying case.* After a lengthy search, I finally spotted the case on top of the television set. Then I took them to the repair shop. Unfortunately, when I arrived at the shop I was dismayed to find that I had picked up the wrong pair of glasses; for when I pulled them out of the case they turned out to be my sunglasses. I temporarily gave up on accomplishing the task.

I spent most of the day in completing the remaining chores on my list and working for an hour or so in my shop. I then drove home to spend some time in mental preparation for attending the class reunion. I selected the clothing that seemed appropriate for the occasion and shined my shoes. After watching television for a while, I had a simple dinner at home. Then I took a Tylenol PM and retired to bed.

I nestled my head in the pillow and reflected on last night's dream about the long ago rendezvous with Harriet. I pondered...if the dream had lasted longer...would I have finally scored with her? Maybe tonight I'll be lucky enough to finish the fantasy and nail Harriet...at least in my dreams.

Chapter 15

A full moon was peeping over the eastern horizon when I parked my car under the canopy of a large oak tree bordering the parking lot in front of Northridge High School. Since it was 7:30 p.m., I was fashionably late in my arrival. The event was scheduled to begin at 7:00, so I figured that I was the final old grad to arrive. Although the reunion planning committee had planned for several graduating classes, I was nonetheless surprised at the number of parked vehicles in the lot. It was a good turnout.

For a brief period of time I sat in my car studying the tree-lined campus with its antiquated buildings. The school complex had remained virtually unchanged during the half century since I had graduated. Other than a couple of small additions behind the original three brick buildings, the view before me was identical to the memory that had been forever indelibly etched in my mind. A sudden wave of nostalgia swept over me, carrying me backward in time.

I locked my car and walked up the concrete side-walk that accessed the front steps to the main building. Although the walkway continued around the left side of the structure to the gym in back where the reunion was in progress, I stopped; for I had a sentimental longing to revisit the inside of the old main building where most of my classes had been held. I tried the front door, found it unlocked, and entered.

The main structure was mostly deserted; however, the dim glow of light and the muffled sound of voices coming from the old science room indicated that some kind of mid-summer school meeting was in progress. It was in this archaic building that I had once studied math, English, civics, and science. The second story housed the study hall and library, the oversized room where I had first met Harriet.

I quickly detected the unmistakable, remembered aroma of the interior of my old high school. It stirred within me a feeling of melancholia. If I had been led here blindfolded, I would have instantly recognized my surroundings by my memory of the unique smell.

The sound of my steps in the empty hallway eerily echoed from the walls as I slowly walked through the ancient building. I strolled out the back door into a small yard directly in front of the gymnasium, where the reunion was in progress. As I came nearer to the building, the cacophonous blend of music, laughter, and jumbled conversation that wafted from the open windows grew louder.

A mélange of raucous sounds and activities greeted

me as I entered the building. When I briefly stopped to fill out my nametag, I visually explored the expansive room. The physical layout of the gym had remained unchanged: Bleachers surrounded the basketball court on three sides. Recessed in the center of the wall on the opposite end of the building was the large elevated stage where school plays and band concerts were held. At least a couple of hundred people were in attendance, some of whom were seated in bleachers while others sat in chairs that had been placed around a dozen tables near the stage. Several couples were on the gym floor dancing to the music provided by a stereo system operated by a disc jockey. The velvety voice of Perry Como was crooning a romantic song from the fifties, *No Other Love.* A multi-colored array of balloons surrounded the stage, and a banner on the low wall below the elevated stage lettered in the school colors of orange and black read: "Welcome to the Fabulous Fifties".

My eyes scanned the crowd as I walked around the room in search of Harriet and Dick. I greeted several of my old classmates, many whom I hadn't seen in years. Some were relatively unchanged in appearance, but the ravages of time had rendered many of them unrecognizable to me; for if not for the nametags displayed on their chests, I would never have recognized them.

I finally spotted Dick on the dance floor. He was a good distance away with his back turned toward me, but his gaudy Hawaiian shirt clearly revealed his identity. Although Dick's broad back and the swirling multitude of dancers blocked a clear view of her, I knew that Dick's dancing partner had to be Harriet.

I nimbly circled around the dancing couples and then sidled along the edge of the dance floor until the path of their dance brought Dick and Harriet near to where I stood. Finally, I was briefly afforded a clear view of her. Although Dick usually felt that almost any female was pretty, he had been right on target with his description of Harriet. The lighting was dim and she was still a fair distance away, but I could clearly see that she was indeed a beautiful woman.

Her dress was bright red, and she was wearing high heels. In the dim lighting, her auburn hair appeared darker. As she and Dick whirled gracefully on the dance floor near to me, I was offered an unobstructed view of every angle of her voluptuous figure. *How could this beautiful woman possibly be the same age as I?*

I quickly reminded myself that I had only seen her from a distance. I would reserve my final judgment until I got a closer look.

The music abruptly stopped and the dancing couples gradually dispersed, heading back to their seats. Dick grasped Harriet in a vigorous embrace and they both joined in laughter.

Neither of them had yet seen me. Dick took her hand and led her toward a table. I quickly followed them and yelled, "Harriet! Harriet Dawson!" They both turned toward me. I scarcely noticed Dick, for my eyes were glued to Harriet. The meeting of our eyes brought an instant smile from her. She released Dick's hand and ran to meet me.

"Tom! Oh, Tom! It's so wonderful to see you again!" The hug that she gave me was vigorous and uninhibited. It was as if we had seen each other only yesterday. She released me from her embrace and cradled my face between her hands. Then she planted a playful kiss on my smiling lips. Her seductive aroma excited me.

We stood facing each other on the dance floor, each of us with our eyes studying the other's face. Except for a few subtle wrinkles around her eyes, she looked almost the same as I had remembered her. My heart skipped a beat. I instantly remembered why she had so easily seduced my heart fifty years ago. She was indeed lovely.

"Tom, you look great!" She again hugged me.

I grinned. "I was going to say the same thing about you," I said, "Only *great* would be an understatement!"

"Come on, Tom!" She excitedly took my hand and quickly led me to her table where Dick had already claimed a chair. Harriet took a seat beside him, positioning herself between Dick and me. The table top held a plastic bowl full of ice, a two liter bottle of Coca-Cola and a stack of paper cups.

Dick grinned at me. "Well, ain't you gonna speak to me? Or is Harriet gonna get all your attention?"

"Harriet's a lot better looking than you, Dick," I said. We all laughed.

Harriet flashed a pouting expression at me and peered at her watch.

"Tom, you're about forty five minutes late!" Her feigned stern expression melted into a warm smile. "I was afraid you had changed your mind about coming."

"When a man gets old he kinda slows down," I answered.

"Tom, you're not old! Not yet! Not by a long shot.

You still look good. I recognized you immediately!"

"Yeah? What did you recognize about me?"

"Your eyes! Your steel blue eyes are exactly the same!"

"But I've lost most of my hair. I don't have a full head of hair like Dick has."

Dick grinned proudly. I noticed that his toupee was misaligned toward the left, giving his head the appearance of a lop-sided gourd.

Suddenly he asked, "Do you guys want a drink?"

"A drink?" I asked, "You mean a drink of alcohol?"

"Is there any other kind of drink?" He reached under the table and produced a fifth of Bourbon.

"I thought this was a non-alcoholic event," I commented.

"Then I guess it's okay for us to have a drink, because none of us are alcoholics," he said, with a laugh. His demeanor indicated that he had already had several drinks.

I frowned at him. "Dick, you'd better not set that bottle on the table or we might get thrown out of here."

"They ain't gonna throw out Dick Noble," he answered, "Don't forget, I'm part of the entertainment tonight! Besides, I'm not gonna keep the bottle on the table…I'm gonna keep it on the floor under the table. I'm just gonna mix us a drink. Harriet, do you want yours straight, or do you prefer a Bourbon and Coke? I know that Tom wants his mixed with Coke, because he's a sissy."

"Mix mine with Coke too, because I'm also a sissy," she answered.

Dick displayed a broad grin. "If we run out of booze, I've got plenty more in my car." He proceeded to mix three drinks.

"I think that fifth you have will be more than we need, Dick," I cautioned. "If you've got a part in the entertainment, you don't want to get drunk."

"Hell, there ain't enough booze in Northridge to get Dick Noble drunk!" he boasted.

The music became louder when the disc jockey played the recording, *In the Mood.* Dick quickly stood. "That's a good jitterbug number, Harriet," he shouted over the deafening volume of the fast tune, "Let's show this bunch of old-timers how to dance!"

Harriet stood. "Let's do it!" She laughed. "Excuse us, Tom."

"Sure," I answered. They quickly blended into the crowd on the gym floor.

I sipped on my drink as I scanned the dance floor, looking at the few elderly couples trying to keep pace with the jumpy beat of the music. I watched the dancers, occasionally catching a glimpse of Dick and Harriet. The hectic tempo quickly became too exhausting for many of them, however, and soon they began to gradually leave the dance floor. Ultimately, only Dick and Harriet and one other couple were able to continue the dance until the tune ended.

When they returned to the table, Dick was almost gasping for breath and sweating profusely; however, other than a bit of perspiration on her face, Harriet appeared to be unruffled. In my recollection of Dick's lively activity on the dance floor, I wondered how he had managed to do it with his arthritic knee. I figured that the alcohol that he had consumed had anesthetized him, temporarily inhibiting the pain. When he awoke tomorrow morning, he would probably pay dearly for his impetuous behavior.

We finished our drinks, and Dick wasted no time in pouring us another. The memory of Dick's ancient football heroics drew scores of people to our table. Most of his admirers had long ago moved away from Northridge and hadn't seen him in years. Dick's involvement with his fans created an awkwardness in the relationship between Harriet and me, for without his garrulous banter to serve as a buffer, both Harriet and I began to become strangely uncomfortable in our conversation.

Two former students who were unrecognizable to me pulled up a chair beside Dick as he recounted some of his miraculous feats on the gridiron. Dick basked in the glory of their remembrance of his legendary triumphs. He repeatedly roared with laughter when he narrated some of the funnier stories. Beaming with confidence, he became braver, so he retrieved the fifth of bourbon from beneath the table and set it in plain view on the tabletop. He immediately poured another round of drinks.

"Hey, we're almost out of booze!" Dick shouted over the din of the loud music, "In a few minutes I'll go to the car and get us another bottle!"

"We don't need any more booze, Dick," I said. He ignored me.

Harriet looked at me and smiled. "That song they're playing...*Because of You*... Doesn't that song bring back memories?"

"They all bring back memories, Harriet," I said, "All the music they're playing tonight is from the fifties."

We finished our drinks and I poured another for Harriet and me. Dick had gone to his car to get another bottle. We sat in silence, sipping our drinks until the song ended. I noticed that on the faster music the volume was louder, but was softer on the slower romantic tunes.

A new song began: *Unforgettable,* a Nat King Cole oldie. The sentimental ballad was appropriate for my present mood, for despite my efforts to the contrary, I was beginning to realize that Harriet was unforgettable.

She suddenly turned to me and smiled. "Dance with me, Tom." Her request resembled a command.

"I haven't danced in years, Harriet," I protested.

She stood and took my hand, slowly pulling me up from my chair.

She smiled. "We used to be so good together when we danced. Why are you still so bashful?" I didn't answer.

We walked to the dance floor and I took her in my arms. She was light on her feet. She was so graceful that she seemed almost weightless, as she anticipated my every move, instantly responding to my slightest touch. We pressed our bodies together so closely that we became as one entity. The closeness of her and the romantic lyrics of the song were as intoxicating to me as the Bourbon that I had consumed.

I felt her firm breasts pressing against me, and her velvet cheek caressing mine. As she gently snuggled her head on my shoulder, I became captivated by the stimulating fragrance of her tousled auburn hair. It was as if our bodies were welded together. Our movements were so coordinated that we blended like a symphony; her responsiveness to my every lead caused me to believe that if she ever surrendered to me, our love-making would be as harmonious as our dance. The combination of the lovely song and the essence of Harriet plunged me into an idyllic world of helpless reverie.

When the music stopped, I realized that we had remained silent throughout the song. I started to release her, but she clung to me.

"Let's dance to another one, Tom."

"Only if it's a slow number," I answered, "I can't handle those fast songs. Arthritis, you know."

She looked up into my eyes and smiled as we waited for the new song to begin.

The first swell of music drew a quick response from her.

"Oh, Tom! They're playing *My Foolish Heart!* That's *our* song! Remember?" Her animated expression was like that of an excited teenager.

Once again, the words of the song reflected my current emotions:

> 'The night is like a lovely tune,
> Beware, my foolish heart!
> How white the ever-constant moon,
> Take care, my foolish heart!'

Our song had once again carried me backward in time. If only I had been wise enough to heed these words fifty years ago!

Our bodies again meshed as we resumed our

graceful dance. She withdrew her hand from my shoulder and looked me directly in the eye. It was then that I noticed her tears. Did the sentimentality of the song bring out this much emotion in her? Although I was unsure of her sincerity, I suddenly realized how quickly she could reduce me to putty in her hands. *Beware, My foolish heart!*

She repositioned her head on my shoulder, and I could feel her breath and her lips touching my ear as she whispered, "Tom, did you ever wish that you could go backward in time, and you had a second chance at happiness?"

I was slow in answering her. "No, not really," I said, "We only get one shot at happiness in this life. There's no point in wishing for the impossible."

"I know, honey…but sometimes it's a bitter pill to swallow."

Honey? She called me honey?

We danced for a while in silence. Finally, I commented, "It's been fifty years since you called me that."

"Called you *what?"*

*"Honey…*You just called me *'honey.'"*

"Did I? It just came out. I guess *our song* just carried me back in time. It just seemed natural…I'm sorry, Tom. I didn't mean to offend you."

"You didn't offend me. You just kinda surprised me, that's all."

The song ended, and I escorted her back to our table. Dick had returned with the liquor and was busy refilling our cups. Good! *I felt like having another drink.*

Harriet and I reclaimed our chairs and I quickly

downed another drink. I began to have mixed emotions: On the surface, I felt giddily happy. I was with Harriet, and by some sort of miracle, we were once again young; yet, I was apprehensive…I was fearful of her. A deeper side of me wished that I had never attended the reunion. I felt like getting drunk.

Time quickly slipped away as we continued to drink and talk about times of the past. Dick and I took turns in dancing with Harriet. Because of Harriet's former popularity in high school, scores of former students, mostly men, visited her at our table, laughing and re-telling stories of bygone experiences.

A slap on my back startled me. I turned my head and saw Dummy standing beside me. Although he was dressed in better fashion than usual, the shoulders of the navy blue sport coat that he wore displayed such an abundance of dandruff that it looked as if someone had emptied an ashtray on his shoulders. With an ogling stare, he made a visual appraisal of Harriet. I smiled at him and shook his hand.

"Hello, Dummy," I said, "I didn't know you were coming to the reunion. Where's your buddy? Didn't Head come with you?"

"No, he couldn't make it. He has a bad case of hemorrhoids. I wasn't gonna come either, but I kinda changed my mind."

He again affixed his gaze to Harriet. I introduced them. "Harriet Dawson, this is Floyd Sutton. Floyd sometimes has breakfast with Dick and me."

He and Harriet exchanged hellos and then Dummy turned his attention to Dick.

"Hi, Dick," he said, "I came here because I heard that you had a part in this-here get-together." He removed his jacket and draped it across an empty chair.

Although he was dressed less sloppily than usual, I noticed that his pants were precariously low on his hips. The upper portion of his crack became visible when he took a seat beside Dick.

"Hello, Dummy. By the way, how's Pinky doin'?" Dick took another drink of Bourbon.

"He's doin' fine. He's takin' therapy now. What's that you're drinkin'?"

"Bourbon," replied Dick, "Care for a little snort?"

"Don't mind if I do." He took the cup of liquor that Dick had poured for him and immediately gulped it down. He then expelled an enormous belch.

Harriet laughed and whispered to me, "What a crude Man! Why do you call him Dummy?"

"Because he can't hear very well. He kinda reads lips to understand what you're saying. He's really not a bad guy."

Dick began vocally reliving his football heroics as Dummy attentively listened. Suddenly, the music stopped and the stage became illuminated with brighter lights. Ross Henderson, an old grad who had been captain of our basketball team stepped to the podium. He was master of ceremonies for the evening program that was about to commence. I wondered what role Dick would play, and when his part would begin.

The room became quiet. The emcee introduced a gospel quartet and the foursome immediately began to sing. The chatter of conversation gradually resumed as the congregation of people paid little attention to the singing.

I turned to Dick. "When do you go onstage?"

"Pretty soon," he answered, "It won't be long before I have to go backstage and dress for the part." Both he and Dummy downed another shot of Bourbon.

Dummy slowly stood, pulled up his pants, and retrieved his jacket. "I gotta go and rejoin some friends at another table...I'll drop by and see you again, Dick...after you get through performin'. See ya, Tom. Pleasure to meet you ma'am." He smiled at Harriet.

She laughed as Dummy walked away. "Is that the kind of friends you guys have? Man, that guy is sure a country bumpkin!"

Dick mumbled, "You can take the boy out of the country, but you can't take the country out of the boy!"

Harriet laughed. "How do you come up with those corny sayings, Dick?"

"Just talent, I guess." He poured himself another drink. He was on the verge of becoming drunk, and I realized that I wasn't far behind him.

Harriet appeared to be concerned about him. "Dick, maybe you ought to slow down a little on your drinking." He ignored her comment and cast a moronic grin.

"When do you plan on goin' back to Texas, Harriet?" he asked.

"I don't know. I may decide to stay here a little longer than I originally planned."

"Well, whenever you do go back, Tom and I just might take a little trip down there to see you. I've been tryin' to get Tom to go on a trip with me, but he says he won't go."

"I've told you many times, Dick, that I don't have the money. And I don't want you paying for it!" I was becoming irritated as well as drunk.

Dick stared at me. "Tom, if you insist on payin' for it, you can do it later, when you've got the money. I'll just put it on your tab." He grinned foolishly.

"Dick, we both know that the 'tab' you're talking about never gets paid! Hell, it's just a joke! I probably already owe you a thousand dollars!"

"Now don't you guys start arguing," said Harriet, "Dick, hadn't you better start preparing for your act?"

He looked at his watch. "Oh my God, Yes! I better get movin'!"

He suddenly stood and lumbered toward the door beside the stage, occasionally staggering as he walked. Harriet giggled as she watched him.

Chapter 16

I picked up the bottle of Bourbon and reached for Harriet's paper cup. She shook her head in refusal. "No more alcohol for me tonight, Tom," she said, "I've already had too much."

I shrugged and poured myself another drink. She sniggered and reconsidered.

"Well, maybe one more, and that's all for sure. I don't want to be so drunk that I can't enjoy Dick's upcoming performance. What's he gonna do, anyway?"

"Beats me," I said.

I poured a small drink into her cup and added Coke. Because of the increased light from the recently illuminated stage, I placed the bottle of Bourbon back under the table, out of sight.

The quartet music had ended. Ross Henderson, the emcee, introduced Charlene Stapleton. She began singing our old school song, *Hail to Northridge High*. I figured that it was a prelude to Dick's entrance to the stage for his act, which was to be the grand finale of the evening.

"She has a pretty decent voice," Harriet said, "But her boobs are so big and saggin' so bad it's a wonder that she doesn't fall on her face."

"I hadn't noticed," I answered. Her catty comment told me that Harriet was feeling the booze.

I looked at my watch. "It's 11:40," I said, "This shindig is supposed to end at midnight. Dick's part must not be very long."

"Well, not many people have gone home. They're all waiting to see Dick do his thing," she said.

"Yeah, I guess that's true. You know, Dick is probably the most popular guy to ever graduate from Northridge High. He sure enjoys being the center of attention," I commented.

Harriet again giggled. I suspected that she probably shouldn't have had that last drink; for that matter, the same could be said of me.

In the middle of the song, I saw Dummy staggering toward our table. The drips on the front of his unzipped pants bore evidence of his limited bladder control. He took a seat beside me, once again revealing the top half of his butt. I instantly saw that he was drunk.

"Have a seat, Dummy," I invited, after the fact.

"Hello, Tom…I jes' come over to set wif you to see whut our ol' buddy, Dick is gonna do. Where's the liquor?"

"Hell, Dummy, you don't need any more liquor. You're already stoned!" I said. Harriet giggled.

When the song ended, the room became eerily

quiet. The people sat in excited anticipation, waiting for Dick to appear.

Suddenly, an ear-splitting song began. "YOU AIN'T NOTHIN' BUT A HOUN' DOG"...The words echoed through the gym as Dick made his grand entrance. The sight of him brought down the house and my jaw fell open in disbelief. Dressed in a typical white Elvis jumpsuit and wearing a jet-black wig, Dick pranced and gyrated around the stage, lip-syncing the words to the throbbing music; however, it was not the routine impersonation of Elvis that shocked me, but it was Dick's physical likeness to Elvis that was so uncanny. Over the years I had seen many Elvis impersonators, but never before had I seen an imitator who more closely resembled the music legend. I had always thought that Dick's handsome face reminded me of someone; but never until now did I realize who it was. In appearance, Dick had always been a fair-haired, older version of Elvis. His blond hair had previously disguised the likeness.

He cavorted around the stage, sparkling like a swarm of lightning bugs as the sequins on his jumpsuit and his unfurled cape reflected the illumination of the spotlight. Instead of a guitar, Dick cradled a football in his right arm. Although it was an out-of-place appendage to the overall theme, it nonetheless reminded the audience that his performance was in honor of two great legends: Elvis Presley and Dick Noble.

The crowd displayed their approval with exuberant cheers mixed with peals of roaring laughter as it became obvious that Dick was completely drunk.

As the pulsating song ended, Harriet and I hugged

each other and laughed hysterically. Dummy stared at Dick in disbelief, then sat down in a drunken stupor with his back to the stage.

Projecting a victorious grin, Dick thrust both arms upward in the manner of a referee signaling, 'touchdown'. Assuming the stance of a quarterback, he cocked his arm that held the football. "Catch this touchdown pass, Tom!" He threw a bullet pass directly at our table. The football was moving at such a high rate of speed that I had little time to react; as a result, the streaking missile struck Dummy squarely in the back of his head. He immediately stood and held up his fists. "Okay, who's the smart-ass that hit me?"

The remaining people in the building laughed and clapped their hands in applause. When Dick staggered off the stage, his feet became entangled in some electrical cord, causing him to sprawl heavily onto the floor. Two stage assistants quickly came out of the wings and helped Dick make a more graceful exit. Just before stepping off the stage, he displayed a drunken grin, and then executed an elaborate bow to the remaining audience.

Dick's grand finale was a fitting conclusion to the event. The bright overhead lights came on and most of the old grads sauntered toward the exits; however, a few of Dick's most loyal fans gathered around our table waiting for him to rejoin us.

When Dick came back to our table, he was mobbed by the handful of admirers who had waited for him. Again noticing his uncanny resemblance to Elvis, I decided that the black Elvis wig that he wore looked better than his own.

He was still dressed in the elaborate white outfit. It appeared that the exertion of his energetic performance had sobered him to a certain extent, a condition that he quickly remedied by swallowing an enormous drink from the remaining booze in the bottle.

Gradually, his hero-worshipers left for home. Other than a handful of people who had been assigned to the cleanup crew, Dick, Harriet, Dummy, and I were the only people remaining in the gym.

Dick flashed an elaborate grin. "How did you guys like my act?"

Harriet hugged him and laughed. "That performance really knocked the crowd off their feet!"

"Kinda knocked Dick off his feet, too," I commented, "Say, Dick, hadn't you better take off that Elvis outfit and get dressed in your own clothes?"

"What's the hurry?" asked Dick, "I don't get to dress like this every day!" It was obvious that he wanted to continue being Elvis for a while longer.

"But we've got to get out of here, Dick. They'll be wanting to lock up before long," I protested.

"You worry too much, Tom," he said, "Let's all go out to the old football field for old time's sake!"

I again protested. "But we'll get locked out of the building, Dick. How are you gonna change into your own clothes if we can't get back into the gym?"

He grinned devilishly. "I've got a key to the building, that's how. I've had it ever since we started rehearsin' for the show!"

Harriet looked at me and laughed. "Oh come on, Tom. Don't be a spoil-sport. Let's go out to the stadium and relive some old memories!"

"Hell, I'm fer it!" Dummy grinned. "Got any more of that good liquor?" He picked up the bottle and drained the remaining contents, then punctuated the deed with a resounding burp.

"Good for you, Dummy!" Harriet said, laughing, "I'm glad that's the last of the whiskey, because all of us have had too much to drink!"

"Hell, I've got plenty more in my car," Dick boasted. He picked up his football and led the procession out the side door toward the stadium, about fifty yards away.

The cooler air ushered in by the late evening moisture felt good on my sweating face. Directly overhead, a bright full moon hung in the clear night sky, it's brilliance so intense that nearby objects could be easily recognized. Dick and Dummy chattered at each other in a meaningless exchange of drunken nonsense as they trudged ahead of Harriet and me. Following behind them, we both remained silent.

I studied her loveliness in the radiance of the full moon. She was as beautiful in the moonlight as she had been on that homecoming night fifty years ago when we were together at our secret rendezvous. Looking upward at the romantic moon, I thought about some of the lyrics of *our* song…

"How white the ever-constant moon…"

It was the same constant moon that had smiled down on us that night a half century ago. Strangely, I somehow felt that the span of time linking then to now had been miraculously erased; for this magical night seemed only a continuation of our long-ago romance. Instantly, I began to experience a deep feeling of guilt; for to erase that fifty year span of time would be to wipe away the wonderful years that I had spent with Jenny.

I need to come to my senses! I considered that perhaps my amorous, sentimental emotions must be the by-product of the Bourbon that I had consumed. At that moment, I determined that I wouldn't let my heart be again seduced by Harriet.

We finally reached the football stadium. The unlocked gate in the fence surrounding the field gave us easy access to the gridiron. We walked through the gate and Dick led us toward the south end zone. A nearby bright streetlight supplemented the moonlight, adequately lighting the south end of the field. We gathered in a careless circle beneath the goal posts with Dick in the center, playfully tossing the football back and forth to each other. In their drunken state, both Dick and Dummy were totally uncoordinated in performing the simple activity.

Weaving unsteadily, Dick caught the football and held it, momentarily halting the playful exercise. "Why don't we play a li'l game of touch football?"

"I'm fer it!" Dummy responded.

I was hesitant. "It's too dark out here, Dick," I said, "Besides, the ground is kinda soft after that early mornin' rain we had."

Harriet laughed and kicked off her shoes. "Yeah, that's a great idea! Tom, you and I will play Dick and

Dummy!" Her playful nature had been enhanced by the alcohol that she had consumed.

"We're liable to get into trouble," I protested, "Besides, this field is a hundred yards long, and there's not any of us sober enough to run that far."

"Hell, we'll just confine the game to the twenty yards on this end of the field," said Dick, "Dummy and I will let the twenty yard line be the goal that we defend, and you and Harriet can defend the goal line. You two can kick off to Dummy and me. But I'm warnin' you, when I get to the five yard line, there ain't nobody can catch Dick Noble!"

"I don't think we should do something this silly," I complained. We lined up for the kickoff. Harriet booted the ball upfield to Dummy, whose pants immediately dropped to his ankles when he caught the football. He tripped over his fallen pants and clumsily fell to the turf. With the exception of Dummy, we all broke into laughter. Harriet clapped her hands with glee. "Isn't this fun, Tom?"

"I'll have to admit, it is fun, but it's also as silly as hell." I was beginning to generate some enthusiasm for the absurd activity. Dummy pulled up his pants and Dick marked the spot where he had fallen.

"Okay, it's first down for us right here on the fifteen yard line," Dick muttered.

We all lined up for the next play, with Dummy standing over the ball. Dick stood directly behind him with outstretched hands, calling the signals.

"Ready, set…Hike! Hike!…Dammit, Dummy, hike the ball to me!"

Dummy finally passed the ball back to him. Stumbling like a drunken gorilla, Dick ran wide to his right, the area of the field that Harriet defended. When he neared her, she left her feet in a reckless dive, landing on his back with her arms around his neck; as a result, Dick lost his footing, causing both of them to fall clumsily to the turf, sliding on the wet grass.

When they got up, Dick was irritated. "Dammit, Harriet! I said we were gonna play TOUCH football, not tackle! Why did you tackle me?"

Harriet laughed. "I thought I was supposed to tackle you! I've never played football before! Isn't that the way it's played?"

I chuckled. "I thought you said that nobody could stop the great Dick Noble when he reached the five yard line!"

"Shit! Look at my pretty outfit!" Dick appeared to be disgusted.

I inspected the clothing of both Dick and Harriet to assess the damage: Although both were smeared with grass stains and mud, the grime on Dick's white costume was more obvious. In addition, because of the unexpected tackle, Dick's black wig had been knocked from his head, causing him to be unrecognizable. He picked up the oversized toupee and repositioned it on his head.

The exploring beam of the flashlight that scanned the area caused the four of us to freeze in our tracks.

"Who are you people?" asked the gruff masculine voice behind the beacon. "What are you doing out here? It's nearly one o'clock in the morning!"

Since I considered that I was the most sober person

in the group, I decided to assume the role of spokesman. I walked toward the blinding light beam that was now riveted on my face.

"We're just out here reminiscing about old times, sir," I answered, respectfully. "We just came out of the gym where we attended our class reunion. Who are you?" I shielded my eyes from the piercing light. My mind struggled to find a way to explain our foolish behavior.

"I'm the night watchman," he said, "I heard some kind of a commotion out here. It sounded like somebody was in a fight!" He had the voice of an elderly man.

"Oh, that was just Harriet tackling Dick," I explained.

"Tackling him? What do you mean?"

"We were playing a little game of football," I said.

He switched the flashlight beam to Harriet. "Ain't that a woman?"

I laughed. "If it isn't, it's a damned good impersonation of one."

He moved the beam to Dick. "Say, that guy in the white outfit looks a lot like Elvis!"

"In the flesh!" Dick boasted, with an elaborate bow.

The night watchman had lost his sense of humor. "You're all drunk! Get out of here before I call the cops!"

"No problem, sir," I said, apologetically, "We're outta here!"

Harriet giggled. Dummy raised a leg and expelled a generous portion of gas.

Harriet picked up her shoes and took my arm. We all hurriedly walked out the gate at the south end of the field near the streetlight where Dick had earlier parked his car. The beam of the flashlight followed us as we made our way to Dick's vehicle.

"Let's get in my car and get outta here!" said Dick.

"Wait, Dick," I said, "You need to go back to the gym and change your clothes."

"Screw changin' clothes. We gotta get outta here before that guard calls the police on us." Dick opened the front car door on the passenger side. "Get in, Dummy."

"I ain't goin' with you," said Dummy, "I'm goin' home."

"How're you getting' home, Dummy?" I asked, "You're too drunk to drive."

"I'm walkin'. I just live two blocks from here." He hiked his trousers and stumbled away.

I opened the rear door and Harriet took a seat in the back of the car. When Dick started to get behind the wheel, I stopped him.

"Let me drive, Dick. I've had less to drink than you have." Although he lamely protested, he quickly reconsidered, for he apparently liked the idea of being in the back seat with Harriet.

I slowly drove away. Looking in the rear-view mirror, I saw the beam of the flashlight disappear. I turned my head toward the back seat, where Dick was engaged in the task of opening another fifth of whiskey.

"Don't drink any more, Dick," I pleaded.

"One more little drink ain't gonna hurt us," he replied.

"Look, Dick...we're all kinda drunk. I'm a little scared of drivin,' so I'm just gonna take it real slow. Lucky for us, it's so late that there's not much traffic. I'm gonna drive you and Harriet home, then I'll drive myself home in your car."

"How about your car?" asked Harriet.

"I'll come back and get it tomorrow," I said, "Right now, we all need to go home."

I felt the cold glass of the whiskey bottle against the back of my neck.

"Have a drink, Tom!" Dick displayed a stupid grin when he thrust the bottle toward me.

I glared at him. "Put that booze away, dammit!" I shouted, "We may all get arrested!" Dick only laughed and took another swallow of the Bourbon.

"Hey, Tom, let's drive over to Bill's Grill where we used to hang out when we were in high school."

"Dick, it's after 1:00 in the morning!"

"What do we care? Hell, they're open all night, remember?" I ignored his suggestion.

I proceeded to carefully drive toward the motel where Harriet was staying. In the back seat, Dick and Harriet had become quiet. The effect of the alcohol that I had earlier consumed was beginning to gradually subside. I figured that the three of us would feel terrible in the morning.

From the back seat came the sound of a vigorous slap.

"Stop it, Dick!" she shouted, angrily. Looking over my shoulder, I saw Dick trying to kiss Harriet. With his hand up her dress, he was practically wallowing on her.

"Cut it out, Dick!" I yelled. He only laughed.

"Tom, pull over and let me out of the car!" she screamed.

"Harriet, I can't let you out of the car here in a strange neighborhood!"

"Stop the car, or I'll jump out while you're driving!" she threatened.

I braked the car and pulled over to the curb. She opened the door and jumped out. She ran to the sidewalk and stopped. Then she turned to face the car, and in a defiant stance, placed her hands on her hips. In a drunken stupor, Dick only eyed her with a confused stare.

I glared angrily at him. "Damn it, Dick, have you completely lost your mind?"

"I'm sorry, Tom," he said. He turned his gaze toward Harriet. "I'm sorry, Harriet. Come on…get back in the car."

"No, I'll just walk!" She removed her shoes and began carrying them as she walked briskly down the sidewalk. I urged her to get back into the car.

"C'mon, Harriet, get in! You can't walk all the way back to the motel. It's too far!"

"No!" She increased the speed of her pace.

Dick also pleaded with her. "C'mon, baby…Get back in the car. I won't bother you anymore…I promise!" She continued to walk.

While Dick remained in the vehicle, I stopped the car in the middle of the street and got out. "Come on, Harriet, get back in the car so we can all go home!"

I walked toward her. When she saw that I was gaining on her, she began jogging. The arthritis in my knee raked my leg with pain when I broke into a dead run in order to catch up with her. It took a half block of painful running before I finally wrapped my arms around her waist as she beat at my head with her shoes.

She was desperately trying to free herself from my

grasp when the police car pulled up alongside us. Before I could release her, two uniformed policemen seized me, one of them with his forearm around my throat, choking me. When they pulled me away from her, she stopped trying to run away, again positioning herself in a stubborn stance with her hands on her hips.

"Are you hurt, Ma'am?" asked the fat policeman.

"No…I'm not hurt!" She glared at him. "We can settle our own differences without you butting in!"

"What's going on here?" asked the skinny cop. I searched my mind for a plausible answer.

"I was just walking the lady home," I answered.

"Then why was she trying to get away from you, and beating you with her shoes?" The fat patrolman was skeptical.

"She didn't want to go home," I explained, "She wanted to stay out later."

"You're drunk!" he said, accusingly.

Seemingly out of nowhere, Dick appeared on the scene.

"Officer, release this man!" He was so unsteady on his feet that he almost fell.

"Where did you come from? Are you with these other two? Who are you?" asked the slim policeman. The heavy officer scanned Dick's face with the beam of his flashlight.

"Hell, don't you recognize him? He's Elvis Presley!"

"Get outta here!" remarked the slim cop, in amazement. "I knew all the time that Elvis wasn't really dead!" He leaned closer to Dick, inspecting his face with the flashlight beam. "I'll have to admit," he said, "You sure are a dead ringer for Elvis!"

Dick raised his upper lip in a surly sneer. "Thanky-vury-much!"

"You're all under arrest!" declared the hefty officer.

"On what charge?" asked Dick.

"Public drunkenness."

Dick eyed him with an incredulous stare. "Don't be ridiculous! There ain't enough booze in this town to get me drunk!"

The slender policeman cast his flashlight beam on Dick's car.

"Which one of you owns that car that's parked in the middle of the street?"

"That's mine," said Dick, proudly, "It's a BMW. You wouldn't believe the deal I got on that car!" Harriet giggled.

Both officers had heard enough. "All right, all three of you get into the back of the patrol car. By the way, which one of you was driving the car?"

"I was," I reluctantly answered.

"That's a tough break for you, sir," said the heavy officer, "You just might be facing a charge of DUI."

The small officer assisted Harriet in entering the police car. "Watch your head, ma'am."

I entered the car next, taking a seat beside Harriet. Dick weaved unsteadily as he waited his turn. He grinned idiotically at the officers.

"Officer, I'll make a deal with you.," he slurred, "Since you're worried about his drivin,' If you'll let us go, I'll do the drivin'." Both officers ignored him.

After Dick was placed in the back seat, the officers climbed into the car. Before pulling away from the curb, the heavy-set patrolman called headquarters, reporting the arrest and instructing the jailer to prepare cells for the prisoners.

"Call the wrecker service and have a wrecker sent out to the 300 block of Walnut Street to pick up a car. Also, we've got three people we're bringing in for public drunkenness. One of 'em claims to be Elvis Presley."

Chapter 17

Other than a sleeping drunk sprawled on a lower bunk on the right side of the cubicle, Dick and I were the only occupants of the small cell. The jailer had taken Harriet to a separate section of the jail that was reserved for women. Dick was now so drunk that he was no longer able to stand, so he immediately collapsed on the lower bunk on the left. A single overhead bulb provided the dim light in the cell.

A glance at my watch indicated that it was now 2:15 a.m. The night sergeant had told us that it would be at least four hours before we could be released. I realized that I would be in total misery until 6:15 or later, when we would be eligible to be bailed out by someone. Since neither Dick nor Harriet had relatives in Northridge, I cringed at the thought that it would undoubtedly be either Marsha or Melissa who would have to be awakened so early in the morning. It would be necessary for me to call one of them.

Dick had immediately passed out, but I knew that for me, sleep was out of the question. The gradual decrease in my drunken state of mind was accompanied by an increase in my feeling of remorse; for both physically and emotionally, my recent behavior had been like that of a child. Not only had I cavorted around in the middle of the night playing football, but I was once again on the threshold of falling victim to the devious wiles of Harriet.

Except for the rasping snores of Dick, the corridor inside the jail complex was eerily quiet.

I was bone-tired, but edgy. As I became more sober, the excruciating pain of my arthritis was once again evident in my right knee. I felt like lying down, but I doubted if I could bear the pain of climbing to the top bunk; as a result, I spent the night either gripping the bars of the cell door while peering down the corridor or painfully pacing the floor.

It was after 8:00 a.m. when the sleeping drunk awoke. He was an elderly man sporting a full head of white hair. A generous patch of white stubble covered his lower face. He stretched as he yawned, then fixed his eyes on Dick, who was lying on the lower bunk across from him. Immediately, he retreated to the corner of his bunk, drew his body into a fetal position, and began to violently shake. His eyes registered a look of terror.

"Good morning," I greeted. Without responding, he only buried himself deeper into the corner.

"What's the matter, mister?" I asked, "Are you sick?"

"Is…is that who I think it is?" He pointed at Dick. It was evident that the old fellow had been experiencing hallucinations caused by his obvious alcoholism. He probably felt that he was seeing a ghost.

The metallic clang of the opening door at the end of the corridor caught my attention. I grimaced as I caught the sight of Marsha being ushered through the open door by the jailer. The stern expression etched on her face revealed her sour mood.

I walked over to Dick and shook him. His only reaction was a resounding snort. I shook him again, this time more vigorously. He slowly rose from his bunk. His black Elvis wig was out of alignment with his head. Its position suggested that someone had tossed it like a Frisbee and it had accidentally landed on his head. Listlessly, he sat on his bunk, staring at me with sleepy eyes that looked as if they were on the verge of bleeding. His confused expression indicated that he had no memory of the events of the previous night, and that he was baffled in regard to where he was at the moment. He wouldn't have been any more bewildered if he had unexpectedly stepped out of a space ship that had just landed on the planet Mars.

The jailer unlocked our cell door while Marsha eyed both Dick and me with a penetrating glare. Dick slowly rose to his feet.

"Okay, fellers, time to go home," said the jailer. Marsha remained silent as the jailer escorted the three of us down the corridor into the small office.

When we entered the room, I noticed that Harriet was already there, sitting in an office chair facing an official who was sitting behind a small desk. She quickly looked at me and smiled. "Hi, Tom."

"Hello, Harriet," I said. She didn't speak to either Dick or Marsha.

Except for the jailer, we all claimed chairs facing the officer behind the desk, who appeared to be about fifty years of age. Over his small bifocals, he peered at us.

"Well, folks, you're three lucky people," he began. "Which one of you is Tom Spencer?"

"I am," I answered.

He turned his gaze to me. "Lucky for you, one of the arresting officers, Deputy Brown, is a friend of your daughter, and called her about your situation. Mr. Spencer, I understand that you were driving the car."

"That's true," I confessed.

"Well, you're *double lucky!"* he said, "Because we ought to charge you with driving under the influence! We're not going to charge you with it this time, but we'd better not ever catch you behind the wheel of a car again when you're drinking!"

"I appreciate that, sir," I said.

He continued. "Since, other than driving the car while drunk, you didn't do anything so terribly bad I'm dropping all charges against all three of you…You can thank your daughter, Marsha for that. She tells me that you people were just celebrating your class reunion."

"That's true, sir," I said.

"How old are you, Mr. Spencer?"

"Sixty-eight. We're all about the same age."

"Tell me something, Mr. Spencer. How can three people your age act like teenage kids? Spencer, your daughter here ought to give you a good lecture when she gets you home!"

"I'm sure she will, sir," I said.

The officer turned to Harriet. "Ma'am, if you don't mind my saying so, you look like a decent lady to me. Maybe you shouldn't hang around characters like these two guys. How did you get that dress so muddy? Did one of these guys get rough with you?"

"No, not really." She seemed embarrassed.

"Then how did you get so muddy?"

"Playing football," she answered. The officer rolled his eyes in amazement. He turned his attention to Dick.

"What about you, Elvis?" he asked, "Were you playing football too?"

"Yeah. We both got muddy when she tackled me."

The officer studied Dick's face. "You know, you could actually pass for Elvis. Maybe you could sing a little song for us. An appropriate song under the circumstances would be *Jail House Rock.*"

Dick again displayed a surly Elvis sneer. "Thankyvury-much." The officer again rolled his eyes.

He then stood and announced, "You're all free to go. You better collect your personal belongings."

He opened a desk drawer and pulled out a large envelope with my name written on the back. I opened it and extracted my personal items as well as the keys to Dick's car. The officer appeared to be puzzled. "That's all I can find that belongs to you people." He looked at Dick. "Didn't you or the lady have any valuables with you when you were arrested?"

"No, " Dick answered, "I left everything in my other clothes, back at the gym."

"How about you, Ma'am? Weren't you carrying a pocketbook?"

"No, I left it in the gym, too."

Dick spoke up. "What about my car? Where is it?"

"It was towed in. You'll have to pay to get it out. It's over at Williams' Wrecker Service, about a block from here. If you'll wait outside, I'll have a deputy take you and the lady wherever you need to go."

Marsha led the way as we filed out of the room toward the street. The officer called to us, "You people go home and act like grownups."

Once outside, I handed Dick his car keys. He turned to Harriet. "Sorry about last night. It was just the liquor, you know."

"I know," she said. She looked at me tenderly and then hugged me. "Will you call me, Tom?"

Instead of answering her, I introduced her to Marsha, who only mumbled 'hello' without further comment.

Marsha and I stepped into her car and she drove away. Her face was an expressionless mask.

"Thanks, Marsha, for getting me out of jail," I said.

"Okay," she answered.

"Do you mind driving me over to the high school so I can get my car?"

"No problem, Dad," she said, with no emotion. Her false non-judgmental attitude made me uncomfortable. I would have felt much better if she had given me hell.

While she drove me to my car, we both passed the time in an awkward, stony silence. When I got out of her car, she finally spoke. "Dad, I'll call you in a day or so. We need to talk."

"Okay, Marsha," I answered wearily. She drove away and I watched her car disappear into the distance.

While driving toward home, I made an assessment of my situation: Physically, I was hung over, and my arthritis was almost killing me. I was nauseated and sleepy, but too nervous to sleep. Emotionally, I was a wreck. My remorse was overwhelming. I was embarrassed about my childish behavior, especially driving an automobile while drinking. In addition, I was frustrated. Since, by nature I was a well-organized person, the chaotic life style that I had been living had filled me with anxiety. But worst of all, I was again beginning to have romantic feelings for Harriet. I deeply regretted attending my class reunion.

I considered that perhaps it was not too late to avoid the trap of falling in love with Harriet. Now that the reunion was over, maybe she would soon be leaving Northridge, returning to Texas. I decided to avoid her. I would bury myself in my work at the shop and refrain from calling her. *Maybe I shouldn't even answer my home phone,* I thought.

When I arrived at home, I realized that I was physically exhausted; however, in spite of my hangover and emotional turmoil, I decided to get busy. I put on a pot of coffee and retreated to the bathroom to shave and shower.

I felt much better after my bath; for not only had I washed away the grime of the jail, but I also somehow felt cleansed of the decadent experience of the prior evening. I poured myself a cup of coffee, carried it into the den, and took a seat on the couch.

The ringing telephone caught my attention. Fearing

that it might be Harriet, I started to ignore it; but I quickly reconsidered, for I figured that she wouldn't be calling so early. Maybe I should have taken Marsha's advice by installing a caller ID. The call was from the carpenter whom I had hired to remodel my den, but since I was not in the mood to deal with him, I stalled him for a few days.

I was living a haphazard existence, for Harriet had once again upset my life. I had neglected my business, behaved erratically, and on a couple of occasions I had even gotten drunk. Never before in my life had I been a drinker. I had also neglected my health. *How long has it been since I have jogged?*

I finished my coffee and proceeded to get dressed. I realized that a hard day's work would help in rejuvenating my spirit, so I decided to go to work in my shop. Unfortunately, I had misplaced my shop keys. I looked for them in various places in the house as well as in my car, but with no results. In disgust, I poured myself another cup of coffee and reclaimed my seat in the den. I decided to rest for a while before continuing the search.

Immediately following a soft rap on the side door, Melissa walked into the room.

"Hi, Dad!" She flashed a radiant smile.

"When did you start knocking?" I asked.

She laughed. "I figured I'd better give you a little warning before barging in on you…Considering your recent behavior, I was afraid you might be having a drunken orgy going on."

"So Marsha has already called you, has she?"

She giggled. "Yeah. What's got into you, Dad?"

"I don't know, Melissa. Maybe I'm crazy."

"Well, I don't think you're crazy, but you're not behavin' in your usual fuddy-duddy style." She took a seat in the recliner.

"Is Marsha pretty sore at me?" I asked.

"No, she's not sore, but she's worried."

"Does your Aunt Jessie know about my getting in jail?" I wanted to take in all the bad news as quickly as possible in order to get it over with.

"Of course she knows! You don't think Marsha would withhold that kind of juicy information from her, do you?"

"I guess not. How do you feel about my behavior last night, Melissa?"

"That depends on what you did, Dad," she said, "I'm kinda worried about you drivin' while you're drinkin.'"

"You don't have to worry about that because I'll never do it again. I was lucky this time."

"What else did you do, Dad?"

"We met all our former classmates, danced a little, and drank a lot…too much."

"Why are you drinkin' so much lately, Dad? I never knew you to drink until recently."

"Well, that's something else you won't have to worry about. I'm not saying that I'll never take another drink, but I'll sure not be getting drunk again."

"Good." She smiled mischievously, "What else did you do, Dad? Did you do something with that woman, Harriet?"

"Yeah. Harriet and I played football."

"Played football? Where?"

"On the Northridge High School football field. Where else? Dick Noble also played."

"Were you drunk?"

"Of course. Why else would I play football with a woman in the dark at 1:00 in the morning? Harriet used to refer to herself, Dick and me as *The Three Musketeers. The Three Stooges* would have been more accurate!"

Melissa broke into a raucous laugh. "Wasn't there a little bit of romance going on between you and Harriet? Come on, Dad, you can tell me."

"Only in my mind," I answered, "I feel a lot of remorse over the silly way I behaved, so don't make it worse."

Her expression became serious. "Dad, other than your drivin' under the influence of alcohol, and drinkin' a little too much, I don't see where your other behavior...dancin,' playin' football, actin' a little silly, should make you feel so remorseful." She again smiled. "How did you get Harriet to play football with you? It's a little unusual to see a woman playin' football... especially after midnight."

"If you knew Harriet, You'd know that it's not that unusual. She's always been spontaneous. She loves to have fun. She's quite an unusual woman. But she's bad for me... I'll be glad when she's gone."

She thought for a long while before commenting. "Why, Dad? Maybe this 'Harriet' is good for you."

"How do you figure that? Look at me! I've been in jail, I've been without sleep for about forty hours, I've got a terrible hangover, and both Marsha and your Aunt Jessie are mad at me!"

"Is all that Harriet's fault?" She looked puzzled.

"No, of course not. It's my fault. But it's the way I react to Harriet, that's all."

"Do you know the reason you reacted the way you did?" she asked, "You're really reacting against that rigid, structured life style that you try so desperately hard to maintain. Don't you remember how Mom was? She was playful and spontaneous… But since she died, you haven't allowed yourself to be playful or to enjoy life. Lately, you've reacted like a steam valve. The pressure that you've built up in yourself by trying to be so perfectly organized finally had to explode!"

I looked at her in amazement. "Would you rather see your dad leading an orderly life, or living a life as crazy as the life I'm living right now?"

She became more serious. "Dad, you don't have to live either of those extremes. There's a middle ground. If you'll allow yourself to have a little fun on a regular basis, the pressure wouldn't build up in you. For some reason, you feel like you have to make perfect plans for everything you do! Not counting last night, when was the last time you did anything spontaneous?"

"But, Melissa, spontaneity means disorder. I like to live my life by planning things," I protested.

"Yeah, Dad, It's okay to plan things. But just leave a little room in your life for unexpected things. Be willing to change your plans. Sometimes our best experiences in life are unplanned. Why don't you just take a spur-of-the-moment trip somewhere? Maybe with your friend, Dick Noble?"

I thought about the dreary life that I had experienced

since Jenny had died. *Could it be possible that Melissa is right?*

The ring of the telephone startled me.

"I'll get it, Dad." She got up and walked to the phone.

"Don't answer it! Let it ring!" I exclaimed.

"Why? Are you crawlin' unto your shell again?" She stopped and turned toward me. "I'm going to answer it, Dad. I've been telling you that you need a caller ID."

"Well, if it's Harriet, I'm not here!" I said.

"Dad, I'm not gonna lie for you!"

"Just tell her that I stepped out for a few minutes. I'm stepping outside, so that you won't be lying." I went out the door just as she picked up the phone.

When I walked back inside, she had hung up the phone and was sitting on the couch. Her look of accusation made me feel guilty.

"It was Harriet. She wants you to call her."

"Thanks, Melissa."

"Are you going to call her, Dad?"

"Probably not. I'll have to think about it."

"Why do you always have to *think about it?* Why can't you just *do it,* once in a while? Why *not* call her?"

"Can't you see why not? She makes me crazy. Besides, I still feel a loyalty to your mother."

Melissa looked disgusted. "Dad, you need to get over your neurotic guilt feelings about Mom."

"So now I'm neurotic, am I?"

"Dad, sometimes I think that you're impossible! Have you had anything to eat?"

"No, just some coffee. I'm too sick to eat. Why do you ask?"

"I thought I'd fix you some breakfast."

"Aren't you supposed to be working at your flower shop?"

"Yeah, I am. But you see, Dad, I'm not like you. Since I'm more concerned about my dad than I am about the flower shop, I figured that I'd allow myself to be spontaneous enough to fix you some breakfast. Screw workin'!"

She walked back to the kitchen while I took a seat on the couch.

"Don't you have any eggs?" she called from the kitchen.

"No, I forgot to buy groceries."

"Well, it looks like I'll have to make out with whatever I can find. Man, your refrigerator is almost empty!" In about fifteen minutes she called me into the kitchen.

"Sit down and eat, Dad. All I could find to fix was some pork and beans, bacon, and toast." I noticed that she had prepared breakfast for herself as well. For a while we munched on our food without talking. Finally she spoke.

"So, Dad… what's the deal on Harriet? Is she goin' back to wherever she lives?"

"Yeah. She lives in Dallas, Texas."

"When is she goin' back?"

"I'm not sure. Soon, I think." We again became quiet. She poured more coffee into my cup.

"Thanks, Melissa," I finally said. "You know what you said about my needing to get more fun out of life? Well, I might just give it a try."

She looked at me and answered sarcastically, "Knowing your nature, you'll probably do something drastic like putting an extra spoonful of sugar in your coffee."

"Surely you don't think that I'm that straight-laced!" I said. She laughed.

We sat for a while at the kitchen table, sipping our coffee. The breakfast had made me feel much better.

She looked at her watch. "Dad, I've gotta go."

"Going back to work?"

"No, I just now made up my mind to take the day off. I think I'll go pick up Stan and go to the mountains."

"Who's Stan?"

"My new boyfriend. I'd like for you to meet him sometime."

"But what about your flower shop?"

"Oh, Becky can handle it. Not much business, anyway. What are you gonna do for the rest of the day?"

"I was going to work at my shop, but I can't find my shop keys."

She reached into the small pocket of her blouse and pulled out a set of keys.

"Could this be what you're lookin' for?"

I inspected the keys. "Yeah! Where did you find them?"

"In the driveway, beside your car."

She grinned, then after kissing me on the forehead, she was out the door.

Chapter 18

Floating on my back near the shore in the buoyancy of the cool ocean water was almost as relaxing as lying in bed. Gently paddling just briskly enough to keep me afloat, I gazed upward at the towering cumulus clouds in the lazy summer sky.

Turning my head to the right, I noticed a thin, vertical blade-like object moving toward me. *What is it? It appears to be a fin. Could it be a shark? In this shallow water?*

In desperation, I frantically thrashed the water in an attempt to swim away from the object, but it rapidly overtook me. Suddenly, I felt the razor-sharp teeth bite deeply into my right thigh.

With a scream of anguish, I quickly grabbed my right leg and sat up in bed, unsure of whether it was my scream or the severe cramp in my right leg that had awakened me. *Thank God it was just a dream!* I got out of bed and repeatedly flexed my leg until the cramp dissipated, but my leg was still in pain. Since it was 6:30 a.m., I decided to stay up. After relieving myself in the bathroom, I limped to the kitchen and started a pot of coffee. I then took a seat in the den and contemplated the day that lay ahead of me.

Several days had passed since the reunion. I had finally recovered from my hangover, and I was again working fairly regularly in my shop. Later this afternoon I would again resume my jogging routine. I had gradually begun to restore a semblance of order in my life.

It was Sunday morning, and I had decided to stay home from church to read the Sunday newspaper; but the main reason I had avoided church was the fear of meeting Gertrude, who was now back in town. I was not yet emotionally prepared to deal with her. Being confronted by Marsha or Jessie would be even more difficult, since I hadn't yet explained to them my childish behavior at the reunion.

Several messages had been left on my home phone during the days that I had worked in my shop; most were from Dick and Harriet. I had returned Dick's calls, but I had yet to call Harriet, for I was still uncertain about my feelings toward her. To avoid talking to her, I had even stopped answering my business phone.

Oddly, I had received no messages from either Marsha or Jessie. Their strange silence was unnerving to me. *Are they avoiding me?* I found myself wishing that they would confront me about my recent misconduct so I could finally put the embarrassing incident behind me.

In spite of the fact that I hadn't slept well, my arthritis was no longer bothering me; in fact, other than being sleepy, I felt better than I had in weeks.

I decided to start answering my telephone; after all, I couldn't avoid Harriet forever. Besides, I was hoping to hear from Marsha or Jessie so I could take my tongue-lashing from them, enabling me to get on with my life; also, Dick was supposed to call me this morning.

I decided to take a nap. With the realization that a nap invariably induces phone calls, I transferred the cordless telephone from the bedroom to the coffee table in the den beside the couch where I would be napping. Using the TV remote, I softened the volume of the television program in progress. I then lay back on the couch to take my nap.

The soft choir music on the TV morning worship program that blended with the monotonous drone of the air conditioner slowly began to soothe me. In the ambiguous zone of near-sleep, I began to think of Harriet. My recent association with her had proven that her former playful nature had remained intact; yet, something about her personality was different. *What was it?* She had a certain mystique about her that made her even more appealing than when I had known her before. My mind slowly drifted into the nebulous brink of sleep. Reality blended with fantasy in the twilight region of semi-consciousness; I drifted deeper until finally, in the realm of dreams, she was again in my arms. Her imaginary tender touch was more tangible than reality itself; and yet, I sensed a mysterious, murky barrier separating us; a dark, indistinct force that would somehow forever prevent us from being together. The image of her began to fade away as I attempted to maintain my grip on her evaporating body. I reached for her…In my soul, I ached for her…Then she was gone.

The ringing telephone awakened me. I picked up the instrument and pushed the button.

"Hello?" The TV screen went blank and the phone continued to ring.

"Hello?" I repeated. Another ring. Instantly, I felt like an utter fool, for instead of the phone, I was talking into the TV remote.

After regaining my somewhat questionable mental faculties, I picked up the actual telephone.

"Hello?"

"Hi, Tom." It was Dick. "Did I interrupt anything?"

"No, not really. I was just taking a nap."

"Oh, sorry, pal."

"No problem," I said, "Actually, I was kinda waiting for you to call me. What's up?"

"Same ol' stuff. Where have you been hidin'? I was hopin' that we could get together."

"I've been busy, working in my shop. I'm trying to get my life back into some kind of order, Dick."

"Oh, you and your obsession with order! What you need is some fun in your life."

"Like the fun we had at the class reunion? That fun almost killed me!"

"Oh, hell, Tom. Why don't you lighten up?"

"Lighten up? I don't see how you had any fun after it was over. I'll bet your arthritis hurt like hell after all that dancing and playing football!"

"I don't have arthritis, but my football knee hurt me for a couple of days. It was worth it, though. I had a ball at the reunion!"

"Yeah, well, I *thought* I was having fun, but it was just the booze. I wasn't really having all that much fun. I shouldn't have gotten drunk!"

"Hell, if you *think* you're havin' fun, then you're havin' fun! Besides, gettin' drunk was the best part. By the way, what's up with you and Harriet?"

"What do you mean, *what's up?* Nothing."

"That's what I mean, Tom. *Nothing*. She's heard nothing from you since the reunion."

"I have nothing to say to her," I said.

"Why? She's been askin' about you. Are you mad at her about something?"

"No, I'm not mad at her. It's just that ever since she came back here, my life has been in a mess. When's she going back to Dallas?"

"That's one of the reasons I called you, Tom. She's goin' to stay for a while longer in Northridge. She moved out of the motel and rented an apartment a couple of days ago."

"Where's her apartment located?"

"It's out on the west end of town near the city park. Do you know that big brick apartment complex near Shoney's on Highway 321? Well, she rented an upstairs apartment from Old Man Bishop. He lives in the downstairs apartment."

"You mean Oliver Bishop? I thought he was dead."

"Well, not quite. He just has one foot in the grave."

"How long is she gonna stay here?" I asked.

"You act like you can't wait for her to leave," he said, "She said that she'd called you a couple of times and left a message, but you haven't called her back."

"Dick, I've been busy."

"But you weren't too busy to call *me* back. And why haven't you been answerin' your business phone?" I ignored his question.

"When have you seen her?" I asked.

"We had a date the other night," he said.

"Wasn't she mad at you for getting fresh with her?"

"Nah, she knew that it was just the booze. You know how Harriet is. She never stays mad for long."

"Did you have a good time on your date with her?"

"Hell no! She spent most of her time askin' about you. Why don't you give her a call, Tom?"

"I don't know. I'll have to think about it."

"Oh hell, forget it, pal. Do you want to play some golf? I can get us a tee time for Wednesday. And don't tell me you'll have to think about it."

"I don't know. I'll have to…look at my schedule on my calendar."

"Shit! Don't tell me you've gone back to keepin' schedules and calendars again!"

I turned my head toward the knock at the front door. "Dick, I'll have to call you back. Somebody's knocking at the door."

"You better answer it. It has to be somebody on official business. You know it's not your family, because they never knock. Call me about the golf date."

"Right. See ya' Dick."

After hanging up the phone, I walked to the front door and opened it. Marsha was dressed in an off-white, fashionable pants suit. Her aura introduced the subtle aroma of expensive perfume. She probably just got out of church, I figured.

"Come in, Marsha," I invited.

"Hello, Dad." she walked into the den and stiffly took a seat on the couch.

I smiled at her. "Why so formal?"

"What do you mean?" she asked.

"You entered through the front door instead of the side door. Also, you knocked before you entered. I thought that I'd be opening the door to a stranger."

"I'm just trying to honor your new set of rules, Dad."

"What new set of rules?"

"You know. A while back you said that you were taking charge of your life. You complained about all of your relatives just walking into your house whenever we wish, without knocking. I'm just trying to show you some proper *respect!"*

Her last word was saturated with sarcasm, probably implying that after my recent misbehavior I didn't deserve any respect. In my attempt to discern her general attitude, I carefully inspected her demeanor; however, because she was a master at disguising her feelings, her nonchalant manner revealed nothing, other than the fact that to reveal nothing about her feelings was precisely her intention. Her cool attitude suggested that our relationship was limited to only a casual friendship.

"What brings you here, Marsha?" I wanted to quickly get to the point.

"I thought that we should talk," she said.

"Good idea. I haven't heard from you in a few days…or from your Aunt Jessie, either, for that matter."

She started to answer me, but her response was interrupted by the ringing doorbell.

"Excuse me, Marsha," I said, "My house is getting to be a busy place today."

When I opened the door, my surprise at seeing her was only surpassed by my awe of her loveliness. Harriet was wearing a short-sleeved kelly green blouse tucked into a tight-fitting pair of white shorts that revealed the entire length of her bronzed legs. Her jogging shoes and the baseball cap that covered her locks of auburn hair gave her the appearance of an athlete. She smelled heavenly.

She displayed a friendly grin. "Hi, Tom."

"Why, hello, Harriet." I found myself caught in an awkward situation. Not only would I have to explain my past behavior to both Marsha and Harriet (for different reasons) but I also had a distinct gut feeling that neither of them would be able to tolerate the other.

She pointed to Marsha's car in the driveway. "Did I come at a bad time? I see that you have company."

"No, that's okay, Harriet. Come on in." I was curious in regard to the purpose of her visit.

When she walked into the den, Marsha, in character with her impeccable manners, immediately stood. I introduced them.

"Harriet, this is my daughter, Marsha... Marsha, this is Harriet Dawson, a former school mate of mine." Remembering that they had briefly met at the jail, I continued, "Of course, I realize that you have previously met, in a rather informal way."

Harriet walked to her, smiling. Marsha took her extended hand.

"Hello, Ms. Dawson... or is it *Mrs.?* Yes, I remember meeting you. It was at the *jail,* wasn't it?"

Harriet was quick to pick up on her emphasis on the word 'jail'. Her forced smile contradicted the icy stare that she gave my daughter. She ignored Marsha's scornful comment. "Hello, Marsha," was her only response to her.

She turned to me. "Tom, I'm afraid that I have caught you at an inappropriate time. Maybe I should leave and come back later."

Marsha immediately spoke up. "No, don't do that, Ms. Dawson. I was just about to leave." She started for the front door. "It was a pleasure to meet you again, ma'am. I'll catch you later, Dad,"

Harriet remained silent. From the front window, I watched Marsha walk to her car. The unexpected arrival of Harriet had granted me a brief reprieve from hearing her condemnation.

I turned toward her. "Have a seat, Harriet. Can I get you something to drink?" She remained standing, ignoring my question.

She exposed her beautiful white teeth in an expansive smile. "Want to go on a picnic?"

"A picnic?" I was surprised.

"Yeah, a picnic."

"Actually, I'm a little busy," I explained.

"Busy? This is Sunday!"

"Yeah, but I was going to do some chores around the house and make a list of things that I'm supposed to do tomorrow."

"Forget the list, Tom. Come on, let's go on a picnic

together." She delivered a playful slap to my shoulder. "Who knows? You might even have some fun!"

Her beauty was radiant. In her closeness to me, her tousled auburn hair exuded the fresh, fragrant aroma of shampoo. Against my better judgment, I decided to go on the picnic with her.

I smiled at her. "Well, okay. Why not? A picnic sounds like fun. But do we need to pack some kind of lunch? I haven't bought groceries, so we'll probably need to go to the market."

"Everything's already packed. I have the picnic basket in my car. You don't think I'd invite you on a picnic without preparing for it, do you?"

"I'll have to change clothes and shave."

"Fine, I'll wait for you. But don't be too long, because I don't want the food in our picnic basket to spoil."

"Bring it inside and put it in the 'fridge."

"No need for that," she said, "just hurry."

She waited for me in the den for about fifteen minutes until I joined her. She smiled at me, took my hand and led me outside toward the white vehicle parked at the curb.

"Nice car," I commented, "A Honda, right?"

"Honda Accord. I bought it used a couple of years ago. Still runs like new."

I slid into the passenger seat in front and she drove away.

"Where are we going?" I asked.

"You'll see. It's a surprise. Do you like surprises?"

"Sometimes. But not usually."

"You'll like this surprise." She turned toward me and grinned.

"At least give me a hint," I said.

"No hints. A hint would ruin the surprise."

"Okay, then. Surprise me."

Her expression became serious. "Your daughter, Marsha. She doesn't like me." She turned the vehicle to the left, southward on Maple Street.

"I wouldn't say that she doesn't like you. She doesn't really know you. Because of our outrageous behavior at the reunion, she probably thinks that you're a bad influence on me."

"What about you? Do you think I am?"

"I don't know. Even if you are it's my fault, because after all, I have a mind of my own. She also thinks that Dick is a bad influence on me."

"Who is Marsha to judge you?" Her tone seemed resentful.

"You've got to remember, Harriet, she's my daughter. She loves me and feels protective of me. Marsha is not a bad girl. She's a good woman. I know that she's a little judgmental, sometimes, but she has my best interests at heart, and I love her….and Melissa, too." I felt that she was intruding. She only smiled.

She changed the subject. "Your daughter, Melissa…what's she like?"

"Kind, playful, mischievous, and unpredictable. She's also very talented."

"Quite the opposite of Marsha, right?"

"Yeah, but that doesn't make either of them right…or wrong, either, for that matter. Each of them, in their personality, seems to need a little of what the other one has. If there was just some way to blend their opposite personalities together, they'd both be just right."

"But if we started blending people together, we'd end up with a lot of boring people, Tom. Differences in personalities, even to the extreme, are what make people interesting, don't you think? For instance, sometimes when two people with opposite personalities marry, it creates a good balance, and makes for a good marriage."

"Yeah, but sometimes it also makes for a pain in the ass."

She laughed, and turned right on Highway 321. We had now left the city and were traveling in open country, skirting Kingsley Lake on our left.

"How much further?" I asked.

"Only a little way, now."

"I'll bet you're headed for Greenfield Park."

Her face registered disappointment. "Dang! Now you've spoiled the surprise!"

She swung the car into the broad parking area and parked in the shade of a large oak tree.

"Here we are! Isn't it a lovely day?" She was bubbling with excitement.

We got out of her car and scanned the area in search of a good spot for a picnic. From the back seat, I lifted out the large picnic basket.

"Should we take the blanket with us?"

"Of course," she said, "Whoever heard of having a picnic without a blanket?"

It was an ideal day for a picnic. The sunlight was brilliant, but the air was unseasonably cool. I carried the basket of food and the blanket, while she carried a small portable radio. We slowly strolled through the sun-drenched expanse of grass that stretched ahead of us. Under the protective canopy of a large maple tree was a picnic table. When we reached the shade of the large tree, I started to cover the picnic table with the blanket.

"Wait a minute, Tom. Why don't we spread the blanket out in the grass and have our picnic on the ground?"

"Do you think we'll be comfortable?" I asked her.

"We'll be *more* comfortable. We can relax after we eat, and then lie on our backs and look at the sky through the tree branches. And we can look for castles and animals in the clouds. Did you ever do that when you were a kid?"

"Sometimes," I said.

I picked a level place and spread the blanket out under the maple tree.

"Is this spot okay?" I looked at her, seeking her approval.

"Perfect!" she said.

I placed the basket of food on the blanket and we both took a seat, crossing our legs, facing each other.

"What did you make for our lunch?" I asked.

"I'm not tellin' you," she teased, "I want you to be surprised. Close your eyes and make a wish!"

"Make a wish for what?"

"For what you would like to find in the basket."

"But I might wish for one thing and get something else," I said, "Then I would be disappointed."

Her laugh was child-like. "But you also might find something better than you wished for." She hadn't changed in her child-like penchant for playing games.

"You must have prepared something pretty fantastic

for us," I said, "Since you're trying so hard to surprise me."

"No, not really. The fantastic part is the discovery of it…the unexpected surprise, the mystery of what's in the basket. Don't you like surprises, Tom?"

I thought about the surprise that she had sprung on me when she jilted me fifty years ago. "No, I don't particularly like surprises, Harriet."

We remained quiet as I dug into the basket. I pulled out the usual assortment of paper cups, napkins, and disposable utensils. Then I removed a container of barbecued chicken, a couple of Cokes, a small, mostly melted bag of ice, a container of potato salad, and a bunch of grapes. At the very bottom of the basket was a bottle of wine.

"Wine? Well, I *am* surprised!"

" I hope you like wine, Tom. Do you?"

"Sure, I like wine," I said.

"Wine is a kind of romantic drink," she flashed a sexy smile.

I responded with sarcasm. "Is that what we're doing? Getting romantic?"

She ignored my question. "I barbecued us some chicken. I brought a chicken breast and two legs. Would you rather have the breast, or the two drumsticks?"

"I'll take the drumsticks," I said. She became lost in thought.

"A penny for your thoughts," I said.

"Tom, you seem to be trying to create a distance between us. Why are you sarcastic with me?"

"Oh, was I sarcastic? Forgive me for behaving in a way that's not perfectly pleasing to you!" For some reason, I couldn't resist being sarcastic.

I munched on a chicken leg as an awkward silence enveloped us. She turned her head to the left, toward the lake, surveying the sailboats that lazily moved through the calm water. She appeared to be brooding.

I carefully studied her graceful posture and voluptuous figure, amazed at how a woman of her age could be so beautiful; but she was not completely devoid of the blemishes of old age. Her decision to wear shorts had enabled me for the first time in fifty years to examine her shapely bronze legs. Her thighs displayed a sprinkling of cellulite and an occasional spot of spider-veins. Around her lovely brown eyes and full lips were suggestions of tiny wrinkles, accentuated by the bright sunlight. In spite of these imperfections, however, her appearance was that of a beautiful, much younger woman.

She sat silently, munching on the chicken breast, apparently pouting at me.

"What's your secret, Harriet?" I abruptly asked. I popped a grape into my mouth.

She quickly turned to me. "My secret about what?" She took another bite of the chicken breast.

"You're about the same age as I am, but you look twenty years younger," I said.

Her cheerful expression returned. "Do you want to know my secret for staying young? Well, for starters, it's tons of Clairol, numerous Botox injections, silicone, and tooth implants. But mostly, it's the result of about forty years of hard workouts in a health club, and thousands of miles of jogging. I didn't get to looking this way from sitting around in night clubs drinkin' mint juleps."

I began to admire her perseverance. "No plastic surgery?"

"No, I would never resort to that. Don't you see these horrible wrinkles on my face?" Her face looked lovely to me.

I changed the subject. "Dick called me this morning. He said that you had rented an apartment."

"Yes, when you have time, I'd like to show it to you."

"How long do you plan on staying in Northridge?" I asked.

"I'm not sure, Tom. Sometimes I think I'd like to move back here for good."

"Dick tells me that you rented the apartment from that old guy, Oliver Bishop."

"Yeah, he is really old. He must be pushin' ninety! He can hardly get around. The way he looks at me kinda gives me the creeps. He lives alone in the apartment below me. If he wasn't so old and helpless, I might be afraid of him."

"Oh, he's probably a harmless old goat. Care for some potato salad?" I asked.

"Yes, thank you. Would you please open me a Coke, too?" I dished out equal portions on two plastic plates, handing one to her along with her opened Coke.

A gentle breeze caressed us as we nibbled on the food. I watched her as she hungrily consumed the chicken breast. Her face reflected curiosity when she turned toward me.

"Tom, I don't want to get too personal, but what was Jenny like?"

"Jenny was a great wife to me and a wonderful

mother to the children. I loved her very much."

"Yes, I knew that, but what was her personality like?"

"She was like Melissa, only more settled. Friendly, fun-loving, spontaneous, and witty."

"A lot like me, huh?"

"In some ways, yes. Only she was more predictable than you. Sometimes I don't know what you're going to do next."

"Then, Melissa is a lot like her mother, and Marsha is a lot like you."

"That's generally true, but Marsha and I are not exactly alike," I said, "In many ways, we're different."

She again laughed. "Are you kidding me? Marsha is a carbon copy of you in her personality."

"In what way?" I asked.

"She is concerned about her family. She's a worrier. She is rigidly structured and cautious. And she gives a lot of thought to everything before she's able to make any kind of decision."

"You determined all that about Marsha after only briefly meeting her a couple of times?"

"Yes, to some extent, but Dick has told me a lot about her, and Melissa, too."

I took a sip of Coke. "I tried to teach both of our kids to live a responsible, structured life. Unfortunately, in Melissa's case it didn't stick."

"But in Marsha's case, you've taught her well."

She had finished eating her chicken and potato salad. With a playful smile, she held the breastbone in front of me.

"Take hold of the wishbone, Tom. Close your eyes and make a wish."

With my forefinger and thumb, I gripped my end of the bone. "On such short notice, I don't know what to wish for. There are so many things."

"My God," she exclaimed, "Don't think about it for an hour, just make a wish! Come on, close your eyes, and don't peek!"

I closed my eyes but made no wish, for my mind seemed to be blank. We pulled on the bone until it snapped. When it separated, I was holding the short end. She dropped her fragment of the wishbone and gleefully clapped her hands.

"What did you wish for?" I asked.

"I can't tell you that!"

"Why not?"

"Because if I tell it, my wish won't come true! What did you wish for?"

"Why should I tell you? You wouldn't tell me what you wished for."

"But it wouldn't matter if you told me, because you lost. Your wish won't come true, anyway."

"But what if we wished for the same thing? Wouldn't my wish also come true?"

"Don't get so analytical about it, Tom. It spoils all the fun."

Her expression became more serious. "Tom, tell me something. Are you glad that I came back to Northridge?"

I thought about her question. "Why are you asking me that?"

"It just seems that sometimes you try to avoid me. You didn't even return my calls."

"It's not that I don't enjoy your company, Harriet.

It's just that since you, Dick and I have gotten back together I have neglected most of my responsibilities. For instance, I like to stay in shape, but I haven't even jogged in days."

She quickly rose to her feet and grinned. "Let's go jogging now! We've finished our lunch, and we can sip on the wine when we get back! Look over there by the edge of the lake...Isn't that some kind of trail? We can jog there!"

"But we'll get all sweaty!" I protested.

"Who cares? Come on, Tom!" She took my hand, pulling me to my feet. Excitedly, she briskly tugged me along behind her to the bike trail at the edge of the lake.

"Okay, let's start," she said.

"Hadn't we better stretch first?"

"No need for that," she said, "We'll just start out walking to warm up."

For a couple of hundred yards the winding trail generally conformed to the contour of the lake's edge; then it abruptly veered to the right, up a shallow incline into a heavily wooded area. The course became straight and level, disappearing deeper into the forest in a patchwork of alternating splotches of sunlight and shade that blanketed the trail. For more than a quarter of a mile we walked in silence, enjoying the gentle breeze that caressed our faces.

Finally, she spoke. "Are you having fun, Tom?"

"Yes," I admitted.

"Ready to start joggin'?"

"If you are."

She set the pace, which was a trifle faster than my

usual speed. Due to the grueling tempo, our conversation was sparse. After we had covered about a mile, the trail made a broad loop around a green meadow, and then merged back into the forest in the same path that we had previously followed, so that we were now retracing our initial route in reverse. When we were about fifty yards from our finish at our original starting point, she turned her head toward me.

"I'll race you to the finish line!"

"You're on!" I answered.

We ran neck-in-neck until we were about ten yards from finishing when she gradually edged ahead of me. We finally stopped in the grassy meadow near the lake. Between gasping breaths she gleefully laughed. She walked to me, and in a vigorous embrace, we merged our sweating bodies. Although, by nature I am not a hugger, because the expression was so natural for her, it caused me to respond. I hugged her tightly.

For a while, we stood by the water's edge, enjoying the soft breeze from the lake. She stooped and picked up a small stone.

"Watch this, Tom," she said, excitedly, "How many skips do you think I can get when I throw this rock in the lake?" In side-arm fashion, she hurled the flat stone. It skipped three times across the surface of the tranquil lake before it disappeared. Following her example, I selected a flat rock from the lake bank and slung it. The attempt was a dismal failure, for after only skipping once, it promptly sank.

Since I couldn't seem to get the hang of it, she repeatedly beat me as we continued for several minutes to hurl stones into the lake. Eventually, we tired of the frivolous game and returned to our blanket under the shade of the maple tree. We collapsed on the blanket, lying on our backs, gazing through the leafy branches at the lazy summer sky. She found some music on the portable radio and lowered the volume. As I listened to the raspy tune, I realized how badly the younger generation had screwed up music.

"Want some wine?" she asked.

"Not right now…maybe later. I'm pretty content at the moment just lying here on the blanket." For several minutes we rested on our backs without speaking. We were lying close together with our bodies touching. She playfully placed her right leg on top of mine.

She finally broke the silence. "Tom, I kept up with your life for all of these years. Did you ever wonder about me?" Her searching eyes explored the branches that hovered over us.

"Yes, especially for the first couple of years, after you…"

"After I jilted you?"

"Yes."

"That was the worst mistake of my life, Tom. I've regretted it for years."

"Why did you do it, Harriet?" I rolled over onto my side, facing her.

"Nothing I could ever say would justify what I did. But… I was mixed up back then." She looked sad.

"Did you marry that older guy for his money? Does material wealth mean that much to you?"

"It wouldn't mean a thing to me now," she said,

"Maybe back then it did. But that's not the only reason I married him."

"What other reason could you have had?" I asked.

"Remember when we agreed to get married? I wanted to get married right away, because I loved you! But you wanted to wait until we finished college. I admit that I have always been impatient and impulsive, but what girl wants to wait for four years? If you hadn't been so cautious, wanting to examine your thoughts for four years, maybe we…"

"So you're saying that it was my fault?"

"No, I know that it's my fault. Or maybe it's nobody's fault. Back then we were so different in the way we saw life, and we were too young to understand our feelings. I felt that maybe you were just putting off marriage because deep down inside of you, you didn't really intend to marry me. Think about it, Tom! Can't you see how that could make a girl feel rejected? I can't believe that back then we saw things so differently!"

"We're still drastically different," I pointed out.

"Yes, but we're also wiser," she said, "We're both extreme in our differences, Tom. But maybe we're good for each other now. Maybe your steady, structured personality is what I need to temper some of my compulsive ways. And maybe some of my spontaneity would be good for you."

I wondered about her past. "Harriet, if I'm getting too nosy, just tell me to shut up. Why did you get divorced?"

"We didn't love each other, Tom. He was good to me, in a way, but I was just a trophy wife for him. He just wanted to show me off to his big shot friends."

"Who asked for the divorce?"

"I did, Tom. I just couldn't take any more."

"Well, he was loaded with money," I said, "I guess at least he left you pretty well-heeled."

"Not really. It's a long story, but I didn't end up with a lot of money. I have enough money to get by, but I'm sure not able to live an extravagant life style. You noticed my used car."

"Why didn't you ever remarry?"

"I never found anyone I wanted to marry. My failed marriage kinda turned me against it."

"But there must have been other men," I said.

She hung her head. "A lot of men, Tom. Look, I'm trying to be completely honest with you, but please don't ask me any more questions."

I ignored her request. "What do you mean a lot of men? Dozens? Hundreds?"

She stared at me indignantly. "I never did sell my body, if that's what you're askin.' Please, Tom, let it rest, okay?"

I changed the subject. I raised to a sitting position and crossed my legs.

"Why don't we have some wine?" I asked.

"I thought you'd never ask!" Her mood quickly brightened. She sat up, crossed her legs and faced me. I poured small portions of the wine into two paper cups and handed one to her.

"Harriet, where does Dick fit into this picture? Back in our high school days, he also had a crush on you." I took a sip of wine.

"I've always loved Dick as a friend," she said, "but

never romantically. His personality is a lot like mine. Also, he is so sweet and generous that anyone would like him. I still consider him a dear friend." She held out her cup and I poured more wine into it.

I chuckled. "He sure got mad at me back then when I told him that you and I were going to get married. He beat the hell out of me."

"That's another reason I left you, Tom. I felt that I had come between you and Dick, and my involvement with both of you had ruined your friendship."

"Yeah, but Dick and I again became best friends," I pointed out.

"I'm so glad, Tom."

We sat quietly, slowly sipping our wine. The cool breeze from the lake grew stronger with the retreating afternoon. She plucked a dandelion from the grass that surrounded our blanket. Holding it in front of me, she blew the downy wisp of tiny blossoms into my face and mischievously giggled.

I smiled at her. "Harriet, I want to thank you for this lovely afternoon. I can't remember when I have enjoyed anything as much."

Her eyes brightened as she flashed a broad grin. "Oh, I'm so happy that you're pleased! After you didn't return my calls, I was afraid you'd refuse to have a picnic with me." I was touched by her child-like response.

We lazily gazed at the lake, drinking the wine in silence. She casually picked a daisy from the grass. I watched her as she methodically removed each petal, one by one. She finally plucked the final petal from the flower. Seemingly pleased with the result, she laughed and winked at me. Impulsively, she pulled my head toward her and planted a passionate kiss on my lips. Taking her into my arms, I returned her kiss. We released each other and she looked into my eyes.

"Tom, do you believe in second chances?"

"Yes, I suppose I do. I guess everyone deserves a second chance."

The earnest look in her pleading eyes indicated to me that she had indeed changed. I felt that decades of passing years had apparently altered her thinking. She was wiser, gentler, more introspective; even remorseful. However, her more serious outlook on life had not diminished her delightful playful nature. *How could anyone not be attracted to this woman?*

This time, I pulled her to me. Our lips enthusiastically bonded in a lengthy, passionate kiss. She slowly released me and placed her head on my shoulder. We sat silently, immobile, as I held her to me. She raised her head and again peered directly into my eyes.

"Marry me, Tom!"

"What?" I asked, in astonishment. I slowly removed my arms from around her, reflecting on her words. I remembered that she had always been impulsive and domineering. "Is that an order?" I asked.

"Oh, Tom, I didn't mean for it to sound that way. Tom, *will you marry me?"*

I didn't answer.

"I love you, Tom. Will you *please* marry me?"

Although I truly believed that she had changed for the better, I was nonetheless wary of her. I felt myself again falling in love with her, but my cautious nature and the guilt that I felt because of my loyalty to the memory of Jenny instilled in me a reluctance to make a commitment.

"I don't know, Harriet. I'll have to think about it." I finally answered.

She was embarrassed. "I guess you're kinda turned o ff by my impulsiveness."

"Harriet, sometimes in little things, I'm attracted to your impulsive nature. But in important issues, you make spur-of-moment judgments that are often life-altering decisions. I like to reflect on important decisions, and make plans."

"Tom, John Lennon once made a profound statement. He said that *life is what happens while we are busy making other plans.* Sometimes we can get so caught up in making plans that life passes us by. How many more years do either of us have to ponder over our decisions? We're nearing the end of our lives. If we're to find just a tiny bit of happiness in the time we have left, we'd better latch onto it quickly."

I changed the subject. "More wine?" I poured more of the beverage from the bottle into our cups. We sipped on the wine without talking, peering at the setting sun in the west. She again reclined on her back. To afford her a clear view of the lake, she raised her upper body, bracing herself with her elbows behind her. For several minutes she viewed the peaceful lake. She remained quiet as I carefully studied her. I wondered what her thoughts were at this moment. *Does she feel rejection about my evasion of her marriage proposal? Is she humiliated?* I began to feel sympathy for her.

"Harriet?" I mumbled, hesitantly.

She turned her head toward me. "Yes?"

"When you asked me to marry you, I didn't say 'no.' I just said that I wanted to think about it."

"I know, Tom."

She rolled over onto her knees and began packing discarded items into the empty picnic basket.

"It's gettin' late, Tom. Maybe we'd better be goin' home."

I handed her the bottle with the remaining wine, and she placed it in the basket.

"You're not mad at me, are you Harriet?"

"No, I'm not angry at you."

We quickly cleaned up the area and I folded the blanket. We walked to the car in silence. I placed the basket and blanket in the car, got inside, and she slowly drove away. I felt a wave of melancholia when I stole a final glance at our picnic spot and the winding bike trail silhouetted by the setting sun. Today had been the first time since the death of Jenny that I had really enjoyed the companionship of a woman.

We both experienced a sense of awkwardness as she drove toward my house. We spoke only occasionally, with most of our conversation limited to trivia. Finally, she pulled into the driveway of my home. Looking toward the living room window of my neighbor's house next door, I saw the bulbous face of Silas Wooten spying on us as Harriet parked the car. Her failure to shut down the car motor after parking was a strong indication that she wanted to end our afternoon date.

"Well, goodbye, Tom," she said, "I had a real nice

time." She obviously expected me to get out of the car.

"Turn off the engine, Harriet,"

"But, Tom, I…"

Before she had a chance to finish her sentence, I gently pulled her into my arms and passionately kissed her. I slowly released her and looked into her eyes.

"Come inside with me for a while, Harriet," I pleaded.

She turned off her engine. "But, Tom…what if Marsha drops by while I'm inside your house with you? She doesn't approve of me, you know."

"Don't worry about that. Marsha's mad at me. Anyway, she won't come back here until after she carefully plans her method of attack on me."

With a trace of hesitation, she got out of the car and took my hand, allowing me to lead her toward the house. Before stepping through the door, I turned, and with my uplifted middle finger I shot a bird at Silas Wooten as he peered at us from his window.

Once inside my den, without uttering a word, I pulled her to me. The passionate manner in which I kissed her left no doubt in her mind about my intentions. At first she displayed a slight hesitancy, but as I persisted, she gradually yielded to me in complete surrender.

Without wavering, I led her through my house to my bedroom, stopping beside the bed. She offered no resistance to me when I slid my hand behind her shoulders and unfastened her bra. I moved closer to her, feeling her full breasts pressing against me. Her tousled auburn hair brushed against my cheek; teasing me, exciting me, its fragrant aroma arousing me. My heart raced so rapidly that I became short of breath.

"It's been a long time, Harriet," I said, in a quivering voice.

"For me too!" She was wildly excited.

I kissed her again, this time more lustfully. She enthusiastically returned my kiss as we seemed to merge into a single smoldering entity.

In the middle of our passionate kiss, I gently pushed her backward until she collapsed on the soft bed. I clumsily tugged at her shorts while she joined me in our frenzied effort to remove them. She quickly slipped off her panties and frantically kicked off her shoes. She wildly coursed her fingers through my wispy strands of hair; then, fiercely gripping my shoulders, she pulled me down on top of her. I was clumsy in my efforts, for I was badly out of practice in such an activity.

I worked feverishly to unbuckle my belt. My mind was a burning hotbed of lust, and my heart pulsated wildly. I became lost in a world of ecstatic reverie as we continued to ravenously kiss. I kissed her mouth, her face, and her neck. The intoxicating aroma of her disheveled hair incensed me. In our intense desire, our tender love scene had quickly evolved into a frantic mission to satisfy our mutual longing.

While I continued to kiss her, I kicked off my shoes and struggled to pull down my trousers. In the process, my legs became entangled in my pants, causing me to clumsily slide off the bed and crash onto the floor like an animal caught in a bear trap. From my kneeling position, I hurriedly stripped away my pants and crawled back in bed on top of her. Feeling with my hand, I noticed that my erection was dissipating. *What a terrible moment to experience erectile dysfunction!* Never before in my life had I been impotent. I had heard of other men who had suffered from this malady, although it had never happened to me. I now knew what was meant by performance anxiety. It's an appropriate name for the condition, for the more I anticipated the performance, the worse my anxiety became. My long awaited moment had filled me with apprehension. With my right hand, I again examined my lower extremities: *I was now as limber as a dishrag!* I had always hoped that when recalling our first sexual encounter, Harriet would remember me as a virile, stalwart stallion; but if I proceeded in my present benign condition, my performance would probably conjure up visions in her mind of a harmless, anemic earthworm.

"Take me now, Tom! Now!" She sounded desperate. To stall for time, I continued to kiss her; but the longer I avoided the act, the more impotent I became.

The sound from behind me of the opening bedroom door startled me. Turning my head, I was shocked to see Melissa standing in the doorway. Harriet was completely unaware of Melissa's arrival. She again called out to me, "Tom! Now, sweetheart!"

I was now in a state of total panic and confusion. In order to both silence Harriet's pleas and avoid the incredulous stare of Melissa, much like an ostrich burying his head in the sand, I again turned my lips to those of Harriet's. My mind desperately searched for a plausible explanation to Melissa of my compromising situation. I even gave a fleeting thought to telling her that Harriet had experienced a seizure, and the placement of my lips to hers was only my attempt at mouth-to-mouth resuscitation; however, since it would be impossible to explain our state of undress, I quickly abandoned the idea. Realizing that I couldn't sustain the kiss indefinitely, I raised my head and turned to face Melissa.

"Oh, hello, Melissa," I said, casually, "What brings you here?" My fake attempt at nonchalance would have been effective only in the unlikely event that she hadn't noticed anything out of the ordinary. She only turned away from me, giggled, and hurried through the door out of the bedroom.

Harriet was now fully aware that our tryst had been discovered. She scampered from the bed and began to hurriedly dress.

"Oh, my God, Tom!" she gasped, "Was that your daughter, Melissa?"

"Yeah, Harriet, don't sweat it! Just get dressed and stay here in the bedroom. I'll go and explain it to Melissa."

"How in the world will you explain it?"

"Don't worry, I'll think of something." I hurriedly got dressed and left the bedroom in search of Melissa.

Melissa's intrusion was a mixed blessing, for while it had embarrassed me, it had also rescued me from an even greater humiliation; because if I had further attempted to consummate my renewed romance with Harriet it would have been like trying to shoot pool with a rope.

I found Melissa in the den calmly sitting on the couch. She looked up at me innocently. Then she turned her head away and in order to hide her smile, covered her mouth with her hand.

"Melissa," I said, "I guess there's no need for me to try to come up with some ridiculous explanation about what you saw."

She laughed. "What are you talking about, Dad? I didn't see anything that you would need to explain."

I reached for her hand. "Come on Melissa, I want you to meet Harriet."

"No, Dad, I'd better leave so she can get out of here without bein' embarrassed."

"No, come on, Melissa, she can't be any more embarrassed than she already is. Besides, I think Harriet will like you."

I took her hand and led her into the bedroom. Upon entering the door, we stopped in our tracks. The bedroom window was open and Harriet was gone.

Melissa slapped me on the back and laughed. "Dad, if you and I keep bringing our dates to your house, you might consider installing steps beneath the bedroom window."

Chapter 19

As I sat reading in my den, the ringing telephone gave me a start. I rose from the couch, walked to the phone and picked it up.

"Hello?" The only response was the dial tone.

Again, I said, "Hello?"

The telephone continued to ring. I felt like a complete idiot when I realized that the sound of the ringing telephone was coming from the morning movie that was in progress on my TV set.

I hung up the phone, grateful that my solitary presence at home prevented anyone from witnessing my senility.

Three days had passed since Harriet had left my house through the bedroom window. After her hasty exit, she had immediately called me from her apartment with an embarrassed apology; however, my explanation of Melissa's liberal attitude quickly dispelled her feeling of humiliation. Although in her call Harriet hadn't pressed me for an answer to her marriage proposal, I realized with her impatient nature, she would soon demand some kind of answer from me. I was again deeply involved with her; maybe I even loved her, but I still retained some remnants of caution. Maybe I should tell her 'yes,' that I would marry her. After all, Melissa had advised me to disregard any guilt feelings about Jenny in the event that I decided to marry someone. But once I agreed, there would be no turning back, regardless of the consequences; nevertheless, I owed her an answer.

Sensing her anxiety, I decided to call her. Immediately following her melodious 'hello,' she admonished me for not calling her sooner.

"It's been three days, Tom, and you're just now calling me?"

"I've been busy, Harriet," I explained.

"Doing what?"

"Working in my shop. As a matter of fact, I've gotta work for a little while today."

"When are we gonna get together again?" she asked.

"Soon. I'll have to call you and let you know. But I do want us to get together."

"You're calling me *now!* You can save yourself a phone call by just telling me now."

"I'll have to look at my schedule," I said.

"Your schedule? Are you that busy socially?"

"No…I mean my work schedule."

"Your work schedule? Do you work *at night?"*

"Well…no."

"Oh, I get it. Before you can call me, you'll have to *think about it!* Speaking of thinking about it, have you given any thought to the question I asked you?"

"What question?"

"What question? The question that I asked you at our picnic: The question, 'will you marry me?' You seem to be so scared of the idea that you can't even utter, or think the word, *marry!"*

"Well, I have given it some thought. As a matter of fact, in some ways the idea appeals to me."

"In *some* ways? In other words, there are some ways that the idea doesn't appeal to you!"

"I didn't say that," I protested, "I guess you could say that maybe I'm leaning in that direction."

"Maybe you're leaning in that direction? When will you know?"

"Soon."

"Does 'soon' mean days, weeks, months? Maybe years?"

"Marriage is a serious step for both of us, Harriet."

"In other words, you'll have to *think about it?"*

"I believe that we both ought to think about it," I reasoned.

"Well, when are we going to get together? Maybe we can *talk* about it!" She sounded frustrated.

"I'll call you," I said. A long silence followed. Finally, she spoke.

"Tom, Dick has asked me to go out with him for dinner and a play. Is that okay with you?"

"I guess so. Why would I object to it?"

"I just thought that after our closeness at your house a few days ago, you might not want me going out with him."

"I don't have any claim on you, Harriet. Look, why don't we give our relationship a few days and not rush into anything? I'll have to admit that you've kinda rejuvenated my life. Trust me, okay? I won't leave you hanging forever."

After we hung up, I began to seriously consider marrying her. I needed to weigh the pros and cons: On the plus side, I would have a beautiful wife, I would no longer be lonely, and I would again have a sense of direction for my life; however, the minus side of the situation presented serious questions: What would be the reaction of Marsha and Jessie? Would it damage my relationship with them? Also, there existed the possibility that Harriet would again betray me. *I've got to make up my mind! She won't wait forever for an answer!* I began to experience the fear of losing her…Again.

I felt a pressing urge to go to work. It was after I got dressed while picking up my keys and change from my dresser that I discovered that my wallet was missing. For at least an hour I searched every corner of the house without success. I finally found it wedged behind the seat cushion in my car.

In my shop, I was unable to keep my mind on my efforts. After only a couple of hours' work, I decided to return home.

The vehicles of both Marsha and Melissa were parked at the curb in front of my house. I parked in the driveway, got out of my car, and strolled toward the side door. Before entering I turned, and using my middle finger I made an obscene gesture toward Silas Wooten as he peeped at me from his window next door. When I walked into the den, I stopped in my tracks when I detected the strong odor of Pine-Sol. The room was filled with people. Seated on the couch were Melissa and her Aunt Jessie, while Gertrude was sitting erectly in the rocking chair with a tragic expression etched on her face. Marsha was slowly walking back and forth in front of the others.

She stopped pacing and stared at me. With the exception of Melissa, the look of accusation on all of their faces indicated to me that a family conference was about to take place, with me as the topic of discussion. Since she was the person standing, I concluded that Marsha had appointed herself spokesperson, and had summoned the others to my house with the purpose of censuring my behavior in some way. I correctly assumed that the problem under discussion was my relationship with Harriet.

I was at a loss for words. With the demeanor of a prosecuting attorney, Marsha prepared to present her case. She assumed a dignified, rigid position in the center of the room. She stared at me accusingly as she crossed her arms, an indication that she had dug in her heels and was about to blast me with both barrels.

“Dad, we need to talk to you,” she began, ”I’ll just be candid. We’re very concerned about your recent behavior. When did you take up with that immoral woman?”

“I don’t know what you’re talking about,” I answered, somewhat unsure of exactly where the inquisition was headed.

“What’s your relationship with that woman?” queried Marsha. Her sustained erect posture was an indication of her reluctance to yield an iota in her entrenched position.

"She's an old friend that I knew many years ago." I looked at Melissa. "Have you been telling them things?"

"No, Dad, Marsha just called me and asked me to come to your house for a family meeting."

Marsha pointed her finger at me. "The way you and that woman looked at each other indicates to me that your relationship is not limited to just *old friends,"* she said. She began to slowly pace the floor in the manner of a lawyer in her effort to impress the jury.

"How long have you known her?" She stopped pacing and stared at me.

"What business is that of yours?" I asked, angrily.

Jessie chimed in. "Now, Tom, we just have your best interests at heart. You're just not yourself, lately."

Melissa only smiled as Gertrude's expression became more tragic.

Marsha pressed on. "How did you get so lovey-dovey with her in such a short time, Dad? My God! You just met this woman!"

"No, that's not true," I answered, "Don't you listen? I just told you that I knew her many years ago. As a matter of fact, she and I once had a romantic relationship." I was suddenly amazed that I had the guts to confess such a thing to my accusers.

Marsha looked shocked. "Do you mean to tell me that you once had an affair with that woman? How could you do that to our mother?"

"It was before I married your mother. Anyway, when both parties are single, it's not called an 'affair.'

It's called 'dating.' In addition, I may see her a lot more, because I still enjoy the company of Harriet!" I looked at Gertrude. Her shocked expression had changed to one of despair, and I feared that she might cry.

Marsha placed her hands on her hips and stared at me. "So you're getting romantically involved with that superficial woman," she accused, "Dad, she's not right for you! She's weird and shallow, and she looks about twenty years younger than you. She even got thrown in jail!"

"She didn't do anything bad. Anyway, they dropped the charges." I said. I became more surprised at my courage. "In fact, I may just start going steady with her. Don't I have a right to be happy?"

"Go for it, Dad!" exclaimed Melissa, with a laugh. Gertrude glared at her. There had never been any love lost between Melissa and Gertrude.

"There's no fool like an old fool!" said Marsha. It was unlike her to utter such a hackneyed expression. "What if she somehow makes you lose your head and marry her? She could end up with your money and property!"

"You don't need to worry about that, Marsha," I said, "I don't have enough property for you and Melissa to quibble over. Besides, Harriet is probably better fixed financially than I am. If I decide to marry her, I'll get her to sign a pre-nuptial if it makes you feel better…or maybe we'll just live together!"

"So you *do* have marrying her on your mind!" Marsha was becoming angry. "What about Gertrude?"

I glanced over toward Gertrude, who seemed to be on the verge of fainting.

"Listen," I replied angrily, "I'll do whatever I

want to do about marrying Harriet!" I was now completely astounded at my display of courage.

"Right on, Dad!" cheered Melissa. She suddenly placed her fingers over her lips and muttered, "Oh, sorry, Gertrude." Both Gertrude and Marsha stared at her, and Jessie looked at me with sadness.

As if addressing a jury, Marsha began her summation. "It appears to me that what we have here is a senile old man who has taken leave of his senses," she announced dramatically. She turned to her Aunt Jessie. "Aunt Jessie, we may have to take legal action and have Dad declared incompetent!"

My resolve only strengthened, for now that my courage had been revived, I was on a roll. Besides, Melissa's approval had emboldened me.

I quickly announced with authority, "The more you lecture me about it makes it even more likely that I will marry her!"

Melissa clapped her hands and shouted, "Cool!"

Gertrude fell over in a dead faint.

Chapter 20

After a near-sleepless night, I awoke to a gloomy day. While relieving myself in the bathroom, I listened to the drenching rain as it cascaded down on the roof and spattered against the bathroom window. I peered out the window at the overcast sky and the accumulating puddles of water on the driveway. The dreariness of the morning corresponded with my dismal mood.

I shaved, showered, and got dressed. Then I walked into the kitchen and put on a pot of coffee. I prepared a breakfast of bacon, eggs and burned toast; then I sat down at the kitchen table to eat. *Where is the salt - shaker?* I searched the entire kitchen…the counter tops, inside of the cabinets, even under the table, without success. It was only after I opened the refrigerator to get a stick of butter that I discovered the missing article. I finished breakfast, carried my cup of coffee into the den and took a seat on the couch.

With a desire for silence, I ignored the TV set; for it

would only serve as a distraction to my thought processes while I was mulling over my many problems. Recent events had plunged me into a bleak mood. Marsha's condemnation of me during our family conference was compounded by my indecisiveness in regard to my future involvement with Harriet. Because several days had passed since I had seen her, I felt the urge to call her. I began to worry that perhaps I was being too cautious in trying to decide whether or not to marry her; after all, I didn't want to lose her. I felt a tinge of jealousy when I thought of Dick's recent phone call in which he had told me that he had dated Harriet a couple of times during the past week.

When she answered the phone, the sound of her voice excited me; however, she spoke in an almost formal fashion; although not cold, her voice had the tenor of a curious detachment, lacking in its usual humor and enthusiasm. After we casually greeted each other, I got to the point.

"Harriet, I've done a lot of thinking lately."

"Really? What about?"

"Us."

"What about us?"

"You know. About us getting…back together again."

"Getting back together? Do you mean on a *date?"*

"No…I mean about what you asked me. About us getting…*married."*

"Tom, you're about to choke on the word."

"I just wanted you to know that I've been thinking about it, Harriet…a lot."

"Good for you!" she answered, sarcastically, "Is

that what you called to tell me?"

"No, not entirely. I just wanted you to know that I'm leaning in that direction."

"Am I supposed to start turning cartwheels in excitement?" Her derisive tone frustrated me.

"No, but...Harriet, you're not changing your mind about getting married, are you?"

"Tom, you were right when you said that we ought to think about it. Marriage is not a thing that either of us should rush into." She was casting my own words back at me.

I changed the subject. "Dick tells me that you and he have had a couple of dates recently."

"Why shouldn't we date? Do you have some objection? As you have said, you don't have any claim on me!"

Her attitude worried me. I began to panic at the thought of losing her.

"Harriet, have you changed your mind? If you have, you need to tell me."

After a brief silence, she said, "No...not really."

I sighed with relief. "When can we get together? I'm free about every night this week."

"Tom, whenever you can give me an answer, call me. Then we can get together. Look, I've gotta run, okay? I'll talk to you later. 'Bye, Tom."

"Yeah...goodbye, Harriet."

I had hoped that my calling her would deliver me from my bleak mood, but after hanging up, I was more depressed than before. In her last statement on the phone she might as well have told me, "Don't bother me anymore until you've made up your mind to marry me."

It was difficult to restrain myself from again calling her and telling her that I wanted to marry her immediately; however, my cautious nature prevailed.

Aggravating my depressed mood was the unpleasant task that awaited me in my shop. The complex graphic design that I had laboriously spent the entire previous day in producing had been lost when I had neglected to save it on my computer. It would now be necessary to spend a complete day in reproducing it. In frustration, I drove to my shop, booted up my Macintosh computer and began re-creating the lost design. Unfortunately, in the middle of my burdensome task my computer crashed, causing me to again lose the design. Since I was technology-illiterate, I was left totally helpless; consequently, I called the computer repairman and returned home.

For the next several days I moped around the house, often calling the repairman who hadn't yet set a date to fix my computer, and occasionally returning to my shop to check for messages. I wasn't sleeping well at night, and again I found my mind in emotional disarray.

During an afternoon nap in my bedroom, the ringing telephone awakened me. A glance at the bedside table revealed to me that the cordless phone was missing. I rose from the bed, trailing the sound of the ringing telephone as a hound would follow the scent of a rabbit. I finally located the phone on the back of the commode tank where I had left it earlier that morning.

"Hello?"

"Hello, Tom? This is Dick."

"Yeah, what's up, Dick?"

"Not a whole lot, pal. I've been missin' you lately. Where have you been keepin' yourself?"

"Here at home, mostly. I've been wanting to see you too, Dick. How are our buddies at the Cracker Barrel doing?"

"We've all been missin' you. Pinky's hip is gettin' better, but Dummy's in the hospital havin' prostate surgery. Head is gonna have cataract surgery next week."

"How's your arthritis?" I asked.

"What arthritis?"

"The arthritis in your knee."

"That's not arthritis," he said, "That's just my old football injury that bothers me sometimes."

"How are you and Harriet getting along?" I asked.

"Look, Tom, speakin' of Harriet…I need to talk to you about something. Can you drive over here? I would drive to your house, but I want to talk to you about something personal, and at your house there's the chance that some of your people will pop in unexpectedly."

"Sure thing, Dick. I'll be right over."

The rain fell heavily during the short drive to his house. I was consumed with curiosity about the *personal matter* that he wanted to discuss with me, particularly since he had brought up Harriet's name in connection with his request.

He met me at the door with an elaborate grin on his face and shook my hand in a warm greeting. I claimed the easy chair in his den.

"Want a drink?" he asked.

"This early in the day?"

"Hell, Tom, can't a couple of old retired buddies

have a drink together anytime they choose? What difference does it make what time it is?"

"Well, none I guess,"

He left for the kitchen. Soon, he returned to the den carrying a tray with a fifth of Bourbon, a large Coke, and two glasses of ice. He poured our drinks.

"You take yours with Coke, right?" He grinned. "You always were a sissy." He handed my drink to me.

I returned his smile. "Thanks, Dick."

We tapped our glasses together in a toast and took a drink. Dick took a seat in a chair facing me. He was in no hurry to resume the conversation. He seemed almost hesitant to bring up the 'personal matter' to which he had referred.

I became impatient. "What's on your mind, Dick? What's this personal thing you wanted to discuss with me?"

He seemed to be trying to find the right words. "Tom, there's something that I'm considerin' and I just wanted to run it by you to get your idea about it. How serious is this relationship between you and Harriet?"

"Why do you ask?"

"Well, you knew that Harriet and I have been datin' some lately, didn't you?"

"Sure, that's okay with me."

"Are you sure you don't mind?" he asked.

"Why should I mind? You're my best friend…and I don't have any claim on her. Besides, I know that you and Harriet are just good friends."

He seemed relieved. "Then I'll just lay it out for you, Pal. Here's my plan. I intend to ask Harriet to move in with me."

"Move in with you? Do you mean that you're going to ask her to marry you?"

"Hell no! Who's talkin' about *marriage?* I'd never marry *any* woman! Least of all, Harriet!"

I was shocked. I wasn't prepared for this. "Dick, I wasn't going to tell you this yet, but Harriet and I have been talking about getting married."

"What? Are you kiddin' me?" He seemed to be amazed. "You're not goin' to start playin' that same old tune again, are you? You've always thought that I'm stupid! Well, you're the stupid one! In fact, you're an idiot!" Anger showed in his eyes as he rose to his feet.

I suddenly stood. "You're beginning to piss me off, Dick," I said, "Before one of us says something that we'll both regret, I'm leaving!" I headed for the front door, with him in hot pursuit. He followed me to the front porch, grabbed my arm, and spun me around to face him.

"Don't walk away from me, Tom!"

"Turn loose of my arm, Dick!" I warned.

He ignored my warning. "You damned idiot! You're lettin' that bitch come between us again!"

"Don't call her that, Dick!"

"Why not? She is a bitch, Tom!"

His arm jerked upward and blocked the punch that I threw at him. Then he pushed me aside. When he swung his fist at me, I stepped backward, avoiding the punch; as a result, he lost his balance and plummeted down the concrete porch steps. He groaned and rolled over onto his back in the rain-soaked lawn.

When I saw his crumpled figure at the bottom of the

steps, I was horrified. He was holding his side, writhing in pain, groaning. His hairpiece was barely hanging to his head. His facial expression was one of complete agony.

I ran to him. "Dick! Dick! Are you hurt bad?"

"My side!" he groaned, "I think I broke some ribs, and my back is hurtin!'"

I tried to lift him. "I've got to get you to the hospital!"

He screamed in anguish. "Don't try to move me!" He said. "Call 911!"

After placing the call, I sat by his side in the yard. Ignoring the drenching rain, I tried to comfort him until the ambulance arrived. He was placed in the emergency vehicle and it quickly pulled out of his driveway. I stood in his front yard, staring in sadness as the ambulance disappeared down the misty street.

The following few days were a living hell for me. I was so consumed with worry about Dick that I only occasionally thought about Harriet; anyway, I felt that she had possibly once again come between Dick and me in our friendship, so I decided not to call her.

Dick had suffered three broken ribs. In addition, his doctor suspected that he had injured his back; consequently, he spent a couple of extra days in the hospital undergoing various tests. I visited him often, and on the day that he was scheduled for release, I took a bouquet of flowers to him.

When I walked into his hospital room, he warmly greeted me, but his customary carefree smile was missing, for his face expressed only sadness.

"How are you feeling, Dick?" I asked.

"Not good," he answered. He hung his head. "I

called Harriet, and she came over to see me last night."

"How's she doing?" I asked. "By the way, I need to call her."

He looked sadly at me. "Don't bother to call her, Tom. You know that landlord of hers, that old guy, Oliver Bishop? Well, Harriet married him yesterday! They're on their way to Dallas, Texas!"

Chapter 21

Surprisingly, I had slept well for a change. The banner of golden morning sunlight from the bedroom window that illuminated my bed told me that the summer day was beautiful. When I sat up I felt no evidence of arthritic pain in my knee; nor did I experience any dizziness when I rose from the bed and stood up. I again relieved my bladder in the bathroom and then made my way to the kitchen to start a pot of coffee.

I walked into the den, and taking note of the gloomy darkness of the room, I moved to the window and pulled back the curtains, allowing the morning sunlight to bathe the interior of the room.

When I peered through the window, the moving figure of a man caught my attention. Walking with a pronounced limp, he had the appearance of a homeless derelict as he headed up the walkway toward my house. He was overweight and bald, slumping in his posture as he made his way to my door. He was on my front porch before I recognized him: It was Dick.

Before he had a chance to ring the doorbell, I opened the front door. He stood on the front porch grinning. "Ain't you gonna invite me in?"

I returned his grin. "Come in, Dick. How do you feel?"

"Well, I couldn't play a game of football right now, but I'll survive."

I looked at him in amazement. "Dick, What's happened to you? I hardly recognized you! Where's your hairpiece? And the way you're dressed!" I laughed. "I almost mistook you for a bum!"

He echoed my laugh. "Hell, that was no mistake. I *am* a bum. I got tired of bein' a phony. No more dressin' in gaudy clothes, no more pretendin' to be forty years old...and man, that hairpiece...What a pain in the ass that thing was! You know, Tom, stayin' young has very little to do with a man's appearance...It has more to do with a person's attitude!"

He took a seat in the recliner as I sat down on the couch.

I was concerned about his injuries. "Tell me, Dick, what did the doctor say about your back? Is it going to be alright?"

"Yeah, my back checked out okay...It's just these damned broken ribs that are so hard to deal with."

I breathed a sigh of relief. "Man, I'm glad your back's okay!"

He looked sadly at me. "Tom, I've done some checkin' on that guy, Oliver Bishop. He's a rich old miser. He owns about a million dollars worth of real estate in Knoxville."

"Who's Oliver Bishop?" I asked, facetiously.

"The old buzzard that married Harriet! Hell, get your head out of your ass, Tom! She pulled that same old trick on us again!"

"That figures," I said, "Harriet was always a sucker for money."

Dick sighed. "It looks we've lost her for good, this time, ol' buddy." Then he projected an ecstatic grin. "But man, she was sure one more hot babe in the sack, wasn't she, pal?"

I was shocked. "In the *sack*? Do you mean that you've had Harriet *in bed?"*

He looked surprised. "I don't usually kiss an' tell, but since we'll probably never see her again, I don't see the harm in it. Do you mean that you haven't?"

With the sudden realization of what a fool I had been, I was embarrassed.

"No…no I haven't, Dick."

He looked at me in awe. "Do you mean that you never tapped her even back when we were in high school?"

I hung my head. "No."

"Amazing!" he replied.

I began to feel anger toward Harriet. "Well, I guess she was just a slut," I said, bitterly.

Dick's expression was serious. "Tom, there ain't no such thing as a 'slut.' There's only honest women and dishonest women."

"Damn!" I said, "What a cynical attitude!"

He smiled at me. "It may sound cynical to you, but it's realistic."

I raised my head and looked at him. "Dick, I was a fool to fall for her again."

"Well, there's no fool like an old fool!" His adage was appropriate.

I thought for a while before saying anything else. "Tell me something, Dick...did you have sex with her this time around...since she came in for the class reunion?"

He looked puzzled. "You know, it's kinda odd," he said, "But since she came back to Northridge she wouldn't let me touch her. But it's hard to believe that you didn't make out with her in the old days."

"We got plenty passionate many times, Dick," I said, "But when I got close to scoring, she always pulled away. She said she was 'saving herself for me'. What a joke! I can see now that she never loved me at all."

Dick leaned forward and placed his elbows on his knees, clasping his hands together. "You know, Tom, I know that as far as intelligence goes, you don't think that I'm playin' with a full deck; but in some ways I'm smarter than you are. You're book-smart, but you're sure as hell not people-smart."

His statement puzzled me. "How do you figure that?"

"She wanted you to respect her. She respected your opinions more than she did mine. She had sex with me because she didn't give a damn what I thought of her." He stopped and reflected on what he had just said. "She loved you, Tom, maybe more than you'll ever know. Sure, she loves money and material things. Who doesn't? But she loved you *more.* With the others, it was just a matter of havin' sex, pure and simple...But she wanted to *make love* to you, Tom. There's a difference, you know."

"Yeah, but this time I thought that she wanted to marry me for sure. I'll bet that old miser she married won't live another year. He looks like he's pushing ninety. He practically has one foot in the grave."

"All the better for Harriet, ol' pal. Everyone says that he has no heirs, so after he's gone, she'll be a millionaire. Maybe then she'll come back into our lives. When did you ask her to marry you?"

"I didn't."

"What do you mean, *you didn't?"*

"She asked *me."*

"She asked *you?* What did you tell her?"

"I told her that I'd have to think about it."

He stared at me with an expression of exasperation. *"You'd have to think about it?* Hell, Tom! She *did* want to marry you. My God, man! She *proposed* to you! But you never gave her an answer! Have you ever made a decision in your life without thinkin' about it for years? No wonder she went ahead and married that old rich bastard! She probably figured that you'd be thinkin' about her proposal for fifty years, like you've done about forgivin' me for beatin' you up a half century ago! You know, even the wonderful life that you had with Jenny was a result of an accident. Getting' her pregnant spared you the responsibility of havin' to make a decision. That accident brought about the happiest part of your life, ol' buddy, because it gave you Jenny! If it hadn't been for fate steppin' in, you'd have never made up your mind to marry Jenny...or probably anybody else, for that matter!"

"Well, I'm not impulsive like you...and Harriet."

"Tom, you and I…and Harriet, too, are gettin' old. We don't have that much time left to sit around and think about things forever before we make a decision."

"Yeah, but even when you were young, you've always been impulsive. You've always done things on the spur of the moment."

Dick winced with pain as he leaned back in his chair, reflecting on our past conversation. Finally, he spoke. "You know, Tom, Harriet and I are a lot alike."

"In many ways you're alike, but in some ways you're very different." I was curious. "Be more specific. In what ways are you alike?"

"Both of us are able to love 'em and leave 'em. We both know what we want, and we don't waste any time goin' after it. We're both risk takers, and neither of us ever holds a grudge. On the other hand, Tom, you're just the opposite: You can't ever make up your mind what you want. You're so cautious that you won't ever take a chance or try a new adventure, and when something bad happens to you it takes forever for you to get over it and to get on with your life. I guess you'll always be that way, because you can't teach an old dog new tricks. Another thing, Tom: You think too much. Let me ask you something, pal. When was the last time you were surprised?"

I became restless. I got up from the couch and began to pace the floor. "The trouble with your kind of logic, is that sometimes we can make a bad mistake if we don't think things through before we decide. We might be wrong at least fifty percent of the time!"

He smiled. "That also means that at least fifty percent of the time, we might be *right!* When an opportunity comes your way, you have to have the guts to seize it! We just go around once in this life. We need to act on our gut feelings, and grab the brass ring when it comes around! He who hesitates is lost!"

I spoke up, "Well, another well-known adage is, 'Fools rush in where angels fear to tread'!"

Dick responded, "Yeah, or you could say, 'haste makes waste!'" We both laughed.

I reclaimed my seat on the couch. "You know, Dick, I suppose you were right about Harriet. I guess she is a bitch."

"Tom, as I've told you before, I've got nothin' against bitches. When I said that Harriet is a bitch, it wasn't an indictment…it's just a description. A lot of women are bitches. A man just needs to know how to relate to them."

"Tell me your secret," I said.

He grinned. "Here's my philosophy, Tom. You should treat a bitch like a lady, and you should treat a lady like a bitch."

"Is that why you were always so nice to Harriet?" I asked.

"Sure."

"Dick, that sure is a skeptical philosophy. Maybe you could explain it to me."

"Okay, pal. When a woman is a bitch and you treat her like a lady, she's grateful to you, because deep down inside, she knows that she's a bitch. On the other hand, when you're dealin' with a goody-two-shoes conceited 'lady,' who's used to everybody bowin' down to her, you can shape her up by takin' her down a peg or two."

"Damn, Dick! What a screwed-up formula for getting along with women."

"It's always worked for me," he said, "Say, ain't you got a cup of coffee or a Coke that you can offer a man?"

"How about something a little stronger?" I asked.

"This early in the day?"

"What difference does it make?" I asked, "Can't a couple of old retired friends have a drink together any time they want to?"

He laughed. "I used to say the same thing to you. Remember?"

I walked to the kitchen and fetched a bottle of Bourbon and two glasses. I then returned to the den and reclaimed my seat on the couch.

"It's a good thing that I had this booze for us to drink, because I forgot to plug in the coffee pot this morning," I said. I set the whiskey and glasses down on the coffee table.

He laughed. "Don't tell me you're startin' to forget things! Join the crowd, pal."

"I hope you take yours straight," I said.

"No problem, kiddo. Say, when did you start drinkin' it straight?"

"When I stopped being a sissy."

I poured a generous amount of booze in the two glasses and we toasted before taking our drinks. I thought about my recent involvement with Harriet.

"You know, Dick, I can't believe that I let her fool me again."

"Fool me once, shame on you; fool me twice, shame on *me!*" he profoundly stated.

I reflected on my long friendship with Dick. "Have you ever thought about what a strange hand that fate dealt us? We've been friends for fifty years, and our recent episode with Harriet turned out exactly the same way as it did fifty years ago. We got into a fight again, and we were both jilted by Harriet again. I guess it just goes to show that history does repeat itself!"

"Yeah, but the only difference is that this time I'm the one who ended up in the hospital," he said.

"But, luckily, we do learn from our mistakes, Dick. We'll both know better next time."

"Bullshit!" he said, "If Old Man Bishop dies and Harriet comes back here, we'll do the same damned thing all over again. Only this time, it's your turn to go to the hospital."

"Not me, buddy! Next time I'll run!"

Dick laughed. "Tom, now that Harriet's gone, I guess that's the end of *The Three Musketeers* for good. Since there are only two of us, what'll we call ourselves now?"

"The Odd Couple, Maybe? Or how about *Mutt and Jeff?"* I asked.

"Which was the dumb one? Was it Mutt? I guess that Mutt would be me."

"Don't sell yourself short, Dick. I'm the dumb one."

He cast an inquisitive look at me. "So where do we go from here? What are your plans?"

I took another sip of the Bourbon. "Dick, I've decided to get my business up and running again. It has a great potential, but I really need to put some money toward improvements; and as you know, I'm not really too well-heeled with money."

His face brightened. "Hey, buddy, I just had a brainstorm! Why don't we combine our talents and get that shop of yours hummin'? I'm not hurtin' for loot. I can put some money into it. Just think how well we could do with the popular Dick Noble sellin' for you. We'd make a great team! We could be partners!"

Reflecting on his proposal, I had to admit to myself that his idea made sense.

"I'll have to think about it," I answered.

He sighed. "Well, I guess we can kiss that idea goodbye for about fifty years."

I changed the subject. "Dick, I'll tell you something that kinda surprises me. I don't feel as bad as I thought I would about Harriet jilting me again. In fact, I don't feel bad about it at all. You know, we all have a magical feeling about our first love. I guess that I just had a sentimental curiosity about *what might have been.*"

He took another drink. "I was wonderin' when you were gonna see the light, Tom. Most men would envy you, because in Jenny, you had a wonderful woman. She's the real love of your life. You and Harriet would be a misfit, because water and oil don't mix. She's not the genuine person that you are. In fact, she's not anything like you at all. She's like me: As superficial as hell!"

I was amazed at his admission to the undesirable trait, but I wasn't in total agreement about his appraisal of Harriet.

"Well, she really *isn't* that superficial, Dick. She's just playful, carefree, and spontaneous. Those are the qualities that made me fall in love with her. Ironically, those are the very traits that made it impossible for me to marry her."

Dick was right about Jenny and me. I had previously held the mistaken belief that to mentally outmaneuver Dick was as easy as shooting fish in a barrel, but now I was beginning to be amazed at his insight. Dick was right on target. Jenny was the real love of my life. Although there was a part of Harriet that I would always love, the mere memory of her made me feel uncomfortable. But the memory of Jenny's vibrant spirit would comfort me always. I suddenly realized how much my marriage to Jenny had enriched my life.

Dick gave me a compassionate look. "Tom, you and Jenny raised some fine daughters. You should be proud of both of them."

I was surprised at his remark. "But Dick, I didn't think you liked Marsha very much. After all, she doesn't seem to approve of you, sometimes."

"Just because she doesn't approve of me doesn't mean she's not a good person. Look at how well she raised that grandson of yours. She must be doin' *something* right! Hell, you were just like her when you were young! Don't you remember? Actually, back when I was young, I should have married a level-headed gal like Marsha. Maybe she could have made a more decent man outta me. The trouble is, I married women with personalities too much like mine…and you can see what disasters my marriages turned out to be! Sometimes, differences in personalities make a good blend for a marriage. But in the case of you and Harriet it would never have worked, because you're just *too* different!"

"Well, speaking of Marsha…she's a good woman and I know that she loves me, but sometimes she almost smothers me to death!" I said.

Dick took a sip of his booze. "That's because she is concerned about you. She loves you, Tom, and that's the only way she knows how to show it. You're a lucky man to have two daughters that love you so much. Your sister Jessie loves you, too. I just wish that I had someone who was that concerned about me. I don't have any family left, Tom. All I've got are those jock-sniffers who remember my glory days in football...and they've all just about died off. You know, outside of you, there ain't nobody in the world that really gives a shit about me!"

I experienced a deep sorrow for him. At that moment, I knew that I truly loved Dick like the brother that I had never had; also, I realized that he was right in his evaluation of my daughters. *I am indeed a lucky man!*

He grimaced with pain as he shifted his weight in the chair. I knew that his broken ribs were giving him a fit. I felt remorseful about our recent altercation.

"Dick, I'm sorry about our fight. I shouldn't have tried to hit you." He didn't answer.

I eyed him curiously. "Can you ever forgive me?"

"I'll have to think about it," he mumbled.

"Shit!" I said. I poured us another drink and changed the subject. "Dick, I'm glad that Harriet came to Northridge for the class reunion."

"Yeah, it was nice seein' her again. But I thought you were sorry. Why are you glad?"

"Because in spite of the way it ended, I figure that Harriet did me a big favor. I owe her a lot. She opened my eyes to some things."

"What things?" He finished his drink and poured himself another.

"I learned from her that growing old doesn't mean that we have to give up on having fun. She also taught me that I need to be more spontaneous, and it's never too late to have dreams for your life. Until Harriet temporarily came back into my world, I was leading a dull existence. She re-awakened my yearning for some excitement in my life. She was like a breath of fresh air!"

Dick leaned back in the recliner and crossed his legs. "You know Tom, with your straight-laced nature, you need more people like Harriet in your life. You just don't need to *marry* one of them. Man, she sure has a lust for life! I'm gonna miss her. I wonder if either of us will ever cross paths with her again?"

"God only knows," I said, "By the way, what do you plan to do now? I mean like tomorrow, or next week?"

"Oh, I don't know…maybe I'll take me a little trip."

"For how long?"

"I don't know. Maybe for a week."

"Well, try to be back as soon as you can," I said.

"Why?"

I grinned. "If we're gonna get my business humming again, I'll need your help."

"No kiddin'? Do you really mean it?" He was becoming excited.

"Sure. I told you I'd have to think about it. Well, I thought about it."

"You won't be sorry, pal," he assured me, "Listen, Tom… the last time that Harriet walked out of our lives fifty years ago, we took a little trip together to kinda get over the loss. I'd ask you to go with me this time, but I know that you'd turn me down because you can't afford goin' away on a week's trip. I guess I'll just plan it without you."

I poured both of us another drink. "Why is it necessary to *plan it?* Just *do it!* And can't we make it for two weeks?"

"We?"

"Yeah... You invited me, didn't you?"

"But where will you get the money?"

I smiled at him. "Put it on my tab."

Tom, Dick & Harriet
by Don Pardue

Orders may be made by phone or mail to the address/phone number below.

Please send me the novel of *Tom, Dick & Harriet* by Don Pardue.

__________@ $12.00 = __________
(quantity)

Shipping and handling* = __________

Total enclosed = __________

*Please enclose $4.00 to cover shipping and handling, or $6.00 if order is more than $20.00.

Please pay by check or money order and make payable to:
Tom, Dick & Harriet.
Sorry, we do not accept charge cards at this time.

Send your payment with the order form above to:
Don Pardue/TD&H, P.O. Box 521 Lenoir City, TN 37771
865-986-8812 or 865-988-6644.

Prices subject to change without notice. Please allow 4-6 weeks for delivery.